The Gregg Press
Science Fiction Series

The Devil Is Dead
by R. A. Lafferty

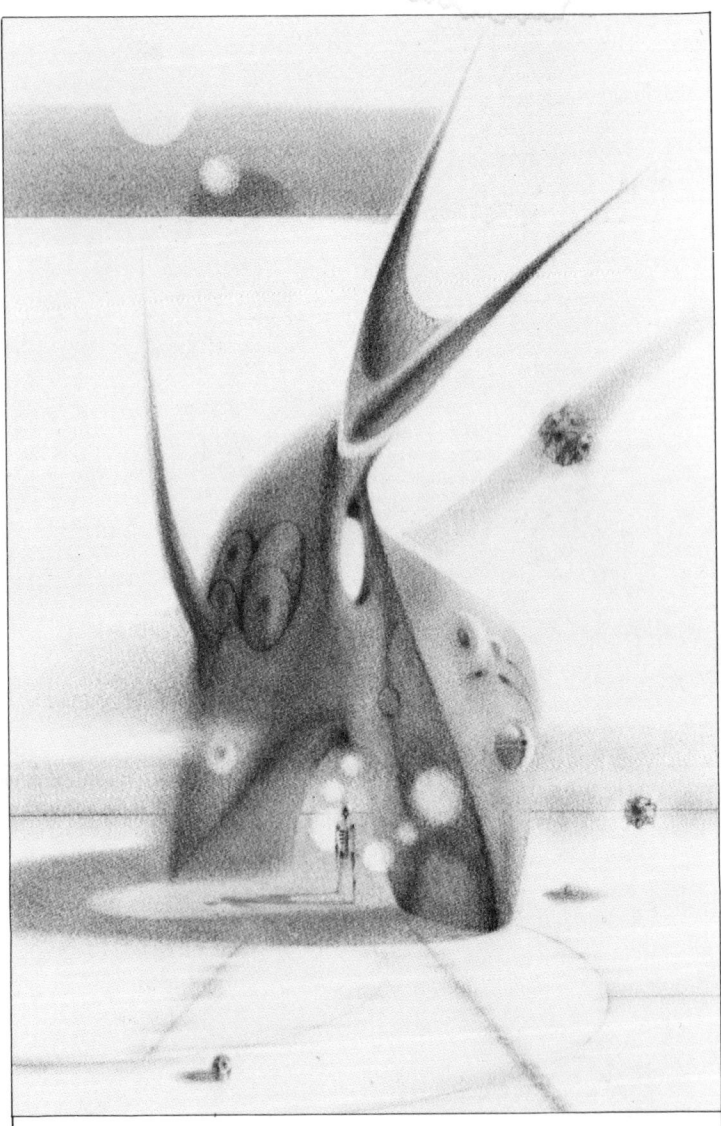

The Gregg Press Science Fiction Series
David G. Hartwell, *Editor*

The Devil Is Dead

R. A. LAFFERTY

With a New Introduction by
CHARLES PLATT

GREGG PRESS
A DIVISION OF G. K. HALL & CO., BOSTON, 1977

This is a complete photographic reprint of a work first published in New York by Avon Books in 1971. The trim size of the original paperback edition was 4⅛ by 7 inches.

Text copyright © 1971 by R. A. Lafferty.
Reprinted by arrangement with the author.
Introduction copyright © 1977 by G. K. Hall & Co.

Frontispiece illustration by Richard Powers.

Printed on permanent/durable acid-free paper and bound in the United States of America.

Republished in 1977 by Gregg Press, A Division of G. K. Hall & Co., 70 Lincoln Street, Boston, Massachusetts 02111.

First Printing, June 1977

Library of Congress Cataloging in Publication Data

Lafferty, R   A
    The devil is dead.

    (The Gregg Press science fiction series)
    Reprint of the ed. published by Avon Books, New York.
    I. Title.
PZ4.L1627De3   [PS3562.A28]   813'.5'4   77-5038
ISBN 0-8398-2364-9

Introduction

THE DEVIL IS DEAD was first published as a paperback original by Avon Books in 1971. It is an idiosyncratic, playful book that defies categorization and evades analysis. It takes liberties with plausibility, plays games with reason, and draws on a grab-bag of mythic and Catholic source materials to stage its unserious entertainments. Those who expect something comparable to other science fiction and fantasy will not find it here. Those who expect rational explanations for paradoxical events will not be well pleased either (they will be thrown only an occasional scrap of pseudologic to ease their hunger for something that makes sense).

But those who enjoy individualism in a writer, lack of artistic compromise, and (on a simpler level) tall tales told for their own sake, will find *The Devil Is Dead* pleasing, entertaining, and in every way delightfully unusual.

Lafferty is an unusual writer. Born in 1914 in Iowa, he settled with his family in Tulsa, Oklahoma—his "favorite city in the world"[1]—where he spent most of his life working in the electrical wholesaling business. He joined the army when he was 27 and saw Australia, New Guinea, Indonesia, and the Philippines; after five years he returned to his electrical business, though he had clearly developed an interest in travel. He did not start writing until he was 45 years old (circa 1959), and took it up "to try to find a hobby that would make a little money instead of costing a lot, and also to fill a gap caused by cutting down on my drinking and fooling around." He sold his first short story in 1959 and his first novel in 1967. He retired from the electrical business in 1971, and has been writing ever since. In 1973 he won a Hugo Award for "Eurema's Dam," a short story, and he has achieved wide recognition for the quality of his work in the science fiction/fantasy field.

He says he has been influenced by Robert Louis Stevenson, Mark Twain, Bret Harte, Herman Melville, Hilaire Belloc, G. K. Chesterson, Dickens and Balzac, among others (he mentions no science fiction authors as influences). In addition he says: "there's a lot of the American tall tale in my background.... The three best tall-story tellers I ever knew, Hugh Lafferty, my father; Ed Burke, the brother of my mother-to-be; and Frank Burke, her cousin, homesteaded near Snyder, Oklahoma, in the 1890s." And it is their influence that is probably most noticeable in *The Devil Is Dead*.

The telling of tall tales is not a modern art. It harks back to a period when there was time to kill, as opposed to the contemporary feeling that there is never enough time to spare. The tall tale, surely, is best suited to a family sitting around a fireplace in the evening, needing some kind of diversion; or some old friends hanging out in a bar together, looking for a conversational topic beyond their own true lives. The tall tale has elements of ritual, game, and myth; like any good mythic form, it contains its share of wonder (amazing incidents, far-flung travels, larger-than-life events), but unlike most myths, it never takes itself entirely seriously.

Lafferty's unusual mixing of classic American tall tale methods with archetypes drawn from more conventional mythic sources, plus a few elements of conventional science fiction and fantasy, gives his work its unique flavor. It is hard to compare him to any other writer whose work is being published today under the usual genre labels. In some ways, there are similarities to Lewis Carroll (whose fantasies showed the same enjoyment of paradox, illogicality, semantic games, and surreal events occurring in the course of a quest). But where Lewis Carroll is distinctively British and wrote about, and for, children, Lafferty is distinctively American, and his recurring themes tend to involve booze and barmaids (in that order) in an unconventional Catholic America, rather than conventional children's story fare.

The difficulty in classifying, categorizing, or comparing Lafferty's work is associated with some difficulty that he has had in seeing his work published. The practical end of literature—getting books into print and keeping them in print—is an aspect commonly ignored in introductions such as this one, but it seems to me that these practicalities are very relevant here. At the time of this writing, R. A. Lafferty has no fewer than *nine* complete novels in manuscript form, unsold, looking for a publisher; two novels that have been accepted for publication; and ten that have actually been published. But of these ten, how many are still in print? And of the unsold nine, how many will *ever* see print? To deal with these depressing and distressing questions it is necessary to digress for a moment into some sordid facts of genre fiction publishing.

In his history of science fiction, *Billion Year Spree* (1973), Brian W. Aldiss writes: "It is easy to argue that Hugo Gernsback ... was one of the worst disasters ever to hit the science fiction field. Not only did the segregation of science fiction into magazines designed especially for it, ghetto-fashion, guarantee that various orthodoxies would be established inimical to a thriving literature, but Gernsback himself was utterly without literary understanding. He created dangerous precedents which many later editors in the field followed."[2]

The suggestion that Gernsback retarded development of the science fiction field can be debated endlessly and is not the focus of our concern here. What seems to me important (and beyond any debate at all) is Aldiss' inference that Gernsback, in 1926, was solely responsible for identifying and creating a new genre: scientifiction or science fiction (the exact term is irrelevant). What mattered was that, once labelled, the majority of imaginative fiction could never again be lost in the amorphous body of contemporary literature. Thenceforth, it was to be segregated.

In Gernsback's time, the pulp magazine field was of course already subdivided into other categories (westerns, mysteries, etc.). Creating a new category for science fiction made reasonable magazine publishing sense, especially since most of the fiction then to be published under that label was really much the same in character, and was no better than the pulp image that came to be associated with the label.

But when science fiction started developing in the 1950s, and some writers sought to transcend the pulp image of the genre, they found it was too late. The "Flash Gordon/Buck Rogers" image was established. The new paperback-book publishing industry of the 1950s was employing the same categories as magazine publishing of the 1930s. Editors considered science fiction a juvenile market where higher literary values might be more of a burden than an asset. And the general reading public did not of course take science fiction seriously at all.

Before the creation of the discriminatory science fiction label, under which the small amount of good writing ended up packaged identically to the bad, this problem did not exist. Victorian and Edwardian "scientific romances" were part of the main body of literature; H. G. Wells and Jules Verne were not segregated on a separate shelf, under a separate label, at the backs of bookstores.

But by the 1960s, an author such as Kurt Vonnegut, Jr. was treated differently. *He* ended up waiting more than ten years for recognition (that came via *Slaughterhouse Five* in 1969) before his earlier books were brought back into print, decategorized, and moved out of the science fiction section into the public eye. And there are other good writers for whom it still has not happened. They remain victims of the category system invented by the "father of modern science fiction."

To be fair, even if Gernsback had never created a category for science fiction, some other editor or publisher would probably have done it. Modern publishing is wedded to the concept of categories in general. Modern sales practice requires it. Booksellers expect it. Readers, too, are supposedly programmed to respond to categories: show a bunch of book buyers a novel without a label (the theory goes) and they will not know what to make of it, but show them a "mystery" or a "historical romance" or a "bestseller" (often printed on the cover of this category, reflecting expectations, not actuality) and they will know right away what they can expect and whether they will enjoy it or not.

Categories eliminate some of the uncertainties and indefinables of publishing. Sales become more predictable, because books are packaged like each other within each category. More and more, you *can* judge books by their covers. Ideally, literature will one day become as easily marketed as products on supermarket shelves—the contents of gothics, detective novels, and westerns will be as programmed and predictable as the contents of boxes of breakfast cereal, laundry detergent, and cake mix. Publishers and distributors and sales representatives and bookstore owners will then sigh with relief, having drastically reduced the risks of their business.

We have not yet reached that utopia, but we are more than halfway there. As a result, it is getting harder for the unconventional, non-category novel to see publication.

An editor who is faced with such a non-category novel has three choices. His first choice is to publish the book without categorizing it, in a package that truly reflects the subtleties of what the book is really about; in which case the sales department will complain that its appeal is impossible to evaluate, and the editor's own associates may give him a hard time in that week's editorial conference. His second choice is to put the book under one of the existing category labels, and package it like all the others in that category, even though this is not really appropriate. His third choice is to reject the book on the grounds that it has no defined audience or market, does not conform to the parameters of what is generally being published, and therefore will probably not sell. (Interestingly, according to this argument, a book like Jonathan Livingston Seagull should not have sold 7 million copies; it should have been a disaster.)

George Ernsberger, the editor who bought *The Devil Is Dead,* chose the second choice of the three I have listed above. The first edition of Lafferty's novel is clearly labelled "Avon science fiction original" and was distributed to the science fiction racks in bookstores and newsstands.[3]

On the other hand, in keeping with the real nature of the book, it was "tastefully packaged"—which is to say, it did not have a garish cover showing pictures of monsters or spaceships or naked women. It had a gentle, whimsical, artistic cover; this was a nod in the direction of choice number one.

The marketing strategy was well-intentioned but unsuccessful. Probably the diehard science fiction fans who saw the book found that its cover art and back-cover blurb did not fit their preconceptions about what science fiction should look like. It was unfamiliar. It did not feel right. Conversely, the buyers of "general fiction" who might have wanted to read the book, had they known it existed, never saw it, because its tasteful cover was buried among all that garish, juvenile science fiction at the back of the store.

So this enchanting, amusing, eloquent, original, clever novel never reached its potential audience and was allowed to go out of print,[4] because publishing is a business of categories, and also because readers have come to think in those categories just as much as the publishers themselves (though the thinking may not be on such a conscious level).

Authors, too, are now motivated to think and work in category terms; and this is surely the most depressing aspect of all. For every author who sits down and thinks, "What do I want to write?" there must now be at least 20 who sit down and think, "What can I sell?" Correspondence courses that teach people how to write have a term for this kind of thinking. It is called market study. It means that you write to suit the categories and preconceptions of the media, rather than to express your own individuality.

It is because *The Devil Is Dead* is such an exception to this pattern—such an individual, idiosyncratic book—that I am so pleased to see it made part of the Gregg Press series, where it will achieve far more permanence than in any paperback edition. And for the same reasons, I feel especially pleased to write this introduction, emphasizing what a rarity it is. R. A. Lafferty is that one writer in 20 who does not seem to have heard of market study, and seems never to think "What can I sell?" when he begins work. (If he did think it, he might have fewer than nine completed-but-unsold novels looking for publication.)

Lafferty himself comments: "I don't compromise very much on what I write. That's partly because of stubbornness and partly due to principle, and partly to circumstances. I didn't begin to write till I was forty-five years old, and I never depended on writing for a living. That does make a difference. One or two of my unsold novels might have been sold if I had compromised a little bit, but for most of them it's just that they are a bunch of misfits that do not fit into any category...."[5]

As for the editors who work within the science-fiction category, Lafferty remarks, "Science fiction editors are as uncom-

Introduction xi

prehending of anything outside the field as are mainline editors of science fiction." And his own regard for the bulk of science fiction is quite critical. He feels there are periods in science fiction when "almost all the stories that are published are rotten, but there are a few good ones to be found"; and other periods when "all the stories are rotten and there are not *any* good ones to be found." As of 1975, in his view, "We are presently in a Type 2 period."

He is no less critical of his own work. For example, he believes that his story "Eurema's Dam," which won the Hugo Award, was not necessarily worthy of it. He felt "considerable exasperation at the two worst short stories [on the ballot] . . . tying for the award, and one of them being mine. This isn't a put-on. I had come in second the year before with the best short story in the group. . . . And in the fateful year [when he did win the award] I had at least five short stories published that were much better than 'Eurema's Dam.' "

If these statements and anecdotes add up to an image of R. A. Lafferty as a science fiction writer who is an individualist and a little alienated from his contemporaries, the image could be accurate. He certainly seems as unbothered by appearing a "misfit" as he seems unbothered by his unsold novels being "a bunch of misfits." In fact, in his work, he seems to delight in playing up the idiosyncracies and evasiveness that make his writing hard to classify and difficult for some readers to accept. By "evasiveness" I mean his tendency not to play entirely fairly with the reader; it is always hard to tell what to believe and what not to believe in Lafferty's work. In his "promantia" in *The Devil Is Dead,* he promises the specific location of the "Terrestrial Paradise" . . . and delivers on his promise, but in such a way as to disappoint rather than reveal. He pretends willingness to expose his influences and sources, in italicized quotations at the head of each chapter; but it turns out that many of the quotations are credited to names of characters whom Lafferty has created himself, in his other novels. ("After all," he says, "if you have characters who are more erudite than yourself, you might as well cite them. Several of the quotations are genuine: Asimov, Aquinas, Numbers, Genesis. Most of them are made up.")[6] Even the title of the book, and the "name on the tombstone where the Devil is buried," are come-ons in a sense, ultimately deflating the reader's initial expectations.

In a way the whole art of telling tall stories entails maintaining a distance between the reader and the narrator. The tall-tale teller must keep the truth about himself as mysterious as the pseudo-truth of his tales; the audience must be tempted with apparent facts (which can never quite be proven or disproven) and encouraged with apparent sincerity, while the narrator keeps himself and the real truth of the matter just out of reach. In this way, the reader is tantalized, just as the audience at a magic show is tantalized by not knowing exactly where the sleight of hand is employed. But, after all, it can be enjoyable to be tantalized (and magic tricks are never much fun when you know how they're done). That is the whole appeal of the game.

Appropriately enough, this book that is something of a misfit, written by a man who projects an image of being something of a misfit himself, is a story *about* misfits. Some of them are good-natured misfits; some of them are evil ones who like to infect other people with their evilness, causing riots, insurrection, and mayhem as a result. At one point the character named X explains: "The whole clique is a catastrophe looking for a world to happen to." Another character, Don Lewis, suggests elsewhere in the novel that the evil-doers are motivated out of jealousy toward the rest of humanity, who are not evil (but who *are* wholly human).

This touches on that most familiar science fiction theme, alienation—a condition where loneliness and withdrawal are balanced by cameraderie with others who are alienated, and a notion that the alienated minority could really be *superior* to the rest of the world. The evildoers and the "halfbloods" in Lafferty's story, mixed up together on their global cruise, are all social rejects with ambivalent feelings toward the world at large. They have a divine discontent that leads them to forsake even the island of paradise, after a while. They feel most at home, it seems, in the social microcosm of a bar room, in the exclusive company of bottles of booze and the occasional friendly barmaid.

The Devil Is Dead tempts much more analysis—in mythic rather than psychological terms—but the temptation is dangerous, because any would-be literary analyst, confronted with such a mess of tall tales, cannot hope to be sure where the author has involved his own psyche, where he has drawn from outside sources, where he has played a game, and where he has exposed his true feelings about how the world works. There are tricks and traps, from the false quotations to the tantalizing little poem at the end of the book, with its last line hinting at a kind of circularity. What is to be taken seriously? What is to be believed?

My own feeling is that it is not really important whether (for instance) the voyage of Saxon X. Seaworthy is really symbolically equivalent to the Voyage of Sindbad. Nor does it matter whether this book is really trying to be profound about questions of reality and identity (but perhaps a frighteningly analytical graduate thesis could be written comparing Lafferty's thoughts on the subject to Carlos Castaneda's dialogues on the same topic; the mind boggles). I think it would be equally irrelevant to start a discursive study of the obsession with death in Lafferty's story (in which many of the anecdotes and premonitions are concerned with dying, and more than half of the characters do die, in more ways than one). Nor do I have the initiative to begin a point-by-point comparison of Lafferty's deceptively simple prose style, false trails in the plot, and sense of humor, to similar traits in the earlier work of Kurt Vonnegut Jr. (such as *The Sirens of Titan,* 1959). And I would certainly refuse to start asking nasty questions about the role of women in *The Devil Is Dead* (they are accessories to the men, every one of them; loveable but no more highly motivated than barmaids—two of them *are* barmaids). The feminist reader might note that these adorable creatures are strangely attracted to our hero, Finnegan, a derelict type with an unprepossessing physical appearance who hangs around getting drunk and sleeping on the beach. The feminist might ask what this tells us about the state of Mr. Lafferty's consciousness.

But I think such questions are best left unasked, and definitely unanswered (I mention them at all only to fulfill the expectations of those who like taking or teaching college literature courses in science fiction). *The Devil Is Dead* really isn't suited to that kind of literary analysis. Some of its source material is surely drawn from identifiable myths and legends, and some of its concerns go well beyond simple entertainment. But its essence is in its mood, its characters, its outlook on life, and its language, and all of this is laid out plainly and accessibly enough to be appreciated by anyone, without need for a guidebook. The playful mood has already been described here. As for the characters, they are whimsical, moved by an intuitive sense of "rightness" that transcends rationality, just as a fairytale scoffs at the pedestrian habits of logic and boring real-world necessities. The outlook on life displayed in this book shows equanimity and a simple enjoyment of what is there, outweighing the spirit of alienation and discontent referred to previously. Lastly, the language of the book is immensely refreshing (especially compared to the usual "fantasy novel" written in pseudo-British idiom with no trace of sensitivity to the real magic of words). Lafferty's vocabulary and semantics are just as full of jokes and entertainments as his anecdotes, reflecting the author's fascination with patterns of languages both English and foreign.

Of his stories, Lafferty has said, ". . . almost all of them are indirect results of dreams. The unconscious . . . is a soil out of which all actions and ideas grow."

In that spirit of myth and mystery, this book was written. In that spirit it should be enjoyed.

Charles Platt
New York

REFERENCES

1. All quotes by R. A. Lafferty in this Introduction are taken from an interview with Lafferty in a small-press magazine, *The Hunting of the Snark* No. 10 (1976), edited and published by Robert J. R. Whitaker—except where otherwise noted.

2. *Billion Year Spree: The True History of Science Fiction,* paperback edition (New York: Schocken Books, 1974), p. 209.

3. *Editor's Note:* Shortly after the publication of *The Devil Is Dead,* Charles Platt succeeded George Ernsberger as SF category editor at Avon Books.

4. It was nominated for the Nebula Award of the Science Fiction Writers of America as Best Novel, but lost on the final ballot to Robert Silverberg's *A Time of Changes.*

5. Quoted from personal correspondence written by Mr. Lafferty to the author of this Introduction.

6. Quoted from personal correspondence with Mr. Lafferty.

Introduction

Here is Lafferty:

"Here is the devil himself with his several faces. Here is an ogress, and a mermaid, both of them passing as ordinary women to the sightless. Here is a body which you yourself may bury in the sand. Here is the mark of the false octopus that has either seven tentacles, or nine. Here is the shock when the very dead man that you helped bury continues on his way as a very live man; and he looks at you as though he knows something you do not. ...

Here are those of a different flesh: and may you yourself not be of that different flesh?"

r.a.lafferty
the devil is dead

AVON
PUBLISHERS OF
DISCUS • CAMELOT • BARD

This is the first publication of
THE DEVIL IS DEAD in any form.

AVON BOOKS
A division of
The Hearst Corporation
959 Eighth Avenue
New York, New York 10019

Copyright © 1971 by R. A. Lafferty.
Published by arrangement with the author.

All rights reserved, which includes the right
to reproduce this book or portions thereof in
any form whatsoever. For information address
Virginia Kidd, Literary Agent, Box 278,
Milford, Penna. 18337.

First Avon Printing, May, 1971

AVON TRADEMARK REG. U.S. PAT. OFF. AND
FOREIGN COUNTRIES, REGISTERED TRADEMARK—
MARCA REGISTRADA, HECHO EN CHICAGO, U.S.A.

Printed in the U.S.A.

Promantia   9

Chapter	1	Seaworthy and the Devil	11
Chapter	2	Mermaid and Ogress	24
Chapter	3	The Furtive Man	37
Chapter	4	The Wives of Sindbad	45
Chapter	5	The Unaccountable Corpse	55
Chapter	6	Luluway is the Plural of Diamond	65
Chapter	7	Habib, I Have Found Something	78
Chapter	8	Anastasia Demetriades	93
Chapter	9	Diana Artemis	102
Chapter	10	Down With the Dead Men	111
Chapter	11	Thirty-Six Thousand Pieces of Paper	123
Chapter	12	Crest and Shatter	135
Chapter	13	Biloxi Brannagan	150
Chapter	14	Company of Fifty	162
Chapter	15	Basse-Terre	174
Chapter	16	Liars' Paradise	183
Chapter	17	Angela Cosquin	197
Chapter	18	Fin in the Graveyard	206
Chapter	19	The Devil Is Dead	215

the devil is dead

PROMANTIA

And they also tell the story
of Papadiabolous the Devil and his company, and of two of the hidden lives of Finnegan; and how it is not always serious to die, the first time it happens.

Here is one man who was buried twice and now lies still (but uneasy of mind) in his two separate graves. Here is another man who died twice—not at all the same thing. And here are several who are disinclined to stay dead: they don't like it, they won't accept it.

Given here, for the first time anywhere, are the bearings and correct location of the Terrestrial Paradise down to the last second of longitude. You may follow them. You may go there.

Here also will be found the full account of where the Devil himself is buried, and the surprising name that is on his tombstone boldly spelled out. And much else.

We will not lie to you. This is a do-it-yourself thriller or nightmare. Its present order is only the way it comes in the box. Arrange it as you will.

Set off the devils and the monsters, the wonderful beauties and the foul murderers, the ships and the oceans of middle space, the corpses and the revenants, set them off in whatever apposition you wish. Glance quickly to discover whether you have not the mark on your own left wrist, barely under the skin. Build with these colored blocks your own dramas of love and death and degradation. Learn the true topography: the monstrous and wonderful archetypes are not inside you, not in your own unconsciousness; you are inside them, trapped, and howling to get out.

Build things with this as with an old structo set. Here is the Devil Himself with his several faces. Here is an ogress, and a mermaid, both of them passing as ordinary women to the sightless. Here is a body which you yourself may bury in the sand. Here is the mark of the false octopus that has either seven or nine tentacles. Here is the shock when the very dead man that you helped bury continues on his way as a very live man, and looks at you as though he knows something that you do not. Here is a suitcase with 36,000 pieces of very special paper in it. Here is Mr. X, and a left-footed killer who follows and follows. Here are those of a different flesh; and may you yourself not be of that different flesh?

Put the nightmare together. If you do not wake up screaming, you have not put it together well.

Old Burton urged his subscribers to keep their copies of the Nights under lock and key. There are such precipices here! Take it in full health and do not look down as you go. If you look down you will fall and be lost forever.

Is that not an odd introduction? I don't understand it at all.

Chapter One

SEAWORTHY AND THE DEVIL

In fact, give a Neanderthal man a shave and a haircut, dress him in well-fitted clothes, and he could probably walk down New York's Fifth Avenue without getting much notice.

—ASIMOV

1.

Finnegan met the eccentric millionaire early one morning. At least he said that he was a millionaire and eccentric. Finnegan told him that he was dull.

"You only believe me dull because you don't know me well," the millionaire said. "I am one of the true eccentrics. Stick with me and you will see that I am."

Finnegan doubted also that the man was a millionaire. He was unshaven and shabby, and he had the shakes. A millionaire will sometimes have one or two of these disabilities, but seldom all three.

The conversation may have begun when Finnegan asked what town they were in.

"The license plates are mostly Texas," said the man. "That is, you can see only one license plate from here, but it's mostly Texas."

They were sitting on the sidewalk in front of a bar waiting for it to open. They were across the boulevard from the graveyard. The millionaire had a scar or tattoo on the inside of his left wrist, and Finnegan looked at it.

"You have the same mark," said the man. "I wouldn't have trusted you otherwise."

"No. I haven't that mark," Finnegan objected.

"It is still below the skin, but I can see it," the millionaire said. "Say, it's chilly for Texas. I wonder what month this is."

"I would guess either spring or fall," Finnegan hazarded. "Probably fall. I remember a summer not long ago. But I am usually in the North when fall hits. Then I have to migrate, often at great pain. You really are a millionaire?"

"Oh yes. As soon as the bar opens we can have a drink. Then we will be well enough to look for other bars and have other drinks. After that we can make plans. By that time I should remember my own name, and you may remember yours. Possibly we will be well enough to look for a bank, and as the day goes along they will be open. When I am in funds I will buy you a pair of shoes."

"If you don't know what town this is, how do you know that you have money in the bank?" Finnegan asked him.

"I am known," the man said. "I even begin to know myself again now."

"Which of us was sitting on the sidewalk first?" Finnegan asked him. "Or which came first, the sidewalk or the people?"

"I don't know. I don't remember how I got here. We were already here and in conversation when I became aware. Your shoes are very bad and your feet have been bleeding. I have compassion on you."

"You are in near as bad a shape," said Finnegan.

"It is different with me. I have always the means of succor. It is just that I am preoccupied when I forget to get a place to sleep, or when I do not eat, or change clothes. When I have been guilty of such a shattering drunkenness as this, I usually have something heavy on my mind. Is the clay and loam of this place not peculiar? It is mixed with sand and old oyster shells. We are both caked with it, you know. We should brush off a little."

Finnegan looked deeply into the man's face, as he had not done before. It was dull, but there was a bottomless depth to that dullness and Finnegan knew that a deeper word would be needed to describe it. It was a lined face made out of old granite. The millionaire was a much older man than Finnegan.

"My cognomen is Finnegan," Finnegan said finally. "I do not yet remember my proper name, but it will not matter; I use it seldom. This amnesia is not new to me. I often have it when I move from one life to another. I have an upper and a lower life, you know."

"Who hasn't! All of our sort indulge in amnesia, of course. With you it is almost as though you do not know what you are. All of us changelings arrive at the understanding late. Finnegan, this is a seaport, it has the atmosphere of one. That being the case, I have some sort of ship here. We will fit it, if it needs fitting, and we will take a trip around the world immediately. I have often found that this clears the head. Will this not prove that I am an eccentric?"

"No. It will prove only that you remember what you were about. Do you remember your name yet, millionaire, or where we are?"

"Saxon X. Seaworthy is my name. I was pretty sure it would be. Yes, I remember everything now, and there is one thing that I forget again quickly."

Well, Finnegan didn't. He didn't remember the pre-dawn adventure, the fearful thing he had been engaged in with Seaworthy before they came to themselves sitting on the sidewalk. The forgetfulness of this event antedated itself considerably; Finnegan realized that there was a gap of several months in his memory before that climax which he could still savor but not remember. 'All of our sort indulge in amnesia,' Seaworthy had said. 'It is an indulgence I had better give up,' Finnegan told himself. But he didn't really want to remember the recent adventure: it had too garish and unnatural a savor.

The barroom opened. Saxon and Finnegan went in and drank beer, Texas beer only, nothing else was cold. And Saxon was angry.

"There should be a punishment to fit the crime," he said. "We did but ask a drink in the name of Christ and you gave us this. It were better in that hour, it were better in that hour—"

"What were better in that hour, little granite face?" the bargirl asked.

"For less than this they did penance in Ninevah. God will punish you for this, young lady."

"Bet He don't. Some of the places handle beer from the states, but I don't know why they bother. Drink it, Mr. Seaworthy. We will calk you up with it and see if you will float. Bet you don't. What have you two been doing to get so bloody and dirty?"

"We don't remember," said Finnegan. "Really, we don't

remember." He wanted to ask the girl how she knew Seaworthy's name and how well she knew both of them.

An hour went by. The club opened, so they went into the club.

Saxon Seaworthy cashed a check. 'Knew he could,' thought Finnegan. He gave Finnegan five twenties, and a little reality trickled into the Finnegan head. There are men who will hand out money to a stranger without reason, but there are not millionaires who will do it. Finnegan was being paid, but he did not know whether for past or future service.

The bargirl ran a wet cloth over the Finnegan face. Then she rinsed it out and did it again. Well, it got some of the blood and the sandy clay off, but that was all. It was a grotesque face and washing could help it only a little. Most of what was on it would not come off.

"Does all this service come with the drink?" Finnegan asked her.

"Yes, Finn the gin, all for free. You are one sorry looking tramp." She led him to a stool behind the bar. She plugged in an electric shaver and went to work on him. "We don't mind tramps here," she said, "It's just that we like clean tramps. Oh, we love clean tramps."

Reality? This was not reality that was trickling back in. Reality was too pale a word for this girl. She was flesh and ichor, but she was also transparent, translucent, transcendent. A conjurer's trick, but not a cheap conjurer's trick.

"Are you always here, or do you sometimes go away?" Finnegan asked.

"Not till the other girl comes."

That wasn't what he meant. He knew that she was real, that she belonged to one of the only two peoples who have ever been civilized, and she wasn't French. But she was something else at the same time. She was a chameleon, and she changed every time he looked at her.

"Where did you meet Mr. Seaworthy?" asked the girl, if she were a girl. Finnegan remembered hearing of another sort of creature that sometimes took that form.

"I don't know how we met, girl. We were sitting on the sidewalk talking together when the sun came up. That may have been the beginning of the world, but I can't prove it. Something like it happened to me on a night several years ago. I talked all night with another man then. It was all strong talk with the horns and hooves still on it. This was up in the north woods and he was a young hobo. He seemed to change in voice and manner as the night went on. We had an open fire there, but the light from it was tricky. But when it was morning, the sun showed that he was a different man entirely from what he had been the night before. He was about forty years older."

"Don't stop there, Finn. What did you do?"

"I got away from there fast, girl, and left him mumbling to himself. Then a curtain came down over it and I forgot all the tall things that we had talked about during the night. But I had not gone a hundred yards from him when I heard a terrible wailing. He had discovered, looking into a pool there, that he had become an old man overnight. It rended my heart to hear that wailing."

"I know that it did, Finn, but what happened last night? I have reason for asking."

"I do not remember last night. I do not remember anything for several months, now that I see the date and month on that arty piece on the wall. But this morning I was with Seaworthy. When I came to myself I was already talking and in the middle of a sentence. If I could know the first part of my sentence it might clear things. I don't know how long we were sitting on the sidewalk. Was Saxon Seaworthy a young man before we had our congress, of whatever sort, last night?"

"No, Finn. He didn't age forty years in the night. He was the same. Oh, Finn, Finn! Look! He's just aged forty years in three seconds now! What is it? He's shaking to pieces."

"So am I," Finnegan shook. Finnegan did not have to look at what presence had just come into the club. He felt the fear of it melting his bones. 'He can't be alive,' Finnegan moaned to himself, 'he has no business being alive.' He didn't remember the thing, but only the aura of the thing. He looked at the now ashen and very old granite face of Saxon Seaworthy, and at the shaking of the millionaire's hands and lips.

But Seaworthy pulled himself together quickly, regained his hard granite color, threw off his deadly old age, and quelled his quaking. He nodded shortly to the presence that Finnegan would not look at. And he was the mysterious and controlled Saxon Seaworthy again.

"Are you drinking, Papa-D?" the bargirl asked the presence somewhat nervously.

"No. I looked in only for a moment," sounded the almost-human voice. "Ah, that all be well even as I am well!"

There was something about the opening and closing of a door. And the presence was no longer present.

"Is he a phoney?" Finnegan asked after a very long pause.

"Papa-D?" the girl asked.

"I don't know any Papa-D," said Finnegan. "It is here that amnesia has its advantages. I mean Seaworthy."

"I suppose he is. How do you mean?"

"Is he a millionaire?"

"He spends like one. Which is to say that he seems to spend a great deal, and doesn't. He carries weight, whatever that means. I guess he is one."

"Does he have a boat in every port?"

"I don't think so. But he has a ship in this one."

"Will it go around the world?"

"It has. They say that he is going again."

"He says that he will take me with him."

"If he says that he will, then he will, Finnegan. I'm going to try to get on too. He will need a barmaid. He had a young Negro boy for bartender when he came to town, but he's disappeared off somewhere. Nobody knows what's happened to him. Will you put in a word to Mr. Seaworthy for me?"

"You must know him much better than I do, girl. I've known him only for an hour and a half."

"It had to be quite a few hours longer than that, Finnegan. And it won't hurt to give me a boost. Just remark what a remarkable little girl I am."

"Yes, you washed me when I was filthy and anointed my wounds with gin and bitters. What is your name?"

"You know it. Anastasia Demetriades. You've been here before. Which will it be, amnesia or me?"

"Oh. Yes. I did know your name. Anastasia, what more apt! I was dead and you gave me life. You brought back my respectability with an electric shaver. Anastasia, the resurrection!"

Finnegan got an odd look at Seaworthy the millionaire. He hadn't, for all his looking, seen him this way before. He had the mark on him, and 'twas not simply the mark on the wrist. A long time before he had met Seaworthy, it had come to Finnegan what the mark consisted of. Finnegan was clairvoyant. Since he had understooood it, he had seen the mark that is not actually a mark on many others, sometimes on a man in a crowd, sometimes on a man alone. But he had never before seen it on a man he was committed to. Seaworthy had that mark.

'He has killed a man, or men,' Finnegan said to himself. 'And he told me that I have the same mark, but what he meant was only part of it. Have I killed a man or men also?'

But Anastasia was talking:

"There is one reason I want to go on the voyage," she was saying. "We will surely go to the Old Country. How go around the world without it? One cannot go around the world and miss the place where the world began. I have never been back, and I was small when I left. There's been trouble there. We aren't sure who of the family is still alive. We aren't a family who writes to each other. It's all a long way behind me, but my mother nearly dies thinking of it.

"There is another reason I must go on the voyage, and you will not understand it unless you have the same reason, Finnegan."

Saxon Seaworthy came over to them.

"I am sorry," he said, "but there is some business that I must take care of, business that I thought was already taken care of. I have seen a man that I had not expected to see. So there will be business that might take me several days. But soon, very soon, we will go on the voyage."

He gave Finnegan another hundred dollars, and he left.

'He buys me and he buys me,' Finnegan thought. And he had another thought. 'I believe that he *does* know where his Negro boy disappeared, and where others have gone. But there is one thing he doesn't know, one man who didn't stay disappeared.'

Finnegan went and got a room while it was still morning. He had a bath. Then he went out and bought a satchel and a few clothes to go in it, and shoes. He had a good meal at a seafood place. He went to a man who had loaned him money on his seaman's papers, and paid the money, and got them back. The name on them was John A. Solli. 'Knew it would be,' said Finnegan. 'Solli I was born, but I'm Finnegan for all that.'

He remembered almost everything now, his upper life with its certain occupations and sets of friends, his lower life with other sets. He remembered the strange division in himself that was not new. But he did not remember anything about the last several months, and he sure did not remember what had happened last night. He went to his room to sleep.

And when he woke he was excited. It wasn't really the smell of Seaworthy's green money that had come to haunt him pleasantly. It was the heady smell of adventure, the high salt aroma of far travel and the iodine tang of menace. He knew already that Seaworthy had a sinister aspect, and that it would not be a bloodless adventure.

The world was Finnegan's coconut and he would have it open. He hadn't lost any of his urge to go everywhere and be embroiled in everything. He was like the old Norse hero who cried out for still more towering oceans where one must always sail uphill. He'd crack the world, he'd have that big fish by the tail!

2.

> "Finnegan said that, Dotty? Did he really? I wonder why he said a thing like that? . . . I never really knew him, Dot. He is my brother and only a year younger, and he was with me more than anyone else. I sort of raised him, but we were always strangers. It's as though he was a changeling."
> —ARCHIPELAGO, Chapter Seven.

The next time they met, Saxon Seaworthy was sober and he passed Finnegan by without seeming to recognize him. This was a disappointment but not a mortal one. Finnegan could open the golden coconut without Seaworthy. He had been busy doing it for several years before he met the man, and his adventures had been more wondrous than any lies that could be told about them. He had felt the tide rising in him, and he could ship out on almost any ship he wished.

Finnegan was working while he waited. He cleaned out bars in the mornings. He had five bars that he opened, with staggered hours, that took him from seven in the morning till noon. At each place he worked about half an hour. Then he would drink a beer and rest till he went to open the next place. He washed dishes from twelve till two and from six till eight, sometimes at the Crystal Palace, sometimes at the Sea Breeze, or at Pier Eleven. He had a dollar for each shift and a dollar for each bar. He snoozed on the beach every afternoon, and he drank in the evenings. He had two meals where he washed dishes, and his room rent was paid ahead; though often he did not use his room. Finnegan seldom slept in beds.

For the rest, he had never let himself go completely broke, and he had not been broke when he met Seaworthy. He had had Miguel; the life of Miguel had been saved by the advent of Seaworthy.

Miguel was a hundred dollar bill. Whenever Finnegan was down to that he knew that he would have to go to work. There had been other bills to bottom his adventures. Before Miguel there had been Jose-Ramires, there had been Hernandez, there had been Aloysius, there had been Gottfried von Guggenheim, a baron. There had been one bill that was never baptized and that had lived for less than thirty-six hours. That bill is now in limbo and Finnegan often thought of its short life with sorrow.

Finnegan was not thrifty, but he understood the economic law of the cushion and the absolute minimum.

There were other intoxicants for Finnegan. He was alive and winning, though he was not sure in what currency. That was the week when all the people were interesting and all the jokes were funny. He won eight hundred dollars dicing at the Little Oyster, and he had a girl straight out of the Arabian Nights. Finnegan had had these intervals before, returning to the world as a complete stranger, believing himself an alien (no matter what his various papers showed him of his past), finding no one he recognized in the world at all. But this time he recognized Anastasia Demetriades. He had known her before he knew her, she was more kin to him than his kindred. He didn't know a thing about her. Well, he didn't know a thing about himself.

They were together a lot that week. They exulted in the town and the beach. She was wry and friendly, often pretty, and sometimes a sort of burlesque of the pretty, for she still changed. She was so wiry that Finnegan could hardly wrestle her down when they clowned on the beach; yet she was very small. A fortune card-weighing machine on the beach showed her at a hundred and thirty pounds, though Finnegan would have guessed her at ninety. He could feel the bones in her, and it was like an electric shock. There is nothing wrong with having bones the way she had them. There is nothing wrong with having a touch of sea-green in the olive and gold complexion, or the paradoxical soft-hardness and cooling-fever that Anastasia always maintained.

When she spoke she set up harmonics as though she were in tune with every shell of the ocean. She spoke now, but as always her first half dozen words tumbled into Finnegan's mind before the sound began.

"The beach isn't quite the same, but the sea is the sea," she said. "I was ten years old when I came to this country. I was born on an island; there is a hill in the center of it, and from there you can see twenty islands and two parts of the main-land. We will go there, I am sure; Seaworthy will not be able to pass it by; besides, I believe that he has mysterious business there."

"The voyage? There will still be a voyage, Anastasia?"

"Yes. And we both will go. Marie showed me both of our names on the ship's papers. You will have to give her more information on yourself, though."

"But Seaworthy didn't recognize me yesterday."

"I know it. When he meets people drunk, he doesn't recognize them again when he's sober. But he remembered your name (if that *is* your name), and that I knew you."

"He does have a boat, and it is going?"

"She is the Brunhilde. I used to have an aunt who looked just like that ship. We'll go see her now if you want to, Finn. The ship I mean. The aunt is dead."

They took a cab across to the bay side with a cabby named Joe Sorrell. The Brunhilde (you knew her already though you had never seen her before) was a rakish queen, a water-going woman, a real old crow of a ship. Long ago she had been the steam yacht of a famous millionaire. Now she was the diesel-snuffling pride of an infamous one.

She was a girl. She had been there and back. If she accepted you, and she accepted Finnegan immediately, she was the friendliest ship in the world. True, she consorted with killers and cutthroats; but she had not to account to anyone for her cronies. There were five crewmen aboard, and Finnegan already knew several of them from fooling around the town. He knew Joe Cross; but the Brunhilde was not the ship that Joe had said he was with, and Joe was an open sort of fellow. And Finnegan knew Don Lewis. Don had several times tried to tell Finnegan something, and always had thought better of it.

Anastasia opened the bar. Well, she was bargirl for the ship. Finnegan and Sorrell and Cross and Lewis went in with her. Two other crewmen stood outside and refused to join them. And a fifth one went away to inform on them.

This fifth crewman was Art Emery, and there was enmity between Emery and Finnegan. "It's pretty, but is it art?" Finnegan had asked someone only the day before as the crewman came into one of the places. Finnegan had already heard the first name. And Art Emery had given Finnegan a look of hatred, and had meant it. And the crewman *was* pretty in an unpleasant sort of way.

The bar was small, six foot long, with four stools; and most of the remaining room was taken up by three huge easy chairs. Anastasia opened the liquor cabinets and fixed their drinks for them. And they spent a quality half hour there.

Then it became very chilly; but it was not with cold that Finnegan was shaking. This was the presence that had affrighted him in the club on the morning when Finnegan had last returned to this world. This was the thing that should not be alive, the thing that aged Saxon Seaworthy forty years in three seconds by a mere glimpse, and turned the granite face ashen.

It was the Devil who came into the ship's bar and put a stop to their quality half hour.

"One drink is enough," said the Devil. "Close the bar, Anastasia. Everybody get back to work."

"Who says so?" That was Finnegan, tempting fate. The

Devil looked at Finn as though he were an idiot. It's a red-eyed trick of his.

"An inane question," said the Devil with some scorn. "I said so. You just heard me. And we don't need you on the ship now, Finnegan. If you do go along, you will come aboard the night we leave, not before."

"Did Mr. Seaworthy put you in charge?" Anastasia asked the Devil.

"Never mind. I *am* in charge. I don't want to have to remind anyone of it. Now get off the ship, Anastasia, and take Finnegan with his bugle nose, and the curious cabby with you."

"I was told to check the bar and the stock and see that everything was in order before we left," Anastasia explained.

"You have checked the bar and sampled the stock, and everything will be in order as soon as you three leave."

They debarked, they debouched, they got back into Joe Sorrell's cab and fled from dockside.

"Who is he anyhow?" Finnegan asked. He knew, and yet he didn't.

"Why, he's the Devil," said Anastasia. "I thought you'd know that, Finnegan."

"Well, I did in a way. I had heard of the Devil, of course, and he is much as I pictured him. But I didn't know that he was in town in his proper person."

(There are those who have seen him and not known him. Yet he is distinctive, and they should have known. He is large and well—but very heavily—made. He has a high purplish complexion and wears expensive purple shirts. He is all but bald; yet there is a reddish fringe around that purple pate. Nor is he really unhandsome; but one would not be inclined to argue with him unless just for the hell of it.)

"He is Mr. Papadiabolous, and we call him Papa Devil," Anastasia explained. "That's really what his name means. He is a devil really, and he may be the boss even above Mr. Seaworthy."

"I thought that Seaworthy was a millionaire."

"One of them is, Finnegan. And they use the same set of pockets."

"If they are associates, why was Seaworthy so startled

when Papa Devil came into the club the other morning?"

"I don't know, Finnegan. They were in there together the evening before, and Papa D said that he would look in on Mr. Seaworthy there the next morning."

"Well, why was *I* so startled when Papa Devil came into the club?"

"I don't know, Finnegan. I don't know why."

"If the Devil is going, then I might not want to go, Anastasia."

"Of course you want to go, Finnegan. What bugle-nosed, salt-blooded young man would miss the opportunity of sailing with the Devil himself?"

"No, no, of course I won't miss the chance. I don't know what I was thinking of."

"I always love to have somebody to hate," Anastasia said. "But Papa Devil may not be so bad nowadays. I'd known them when they were in port once before. He was a real heller then. But this past week, when I talk to him, Papa Devil seems much nicer than he used to be. He used to be kind of mean."

"I like him better when he's all devil," Finnegan insisted. "Do not destroy my impression of the only completely evil man I ever knew. The only except—just possibly one."

It came to Finnegan that Papa Devil might not be as evil a man as his friend Seaworthy. And it came to him that he might have some connection with them both; that he might under certain conditions defend them both; that the two of them seemed like shady uncles of his.

Chapter Two

MERMAID AND OGRESS

We suffer from the disease of abstraction and generalization, and it blinds us to facts. The fact is that persons themselves overlap, as do species. There are degrees of the human and the inhuman, and there are individuals between. There are diverse bloods that stand separate for centuries, and then mingle. There is also a mingling of the ghostly and the flesh. We are many of us possessed by devils, and they cannot be exorcised without our deaths. The children of Ahriman come back onto us like monsters from the beginning, or fearful mutations.

—ARPAD ARUTINOV, *The Back-Door of History*

1.

The Brunhilde sailed on November 7, a Friday morning. The year is uncertain, but it was quite a while ago. Finnegan did not keep accurate account of years, nor did he remember the sailing or getting on the boat.

Finnegan had a premonition that someone had decided to kill him that night. The premonition was a true one. Cannily, Finnegan hid in a bottle, and after a few hours of it he disappeared to himself. He had not been on the stuff seriously since that night one week before when he had become entangled with Saxon Seaworthy. He went on it now, but quietly; he went underground.

At midnight the order had gone out from Mr. Seaworthy that they were to sail at dawn. Anastasia could not find Finnegan. She had left him and gone to work at midnight at the club. Then the call had come, and she had sought Finn at once. He was not in his room. He was not with any of his cronies, but they said that he was on the stuff heavily. He might be in any alley in town.

One hour before sailing time everybody was on board except Finnegan. Seaworthy told Papa Devil to go get him. And he told Anastasia to get his things.

"What if I put his gear on board and he doesn't show up?" Anastasia asked. "He might need his things."

"Papa Devil will bring Finnegan. You bring his things."

In half an hour Anastasia came with a sea bag, a satchel, and a big suitcase, about a hundred and fifty pounds of Finnegan's things. Finn had picked up quite a bit of stuff that week. Anastasia carried them easily, and came on board whistling *anamoné*.

And ten minutes later, Papa Devil came out of another direction of darkness carrying Finnegan over his shoulder. He dumped the Finn heavily on deck, and Anastasia put an old tarpaulin under his head.

Well, Finnegan had made it after all. And he wasn't supposed to. What had gone right?

When the tide is rising in a man you can't keep him down; by his very nature he will come to the top. They were under weigh; they were out in the channel. The ship lurched, and the wheel of fortune took an unaccountable turn. Finnegan was on the top again and some of them were on the bottom.

Almost immediately after they had turned the corner, out of the harbor and around the shoulder of the island, it became very rough. There is sometimes an early morning choppiness there and it is vicious. Some of them were not sailors, and the sailors among them were no better. There was sickness and retching and sudden gloom.

But Finnegan woke to the rhythm of the ship and felt wonderful. The sky was scarlet and the ocean steep and black, and everything was all right. All those not on duty had gone below, and Finnegan went below to resurrect Anastasia.

"Wake up! Wake up!" She wasn't asleep, but he landed on her stomach to be sure she was awake. "Let's open the bar, Anastasia. Let's celebrate. Lord, it's great to have the water under your feet. All is not lost. As long as that old monster can pitch, all's right with the world."

"I'm sick," Anastasia moaned, "and your sitting on my stomach doesn't help. How can you feel so good when you were carried on here only a couple hours ago?"

"Clean living and natural resiliency is the answer,

Anastasia. Let's go topside. It's like being born again to go to sea. Better be sick than be on shore. Seasickness becomes you. I never realized you were so beautiful, but with your new green complexion you are enchanting."

"Off, off, oaf! Oof!" She flung him off and they went out and up a ladder. She hadn't really been so sick. She had seen the rest of them carrying on with it so she did it too.

She opened the bar. They drank sea-green magic of a French name and an ancient flavor while the old witch the Brunhilde pitched and tossed. Then the ship subsided. It hadn't really been as rough as all that either. The ship had just been having fun.

Finnegan mixed a drink and took it to Saxon Seaworthy. It was a subservient thing to do, but Finnegan was a deep enough man to allow a little subservience. He would have done it for the meanest man in the world. Why should he not do it for an unfortunate millionaire? But the fact was that Seaworthy seemed quite startled to see him, one third as startled as he had been to see Papa Devil one week ago. It may be that Seaworthy startled easy, but apparently not in anything except encounters. But he took the drink, thankfully but nervously.

"It's all right now, Finnegan," he said when he had downed it. "I'm glad it's you and not another one, however it's happened. I won't be bothered with any sickness for the rest of the voyage. It only comes on us to remind us that we're mortal; which being the case, I wonder how the other sort took it? Get Papa Devil up if he's down. Get my two cronies also and have them all meet me in the bar."

Yes, Papa Devil was down, but he did not seem to be sick. If the Devil is mortal, he is not bothered by seasickness at least.

"Mr. Seaworthy says for you to come to the bar," said Finnegan, suddenly feeling more like a boy than he was.

"Papa Devil says for you to go to Hell," said Papa Devil, but he arose to go. Now was the time to mention it, quickly, for Finnegan did not believe in allowing questions to fester.

"Why didn't you kill me last night, Papa Devil?"

"I'll kill you when I get ready to, boy," he said looking at Finn suspiciously.

"You were supposed to kill me, and another fellow was supposed to assume my papers and identity. Why didn't he come on board?"

"He did. But he isn't on board any more. Who have you been talking to?"

"To nobody on this. I get hunches and premonitions."

"Forget it, forget it. We'll all be killed in due time. You talk too much, boy."

If possible, Papa Devil was of an even more ghoulish purple hue this morning. And if possible, he was bigger and more menacing than ever. But Finnegan had always wanted to needle the Devil.

"Papa D," he said, following the Devil, "did you kill a man before breakfast this morning?"

"That I did, Finnegan, that I did."

The two cronies of Saxon Seaworthy were William Gerecke and Peter Wirt. Finnegan knew very little about them. They partook of the mystery of the Devil and of Seaworthy. Seaworthy and the Devil and Gerecke and Wirt went into the bar, and Anastasia and Finnegan were dismissed. The Captain, whose name was Orestes Gonof, also went into the bar with the great ones.

2.

The five crewmen of the Brunhilde were Harry Scott, Don Lewis, Joe Cross. Art Emery, and Chris McAbney. And Finnegan was also carried as a crewman.

Don Lewis and Joe Cross were people who belonged, belonged with such as Finnegan and Anastasia, belonged with all good people everywhere.

Harry Scott, Art Emery, and Chris McAbney were people who do not belong, the other sort of people. There are only two sorts of people in the world, and they are these two sorts. Unless you understand this, you belong to the wrong sort, and you can go to Hell with Harry and Art and Chris, and nobody will care; you belong in Hell.

Harry was neat, Art was pretty, and Chris was worse. A name like that, and he wasn't even Irish. He was Scotch ("Scotch and shoder, I shoder every time I see him," Anastasia said; she didn't like him); he was a blue-nosed sinner, the worst kind. It was Chris McAbney who had informed on them to the Devil that first day that Finnegan had come onto ship.

But Don Lewis and Joe Cross were princes: shoddy, it's true, and compromised (as are many who live in the world), but true princes. All of one's friends are princes if one belongs to the first sort of people. It was with Don and Joe that Finnegan cabined.

Joe Cross had burr-short red hair. You'd bet you could strike matches on the top of his head, and you'd be right. Don was dark and handsome, the most handsome man on the ship, just as Finnegan was, well, not the ugliest, just as Finnegan was the most unusual-looking man on the ship; and you must remember that the ship's company included the Devil himself.

A couple of years later, Finnegan doubted that he had ever made this voyage around the world. This was after he had dreamed up many lives and his memory had become confused by his bouts. Then it seemed that these two hundred days were just something from a sequence of bottles, that he had only dreamed of the death of the beautiful Anastasia and of the sinister Papa Devil. Possibly they had never lived at all, and only in that sense were they dead. A lot of things, which he then knew weren't real, seemed realer.

But it was real, and Anastasia was real. She was a water-witch and she was real. It hadn't been her aunt who looked just like that old ship; it was herself. Finnegan began now to understand her true form.

She was not beautiful when you looked at her; she was even comical looking. But she was beautiful when you thought about her. In retrospect and in prospect she was beautiful. Her complexion was olive, and it went from green to golden and was sometimes both at one time. Often her eyes were black, and sometimes they were purple. She was small and slim and particularly full of life.

Anastasia Demetriades! She looked like one of those carven women on the fore of old sailing ships. They dug statuettes of her out of Cretan cenotaphs. Touch her with two fingers and she was real, but what was she really?

3.

But it was not all Anastasia. There was another girl on ship. She was one of those who are very hard to place among the two kinds of people in the world. Oh, she carried a latch-key to Hell, there was no doubt about that. But before she went she would be the pleasant companion of princes. For a while she was both kinds of people. Not everyone liked her, but everyone had to pay attention to her.

Finnegan had seen her before, several nights before the sailing, but he had believed it a dream, the dream of the Golden Ogress. She had simply come and found him in his cups and gotten information from him for the ship's register. It was a simple business, but nothing she did was simple. Like Papa Devil, she had the aura of great power about her. It seemed to Finnegan that when he wrote down his name for her he had signed a mortgage on his soul rather than certain ship's papers; and it seemed that the soul might be forfeit. But he had the memory that she spoke to him with affection.

Finnegan had never seen anything like her. She was Seaworthy's seagoing secretary, Marie Courtois, a magnificent young woman. That the girl was evil was insisted upon by Anastasia who had a better than average perception of good and evil. And Marie also had a distaste for Anastasia, more for what she stood for than for herself. Believing that good and evil are superstitions, Marie could not ascribe evil to Anastasia; she ascribed instead ideological immaturity, chauvinistic disorientation, and neo-fascistic indoctrination. For that is one of the kinds of girl that Marie was.

But, if you think that's all she was, how wrong you are! She would have made two of Anastasia, and there was no letdown in quality. The girls were roommates in a cabin so small that, had it not been for the pleasure and interest of feuding, it would have been confining. As it was, they sharpened their wits and claws, quarreled with spirit, and schemed and devised. And yet they were pretty good friends, except for Anastasia's jealousy of Marie's beauty.

"It isn't that I object to a woman who thinks or tosses the lingo," Anastasia told Finnegan, "but it is unbecoming to one born without brains. With all that other equipment she has it wouldn't be fair if she had brains too. She isn't a lady; she says that lady is a bourgeois conceit. But I am one, even if of the Mehitabel variety, so I can't say what she really is, but the Greek word is *skylla*. She's on a rampage now because I put crotin oil in her martini; I thought she'd like it. Crotin oil is good for sick cats and it should be good for her."

"Little Miss Resurrection, you're supposed to love your enemies," Finnegan said.

"Love them maybe, like them never. The Lord doesn't expect that; He never meant to take all small pleasures from us. Hey, there is a lot of her, isn't there, Finnegan?"

There was at least a foot and a hundred pounds more of Marie than there was of Anastasia; she was the Golden Giantess.

4.

They were going coastwise, and much of the time Finnegan was at the wheel. He knew this stretch, from land, from deep gulf, from shallow coasting, from mixed fishing. They put into port every night. Seaworthy was a man with much mysterious business in many little ports. They put in at Freeport, at Palacios, at Port O'Conner, at Aransas Pass, at Corpus. And Wednesday they anchored off a desolate strip of Padre Island. It had not then become a tourist place, and there were no settlements on the Island. Most of them went ashore in two small boats for a beach party and fish fry. A pit was dug, and mesquite cut and burned down to its aromatic coals. It had a weedy smell with a touch of incense.

They swam in the gulf all morning. Most of them were at home in the water, and all swam well. Anastasia swam like a mermaid. She was a mermaid, a real one, which from a distance resembles a seal. This is the comparison that Anastasia herself made.

And there is this further that Anastasia told about

mermaids, some of it at other times, but most of it that morning in the lulls of the swimming:

The legendary depiction of the mermaid as a breasty creature with flowing yellow hair has long been known to investigators in this field as erroneous. The mermaid is actually close-cropped and boyish in form, and the features are invariably island Greek. The legend of the blond mermaid is just that, a legend. Nobody has ever seen a blond mermaid. Neither can the mermaids live permanently nor breathe under water. Anastasia could not, and neither are those who are fish-tailed. They must breathe air like a porpoise. They are not fishes.

They do not smell any more strongly to people than people do to them. We sniff at the statement (it is Anastasia's) and we are not sure what it means. Do they smell fishy? Well, they announce their presence, said Anastasia. Why should they not? Finnegan realized that this had always been true with Anastasia, but with her it was not an offense.

They do not live in palaces under the water. They live in water-level caves on rock islands. Those who have married landsmen often live in houses.

(How Anastasia could swim, all in full bodily motion! How she could swim.)

Their original home was in the Cyclades only, but very early they were also in the Dodecanese. By the beginning of the eighteenth dynasty there were mermaid beaches on the island of Kos; there is documentation of this. The early mermaids of Crete were captured ones from Naxos. There was not a separate Cretan variety.

By the time of Alexander they were in the Red Sea, but it is not known how they got there. Still less is it understood how they arrived in the Persian Gulf, but they were there by the time of Haroun-Al-Raschid.

(How she could swim, that girl!)

There were Christian mermaids of a small island between Patmos and Lipsos in the second century. They had a chapel dedicated to Our Lady of the Dolphins. The chapel is still there, but not in good condition.

In the Middle Ages they were off Sicily, especially at Salina and Filicudi. They were at Minorca, but no further West. They were not in the Atlantic. They lie who claim to have seen them in the Atlantic.

What the Norse called mermaids and netted in the North Sea and the North Atlantic as late as the tenth century were not mermaids but sea-cows. They were blond and undoubtedly mammalian, but their tails were tapered vertically instead of horizontally as with the true mermaids. There are no New World varieties. Some of the giant Mississippi catfish have human eyes, but that is as far as it goes.

At the turn of the high Middle Ages the mermaids were at their most numerous. Then they began their mysterious decline. Mermaids are no longer in the Persian Gulf, nor in the Red Sea. There has not been an authentic sighting at Rhodes for over three hundred years. They retreat from sea after sea and from beach after beach. Such as are left of them now are found only in the Cyclades, their ancestral home, mostly off Naxos, and the rocks between there and Amorgos. Possibly eighty percent of them are two-footed now, and the fishtail is disappearing. In another thousand years it will be gone.

This information is all from Anastasia Demetriades herself, who knew a lot about mermaids; she herself was of a mermaid family of Naxos. She was a mermaid though she hadn't the tail; the Demetriades had not thrown a fishtail for six generations now.

"It is claimed that sports turn up in the seventh generation," Finnegan said. "I wouldn't give odds on whatever you might give birth to."

"Maybe," said Anastasia. "Wouldn't it be fun, Finnegan, if we got married and threw a fishtail? Finnegan sounds like a fishy name anyhow."

"I have now heard the mother of all fish tales," said Marie, "or of fishtails. Those sea-cows, you didn't put them in for my benefit, did you, Anastasia?"

"Naturally you reminded me of them. But I always have sea-cows in it when I tell the story. I might add a red-headed variety, though."

"Wasn't Lorelei an authentic mermaid?" Marie asked. "She had red-gold hair, probably about the color of mine."

"No. She was a sea-cow. A damned Dutch sea-cow!"

Anastasia, how wrong you were!

5.

For, if Anastasia was boyish of figure, Marie Courtois was not. But there is something to be said of a form such as hers: curvaceous and stately, tall and ample, strong yet willowy, indescribable except by motion of hand; light golden, and topped by that red-gold hair. Marie was stronger than a circus woman, and produced an excitement very like that of a circus.

Though Anastasia called her a giantess, yet it was not so. She might have been twelve inches over Anastasia, but Anastasia couldn't have been much more than five feet. And if Anastasia the mermaid was supreme in the deep water that morning, Marie was so that afternoon on the beach and in the swelling surf. Proud of her strength, she invited the seamen to dive off her shoulders as she stood indomitable, breasting the breakers. Marie also was a legend, and one that all the men remembered with sudden stirring. Larger than life, and of a beauty that has been forbidden for centuries, she was a red-haired primordial creature of limitless strength and dazzling color. Her hair came below her shoulders, too thick to become straggly in the water.

For a while it seemed that a shore and surf goddess was at least equal to a mermaid. Even Finnegan, in momentary disloyalty, abandoned Anastasia and exulted with the iridescent Marie Courtois, losing himself in her hair, and riding on her shining shoulders.

When he went back to Anastasia she was jealous and sulky.

"I thought you were my pet," she said, "and here you go riding that nightmare. You can't be my pet if you do that. What are you looking at? Why do you keep looking at her?"

"It's the color. It cannot be caught except in oils. That old sand shore, and the green shallows, and the blue deep beyond, and that golden movement that is central to it all." (Finnegan was a painter.)

"You forget golden movement," said Anastasia. "See, she's forgotten you."

The seamen were involved in beach acrobatics, and Marie was the sturdy understander for a human pyramid.

"You will have to admit she is beautiful," said Finnegan.

"She is beautiful, and it hurts me. Am I not beautiful?"

"You are an urchin."

"Well, am I a beautiful urchin?"

"You are a beautiful urchin, Anastasia. That is better than to be no urchin at all."

A fish broke water, whistled at them, and disappeared with a great splash. Well, it had been Joe Cross and not a fish, but it was as funny as if it had been a fish.

They were in a cove, Finnegan and Anastasia, where the surf came over the sand strongly, leaving cryptic markings and then obliterating them.

"There are letters on the sand between the waves," said Anastasia. "There are words, and the next wave wipes them away. The wave after that writes the next phrase. I think the waves write in Chaldee. If I could read Chaldee I would tell you what they say."

"I can read Chaldee," said Finnegan. "All clairvoyants can read Chaldee. I know what they say. I am afraid of what they say."

6.

Finnegan and Anastasia were walking inland through the dunes and brush.

"Who are you?" Anastasia asked suddenly. "Your name on the ship's papers is John Solli. Why do you hide behind Finnegan?"

"I don't hide. It's just a nickname I picked up."

"You always look as though you were someone else, Finn. The nose and all."

"The nose is sadly real. It won't come off. I am a gargoyle."

"I knew a story about a gargoyle. I forget how it goes. He had a good heart, though."

"Oh, we have that, we have that."

"Finn, you are a little like Papa Devil. Both of you are so unusual-looking. Maybe he has a good heart too."

"It may be. But he certainly has a vicious liver."

"Are you some kind of spy, Finn?"

"No kind that I can think of. Is everybody supposed to be a spy?"

"Some of us might be. I think Don Lewis is one kind of spy. I think that I am another kind. You were supposed to have been killed, Finn, and another man slip into your identity. Something changed. Now you are taking the place of the man who was supposed to take your place."

"What is this voyage, Anastasia?"

"I don't know. How would I?"

"What is Saxon Seaworthy, and his company, and the Devil?"

"They make these circuits and they check on the apparatus and the men in different towns. It is deep and it is murderous. And you are in it on some level."

"Who is in it deep, Anastasia?"

"Oh, Seaworthy and the Devil and Wirt and Gerecke. They own the captain and the rest."

"And the seamen?"

"They own the seamen too. But Don Lewis is against them and they will kill him when they know it. They own you too, or they will kill you."

"Nobody owns me."

"Seaworthy and the Devil own you. There are no free people on this voyage."

They came back over the dunes to supper.

Papa Devil had an ice chest and drinks and mixes. He had been compounding atrocities, and Anastasia took over. Papa Devil was in a gay mood for him. His eyes lightened up and his gestures were florid.

They ate barbecued pork and fried pork. They had boiled shrimp and fried shrimp, and red snapper and pompano. DePolis the cook left them with it; he hated beach parties and hated anyone else to be cooking.

Joe Cross had worked in a Baltimore raw bar and he knew a lot about seafood. Anastasia had two uncles who ran a restaurant, and she had once been cashier for them, so there was no limit to her knowledge. Finnegan used to hang around oyster bars in New Orleans so he knew a lot about fish and stuff. There were other experts. It was all good. There is really no wrong way to cook a fish.

They ate and talked. Papa Devil spread blankets on the beach and built a camp fire.

And a quarter mile down shore a man entered the water and swam silently out to the Brunhilde.

Chapter Three

THE FURTIVE MAN

Now, there are certain persons who are trying to take away the knowledge of singulars from the perfection of the divine knowledge.
—ST. THOMAS AQUINAS, *Summa Contra Gentiles*

Don Lewis told a campfire story:
"There was a furtive little man I just saw in the gloaming," he said. "Several of us saw him, for all that he was furtive. He reminds me of another furtive little man I once buried."

"Where is the first furtive man?" Finnegan asked.

"Never mind. He cannot have been unseen. Papa Devil is watching from the dunes and he sees everything. The other furtive man I will tell you about; for the fact is, that after I had buried him, I myself became the furtive man."

Saxon Seaworthy sat and watched them with a face made out of tired granite. There was no real interest in that face, but he would weigh all the words of Don Lewis.

"On the morning of October 1, 1944, between ten and ten thirty in the morning, on an island that is sometimes called Pulau Petir and sometimes Willy Jones Island, three American soldiers disappeared, and have not been officially seen since. The three soldiers were Sergeant Charles Santee of Orange, Texas; Corporal Robert Casper of Gobey (Morgan County), Tennessee; and PFC Timothy Lorrigan of Boston. I was one of these three men, for my name is no more Don Lewis than the names of some others here are their real names. These three disappeared from a routine patrol. One of these boys was a coward;

two were not; for this reason I do not say which one was myself.

"I have heard that one of these soldiers got out of the thing alive, that he has told the main part of the story in an unlikely version, and that that soldier is not me. So perhaps I am not of the living; I have felt like a dweller of the middle world since that time. Besides, I do not tell the main part of the story, but only the outré little introduction.

"We saw that day, at the distance of about three hundred yards, a ragged little man who seemed to be a Japanese soldier. He beckoned and the three soldiers beckoned, and they jabbered at each other distantly. Then Corporal Casper said 'Keep the little idiot chattering. I'll get behind him and we'll have him in the sack. I can get behind anyone.'

"Casper went, and he was good at this. In a very few minutes he appeared on a rise another two hundred yards behind the little man; he motioned us to come on. So we closed in on the little bugger.

"But he wasn't in the sack when we pulled the string. We came all the way up to Casper without finding him. And then the little man was standing, as if he had simply reappeared, on another height yet three hundred yards beyond us.

" 'I don't know how he did it,' Casper said, 'but I bet he can't do it again. It's narrower from here on. If I can get behind him again we'll have him sure.'

"We did it again. Casper passed and outflanked the little man and appeared behind him. The little man stood motionless till we were nearly on him. Then he vanished. As we came up to Casper, the little man appeared again, still a long three hundred yards ahead of us.

" 'He couldn't have,' said Casper. 'Nothing could have got by me.' 'We might as well settle him,' said Sergeant Santee. 'He's acting too odd to leave, and we don't want to be led too deep. I don't miss, even at this distance.'

"He didn't, not completely. Sergeant Santee's shot had the little man somewhere. The l.m. shuddered as he was hit and wobbled back out of sight. 'We will have to get him,' said Santee. 'I don't believe in leaving winged game.' 'Oh, let him go,' I said, 'he isn't game.' 'He is to me,' Santee said.

"We followed him a long ways, and most of the time we had him in sight. When we stopped for a short rest, he also stopped, four hundred yards ahead, and sat on a rock. 'We will wait him a while,' said Santee. 'He will stiffen up as he sits there.' We waited quite a while, and it was now late in the day. Santee was right; the little man had stiffened up and was unhappy. He couldn't move with our speed after we started out once more. It wouldn't take long to get him. I lagged behind. I didn't want to see it."

"Not want to see it!" Marie cried in amazement. "All that way and then to miss it? How could anyone not want to see it or do it?"

"Did I say that *I* did not want to see it? That was surely a slip of the tongue. It was PFC Lorrigan who lagged behind and did not want to see it. Santee and Casper went on ahead and killed the little man.

" 'Well, let's make the start back,' Santee said, 'it's late.' 'Not that way, that's not the way,' said Casper. I didn't know the way either. We were lost. We stayed lost. There were a lot of valleys there: there were Cotton-Picker Valley and Pepper-Belly Valley, Hound Dog, and Horse Collar, and Dog-Dirt Draw. There were Rang-Dang-Doo, and Jackass Flats (the most precipitous region I have even seen). There was Little Joker Canyon, and Aching Back, and Slit Trench, and Sore-Head Gulch; there was Little Fat-Head and Big Fat-Head. We knew all the valleys, but we didn't know this one.

"We were still arguing the way when it got dark. We quarreled. Casper said that he would not spend a night in a valley with fools; he went up the walls of the valley to spend the night on one crest. Santee climbed an opposite height to another aerie. I slept in the valley with the little dead man."

"You slept in the wrong place," said Finnegan. "In a valley is in a trap."

"I know it was the wrong place," said Don Lewis. "I had a short-handled pioneer shovel. Yokipoki (likely not his real name) had a little double-edged butcher knife. With those I dug his grave in the mud. 'It isn't the best grave in the world,' I told him, 'but it is the best I can give you. I had better take your boots off; you'll sleep better with them off, and you're going to sleep a long time. And I had better gag you. A corpse is supposed to

39

have his mouth tied. If you began to talk in the night it would make me nervous.' "

Finnegan had reason to remember this part of the story, for, when some weeks later he buried Don Lewis in the sand, he did much the same things for him.

"I put the gag in his mouth," continued Don Lewis, "and also tied his wrists and ankles from some old seemliness. I then bandaged his eyes and covered him up in the mud. *'Requiem,'* I said, 'and *lux perpetua* and all that.' Then, as I had a little left in a bottle, I drank it to him, giving him Christian burial. I bedded down on a little hummock that rose out of the mud.

"I always sleep well, but with a few quick dreams. 'It's a good thing I put the gag in his mouth,' I dreamed. 'If I hadn't, he would be too noisy to tolerate. As it is, that squealing of his is likely to make me nervous.' It did make me nervous, and it woke me up. The little man in the hole was squealing and grunting as he fought with gag and bond. On the threshold of terror one passes into a cold sweat, just before the limbs are completely unstrung and the hair rises entirely off the head. I knew that the tough sergeant or the big corporal would not be afraid of any little man dead or alive, or even half and half. There was no doubt that Yokipoki had been dead, cold dead for several hours. And I was afraid.

"There was a slashing sound down there now with the squeals and grunts. He had his butcher knife down there and was cutting his bonds. I shouldn't have buried it with him, but it was all the property he had. I switched on my flashlight and went to the grave. But when I saw the loose mud heave and pitch, I was completely unnerved. I backed away and fell down and lost my flashlight. The noise became more various. It worked to a climax.

" 'He will be out of there in a minute,' I thought, 'and he will slide along the ground like a snake. He will slash me with the butcher knife, and I will be too paralyzed to do anything about it.'

"And that is what happened. He was out of there and brushed my foot, and I froze. There are ice crystals in my blood from it to this day. Then he slashed me painfully on the ankle.

" 'Be off!' I cried. I knew what it was then, but I was still too scared to laugh. I kicked the rats away, and I knew it had been the rats at the body. They had big mean rats there."

"And rats is all it was!" Marie demanded in incredible disappointment. "He didn't come alive at all? It was only the rats making all that fuss?"

"Do not say 'only the rats.' The reason there are no tigers on those islands is that the rats are too large and fierce and will not tolerate them. Yes, it was only the rats. I have not loved rats since."

"Did you find your way back somewhere in the morning when it was light?" Anastasia asked.

"No. We never did find our way back. I told you that we were officially missing. The next day I was taken into a peculiar custody. I do not know what happened to the other two. I heard that both were killed. I also heard that they returned separately, and each spread a story too tall to be believed. But I came back to my own country by a different way and under a different name; and with a different orientation in my mind, for I am no longer my own man.

"Now I am also a furtive man. I have appeared several times on the hill beyond, and yet it is certain that I will be hunted down and killed. But I have a question about us furtive men. Does anybody know: Are we really forgotten behind God's back? We are singulars: Does God have knowledge of singulars?"

There were fires up and down the coast every mile or so. People liked to come to the sandy place. There were cattle on the island, and horses also. A boat whistle sounded far away. Saxon Seaworthy sat and smoked by the fire. His face was still made out of granite, but more relaxed now; and the fire flickers lighted up the old cliffs of it.

"Were there no happy stories of those islands?" Anastasia asked.

"All island stories are happy," Don Lewis said. "Here is another one that happened on Willy Jones Island, the story of the Big House. Nobody who lives in the Big House ever dies or gets any older; but the visitors who come there are always killed the first night. The people of the Big House take their kidneys and hearts and brains and other organs and make a broth of them. On this they live forever, and they will not die as long as they get one new visitor a year. But if for a year they do not get a visitor, they all age one year.

"A boy named Ali came to the Big House. But first he put two ta'a nuts in his pocket. He planted one in front of the door of the Big House. He kept the other one. Then he went in.

"Ali was given a feast of bird and fish and nuts and fruit, and was made drunk on palm wine. Then he retired with the beautiful daughter of the house. 'I love you,' said the daughter, 'I will feast me on your heart.' 'It is a pleasant sentiment,' said Ali, 'so will I on yours.' 'I will feast me on your brains,' said the daughter. 'Now wait a turtle-egg minute,' said Ali, 'I don't use them much but I would like to keep them inviolate.' 'I would feast me on your kidneys,' said the daughter. 'If this is the way you make love here, you can do without me,' said Ali.

"They came to kill him then, but you can't kill anyone who has a ta'a nut in his pocket. You may not have known that."

"But of course we all know it," said Anastasia. "Why do you think we all carry them?"

"So Ali ran to his room and shut the door and put a log against it. Then he snapped his fingers three times, which made it be morning. He looked out the window; he saw that the ta'a nut he had planted was now a great tree, and one branch came right to his window. So he climbed down it and escaped."

"Knew he would, knew he would!" Anastasia jingled.

"Stop him! Don't let him get away!" Marie cried. She was of a white seriousness.

"What? It is only a story, goldie," Don Lewis said.

"That doesn't make any difference. They shouldn't have let him get away. They shouldn't ever let anyone get away," Marie insisted. She meant it.

"That was the year that they all grew a year older at the Big House," Don Lewis finished it.

"They shouldn't have let him get away," Marie still insisted. "I liked the rats one better."

There was a shocking strength in many of them there as they lounged in the flickering darkness. The strong earthy power in Seaworthy and the Devil, in Gerecke and Peter Wirt, in Marie, even in Anastasia shook Finnegan as he felt it in them. They were people growing out of the ground, full of some old black blood. They were the peculiar people, the other human race.

Was he also? Finnegan had known that many people were startled or afraid of him at first meeting, even at subsequent meetings. There were times when he was even startled at himself: when he had gone through Amnesia's woods and encountered Amnesia herself in the clearing; when the shocking gaps in his memory of events and times could only be filled by dark parable. There had been the weeks in the Green Islands when he had forgotten his own name and personality. There had been the hours with Saxon Seaworthy before the remembered hours with Seaworthy.

Was Finnegan himself one of the under-thing people, in which he himself did not yet believe?

A night-dune imaginary: there was a world full of people with pumpkin-heads for heads, and candles burning inside. Then Seaworthy and the Devil and their spooky crew came along, lifted the top off each head, blew out the candles inside, and put the tops back on. The pumpkin-headed people seemed to get along about as well as before; yet there was a difference.

A furtive man had swum out to the Brunhilde. Another furtive man had been buried in the mud on Willy Jones Island, and Don Lewis had then become a furtive man. So was Finnegan. And now one more whom Finnegan divined about:

In the cabin that Finnegan shared with Don Lewis and Joe Cross on the Brunhilde, behind an upper balk and visible only to one lying in Finnegan's bunk, there was the edge of an envelope. Finn had had many opportunities to take it and see what was in it, but he had not.

And yet the contents had been coming to him, bit by bit, for several days, for he was clairvoyant. It was the writing of the man who was to have replaced Finnegan, assuming his papers and person, after Finnegan had been killed; the papers of the man who had unaccountably been killed instead, leaving Finn to be his own surrogate's surrogate.

"—it is all right you make a bargane with the devil, that you come on here, be the devils finger man. How is it then when the devil change when he be different where are you then. The bugle nosed dago with the irish monikor why is he not dead yet. There is not room for the both of us..."

There was a lot of it there that Finnegan had been able to read without opening it, and some of it he read now, lying in the dunes. The man's name was Pinne, Doppio di Pinne, the seaman known as Dopey. Finnegan had known him slightly.

It had become chilly. All wrapped up in their blankets and went to sleep.

Except Papa Devil who never slept.

Chapter Four

THE WIVES OF SINDBAD

There is a further mystery about Bassorah which is called a port, even the port of Baghdad, in the Nights and other folk-lore. But Bassorah could never have been a port, could hardly have been a town. It is no more than a great rock slab set in the mud shallows, scarred by old fire. It's as though it were used as launching pad for space fleets before they were even dreamed about. It is said that one of the missing Nights recounted Sindbads of space trading from other worlds with the great caliph when the way was more open than now.

—MOISHA EL-GAZMA, *Legends of the Persian Gulf*

1.

The discovery of Manuel on board was gradual, for he was still furtive. The seamen figured he was none of their business. Finnegan knew that Manuel didn't belong there, but the ragged latino looked like his kind of man. Seaworthy surely knew he was there, but assumed he was a creature of the Devil. The other personages didn't even know how many seamen there were supposed to be, nor had they noticed what they looked like.

Anastasia asked Manuel who he was. He was a stowaway, he said. Where did he want to go? she asked. Wherever the ship was going, he said. Besides being a stowaway, he was also a spy, he told her.

It didn't seem too serious to be a stowaway on a little boat drifting down coast. If they threw him overboard he could swim to shore. He could get off the same way he got on.

Papa Devil picked Manuel up, held him out at arm's length, stared him in the eye, and then dropped him. Papa

D did not seem to notice Manuel at all for two days after that.

Papa Devil had seen Manuel before anyone else had. He had seen him come out of the dunes and lie flat on the beach. He had seen him swim out to the ship. He had trained his rifle on the man's head as he swam in the gathering darkness. Papa often sighted his rifle on men, men at a distance, men on shore. He himself had planted the story that he was the best rifle shot in the world, but he seldom shot. It was the aiming, though, that added to his reputation of being sinister.

And yet Finnegan thought that he once caught a flicker between Manuel the furtive man and the Devil himself, as though they were of previous acquaintance.

The Brunhilde stopped at Port Isabel, and the next day at Brownsville. Seaworthy had associates at every stop.

"But what does he do for a living?" Finnegan asked Anastasia.

"He's a ship owner."

"How can he get rich from the Brunhilde?"

"I don't mean the Brunhilde. I mean ships, ships. Greeks always own a lot of ships. They don't own anything else, but they do own a lot of ships."

"Saxon X. Seaworthy is a Greek?"

"The X isn't for Xavier. But I don't know what these voyages are about, Finnegan. He does a lot of work that isn't legitimate. Or he may just be making contacts for something, or setting his trap lines. He does haul funny cargoes, or have them hauled, anything, anywhere in the world. And he's in the deeper business. Often they are people-cargoes he hauls. He makes that pay too."

They were in the estuary of a great river. Manuel came to them, very much afraid.

"But what are you afraid of?" Anastasia asked him.

"That the Devil Papa will kill me and bury my body."

"It's the only decent thing he could do after he kills you," said Finnegan.

"You are joking, but to me it is not a great matter to be killed," said Manuel. "It is only that, if it happens, it will be lost my coming on this boat. I am here as a spy, and I must find out what these evil men are about."

"You keep telling people you are a spy and someone

will believe you," Anastasia cautioned. "Spies and confidence men always pass themselves off as traveling salesmen."

"Coming as I did, ragged, it would not be believed that I was a traveling salesman," Manuel explained. "Besides, sooner or later, you would ask me what I sell. And then what would I say? I would be stunked."

"Stumped."

"The word is stumped and not stunked? There is so much I do not know. But it is only my friends I tell that I am a spy."

"You told Marie," Anastasia protested. "She is a devil of devils."

"The Marie has compassion on me. She may turn out to be my contact. If, that is, Papa Devil does not kill me and bury my body this day."

"Who do you spy for?" Finnegan asked him.

"For myself and others like me. We are a society, a futile society, in my country."

"Mexico?"

"No, no, *mas adelante,* farther south. There is a force there now, as it seems to be everywhere. It runs the guns. It also runs the men. These men are devils. They are not merely anti-clericals and reds; some of them do not even work that road. They are devils literally, and there is a source that turns still more men into devils. There is a source, but we do not know what country it is in or where it gets its particular venom.

"I will find out what the apparatus is and infiltrate it. I am a committee of one to do this because I am the only man I know to be incorruptible. But I will entertain only today's trouble today."

"Which is that Papa Devil will kill you and bury your body?"

"Yes. That would negate any further action by me in this world."

"You aren't what I thought you at first, Manuel," said Finnegan. "You aren't a poor and ignorant man."

"Among my people I am fairly rich and am a lawyer. But I go to infiltrate as a poor man."

Seaworthy and Gerecke and Peter Wirt had gone ashore with a party. Now another party went ashore on the Mexican side in an oar boat: Manuel and Papa Devil, Finnegan and the two girls, Joe Cross who was to stay with the boat. Marie, though she was dressed sumptuously today, took an oar. She used it with amazing power.

"Ah, *la giganta dorada!*" Anastasia breathed.

Marie liked to be called the giantess. She was proud of her power.

Ashore, Finnegan and the two girls trailed after the Devil and Manuel. The Devil said he was looking for a notary, but it was more than a notary he wanted. It was Finnegan, when Papa was at a loss, who correctly supplied the word *un falsario,* a forger; and they were directed to one at once. In some lands it is better to ask a thing directly and with the common word. Finnegan spoke better Spanish than did Papa Devil, who spoke it perfectly but with a stilted perfection that missed the heart of it.

Papa Devil told Finnegan and the girls that they would not be needed there. The second time that he told them so he did it rather testily; so they left the Devil and Manuel with the forger and went on the town.

A crowd of children followed them, and all who followed them were not children. Marie Courtois drew the attention. She was dressed in the high manner today, and her red-blond coloring had never been more vivid. Even Anastasia, in spite of her jealousy, was proud of her.

"*Magnífica,*" breathed an admiring male, "*maravillosa.*"

"She can carry a man on her shoulders," Anastasia told him.

"*Interesante,*" breathed the man.

Finnegan bought from a lady, who cooked over charcoal on a corner, what he said were fried lizards; and they all ate them. They were no such thing as lizards. The lady had affinity with Finnegan; she caught the joke and went along with it, her face like laughing leather.

And now Finnegan was the envy of every man on the street as he walked like an Arabian pirate with his two favorite wives. They went to the Cadillac Bar which was dingy outside and rich within. Most of the customers were Texans. The bar-boys wore white jackets and presided amidst chrome and crystal. The three drank and mellowed.

They left the Cadillac and went to a more Mexican place. It was fly-specked, American, south-of-the-border

Western. The walls were solidly covered with affixed papers, notices, posters, and placards. All of these were very old. None was ever taken down, and there was no room for any to be added. The proprietor was Demetrio, a gray-headed old bandit. He lived wrapped in the mantle of his own great experiences, but he was glad to talk to visiting notables.

"I am a man of the world," Demetrio glowed. "You might not notice this, seeing me here in my little place, and yet you might well have guessed it. In my youth I traveled all over the world and the United States: Alice, Eagle Pass, Uvalde, Beeville, San Angelo, Weimar, even Port Isabel.

"I followed every occupation. I milked goats, I kept bees, I worked in the pickle factory. By all this I learned much of the world. Now in my age I am home again, and have my own bar and am my own man. All sorts of people come to my place, river rats, seamen, cattle and goat men, fruit jobbers, sewing machine salesmen, the factors in the great traffic of two nations. All come to drink in my place."

Demetrio's face was lined with great character, like an old Roman, like an old Aztec at the same time. His was a face off an old coin, and Finnegan could not see a great face without wanting to record it.

Finnegan drew Manuel in ink on the back of a poster. It was not just a sketch; it was a fine portrait, and it took two hours. It hangs behind that bar yet, and some day an art man will come in there and will look at it twice. When he sees the signature he will know it is genuine, one of the random Finnegans; and the heirs of Demetrio will have more for it than the bar takes in in a week.

Even in that present time, everyone acquired a lot of prestige from the portrait: Old Demetrio with the striking and forceful head of himself to hang behind his bar; Finnegan the artist at work; the two girls who were friends of everyone in the place, and of the artist, and of the proprietor. After this, Demetrio gave Finnegan a fine belt, and gave each of the girls a silver ring, all of which he had made himself; for Demetrio also was an artist.

Late in the afternoon they went back to the Brunhilde in the oar boat. It happened that Papadiabolous had not killed and buried Manuel after all. Instead, he had gotten him a complete set of papers, and now Manuel was a member of the crew.

They fished as they went down coast, taking Spanish mackerel, four and five pounds, and very good. During the days they made fair time; but every evening they anchored, and Seaworthy and his group went ashore to the little Mexican ports. They seldom returned until daylight, and sailed immediately thereafter.

They were off Paraiso this day, a little earlier than they usually anchored, and Finnegan was sketching on deck. For a week now he had been working on a project for Saxon Seaworthy: painting the barroom of the Brunhilde. The walls had been readied. There would be nice panels. The paintings were to be of the Voyages of Sindbad the Sailor.

There was a mystique about this. Seaworthy *was* Sindbad. And Sindbad was not so upstanding a fellow as he appears in story. The murky mystery of him has been felt from the beginning.

Finnegan painted in the barroom only in the early mornings, with the doors and shutters open. The bar was port side, and was flooded with morning light as they headed south. But after the sun had risen a while, Finnegan would put away his paints and go to drinking and sketching in his notebooks. And in the afternoons he sketched on deck.

"I cannot draw the roc. I cannot picture the roc at all," he complained.

"Why, it's all in proportion," Anastasia told him. "If you draw Sindbad very small, then you can draw a roc as easily as a robbin."

"No. A roc as big as a robbin could not fly. It would be aerodynamically impossible. It is hard to make a really big bird that can fly. Even God would have trouble doing it. It would have to be built like a pterodactyl, and reproductions of that from skeletons are repulsive. The roc must not look repulsive, even though it is an evil force. Evil with grace and balance is what I want."

"Don't be so fussy. Evil can't have grace. And it doesn't have to be able to fly."

"Of course it has to be able to fly. And evil *can* have grace and balance. Consider Papa Devil."

"How will you do the sea stallions?" Marie asked. "They're in one of the voyages. Aren't they unnatural too?"

"I will just have deep-chested stallions, and have them coming onto the land. But I have to put some signature of the sea on them. I might be able to do this with the convolutions of their manes and hair, and the surge of their lunges. A stallion breaks to a gallop in a manner different from that of a colt or a mare or a gelding. It lunges up and over like a breaker; it's as though every stallion were a sea stallion. It would be impossible to have a sea gelding, of course. I can do the sea stallions, but I can't get the roc off the ground."

"Will you draw me as the fourth wife of Sindbad?" Anastasia asked.

"He didn't have four wives."

"The wife of the fourth voyage, I mean."

"But she died. Shall I paint you dead?"

"Sure. Paint me dead. I want to see how I look. If I don't look good dead, then I'm not ever going to die."

Finnegan suddenly saw Anastasia dead. He often got his pictures all at once. He fixed it in his mind, and he shivered when he did it. She would look good dead. And she was going to die.

"Where will you put me, Finnegan? Down in the common grave with the dead men?"

"Yes, Anastasia, down in the grave with the bodies. I will pull a Dante; he put all his enemies in Hell; I will paint all mine dead and rotten. You, however, I won't paint rotten; just a little bit high. Do you know, Anastasia, you're the only one I'll hate to see dead."

"Take it easy, Finnegan. This isn't for real."

"It is, girl. When I paint them dead, they're dead."

"Finnegan is going to paint me as the wife of the seventh adventure," said Marie, "and she's the happy-ever-after one."

"I thought you thought happy-ever-after was a bourgeois concept," Anastasia protested.

"You thought I thought a lot of things, but this one I intend to be. Sindbad is Seaworthy, and Sindbad was very wealthy when he retired; possibly it was only one of his secretaries who knew just how wealthy. Seaworthy has been to more places than Sindbad ever heard of; he's been

51

shipwrecked more times, in one way or another; he's traded more bales of goods, and talked to more kings and wheels. He has sailed out of more Bassorahs than Sindbad would understand. And I will be the wife of the seventh and last adventure."

"Why don't you paint Marie as an ogress?" Anastasia asked. "Isn't there a place for an ogress somewhere?"

"Paint me as an ogress too," Marie said, "only paint me as I will be when the adventures are over."

"You girls will have to be the wives; you're the only girls I have to paint," Finnegan said. "There were only two women in all the adventures of Sindbad, for his were not ordinary adventures. I'll paint Papa Devil as a man-eating ogre, and William Gerecke will be the Old Man of the Sea. He looks like an incubus."

So he painted Anastasia as the wife of the fourth voyage; and Marie of the wonderful shoulders as the wife of the seventh.

But there was one thing wrong with the sketching, one thing more unnatural than the roc. Finnegan could not draw Papa Devil; and Finn was a man who could draw anything. There was something very wrong when he came to do Papadiabolous. That great purple pumpkin that Papa Devil wore for a head was not unattractive; it was distinctive even; but it was impossible to get it right.

For a long time Finnegan did not realize what the trouble was. There was an inconsistency of color or proportion, an unreality of facial muscle. But it came to him as he analyzed it:

Papa Devil did not really look like that. The Devil was wearing the living face of someone else. Somebody had looked like that, but it wasn't Papa Devil.

It took Finn nearly a week to figure out what Papa Devil *did* look like. But Finnegan had a very shrewd pencil and brush. He made a sketch; then he made a picture. It was the picture of what Papa Devil really looked like. He was very curious to see just who would be startled on coming onto that picture.

All were startled to see it, but it didn't seem to be the startle of recognition, even in Papa Devil himself. All were startled by the power and scope of that face, the face behind the flesh-mask. But none of them seemed to have seen it before.

Many weeks later, when Finnegan saw Papa Devil dead and wearing his own face, it was the same face drawn on the panel in the barroom. It did startle them all then, when they saw the man dead, and then came back and saw the same face on the wall; but none of them understood it, even at the end.

If Finnegan had not earlier solved this appearance, he would not have known who the dead man was, for nobody else knew.

2.

"Do you know who had your bunk for the two days before you had it?" Joe Cross asked Finnegan suddenly one day.

"Sure. It was Doppio di Pinne. Dopey the Seaman."

"How do you know the name, Finnegan?"

"I read it in the air."

"Well, do you know what happened to him?"

"He got himself killed."

"Did you read that in the air too? Do you know how?"

"I can't fake it any longer, Joe. I don't know. I want to."

"Finnegan, you won't believe this. You can whip me. You'll have to if you laugh at this tale. With that nose of yours, you ought to be able to smell it yet."

"The blood? And the fear? Yes, I do smell it yet. After all, this is my bunk here now, this is where it happened."

"Finnegan, Dopey was alone in that bunk in this cabin. I know that. There is only the one door to this cabin. There is no other way in or out. I was standing outside in the passage. Papa Devil came by me. He looked like a ghost in a passion. He went into this cabin. It scared me liverless. He looked like a blind man who knew just exactly where he was going. It was chilly insanity on him, I tell you. He's weird enough in bright day. It had just come on dusk then, and the passage light wasn't on yet.

"Papa Devil went in here and closed the door. Dopey screamed. He screamed a second time, like a terrified animal, like an ass taken by a lion (I have seen that).

"His third scream was cut off short. I stormed in then.

53

Dopey was no friend of mine, but I *will* not have a cabinmate murdered, and I *am* not afraid of the Devil.

"Papa Devil was alone in this cabin, and there was no way Dopey could have gone out. 'What did you do to him?' I gobbled, and swung on him, but he cupped both of my wrists in one of his big hands. 'Boy, there was no one here,' he said, and he looked through me rather than at me. 'Whose blood is that then?' I croaked. 'That little bit of blood? Bug blood, I guess,' he said. He let go me and went out. And it was only the veriest dribble of blood there, to tell the truth. But, Finnegan, there was no way Dopey could have gotten out of this cabin!"

"Maybe he's still here, then, Joe. I feel him sometimes."

"Dammit, Finnegan, did you know him? Dopey?"

"Had him pointed out to me once. We never spoke that I remember. I had been told that he resembled me, that he was sometimes mistaken for me, or I for him. I couldn't see much resemblance, other than our being about the same size and shape and coloring."

"That's because you can't look at yourself sideways, Finnegan. You scare me livid sometimes, when I catch you just in the corner of my eye. I jump like I saw dead Dopey in the cabin here again. But I look at you straight, and you're not too much alike."

"What makes you think I can't look at myself sideways, Joe? I can."

"Finnegan, Finnegan," Joe Cross moaned. "There is only one way out of this cabin."

Chapter Five

THE UNACCOUNTABLE CORPSE

There is one thing that thwarts the highest principle, that of non-contradiction: bodies. And thereby it also negates the ontological principle of sufficient reason. There is not sufficient reason for bodies.
  IGNACE WOLFF, *Gedanken von Leibern*

1.

This may have been at Paraiso, or it may have been at Campeche, or at still another stop. There was a shallow harbor there, with a very old town, and parts of another town only half as old. The Brunhilde had not docked the night before, but had anchored off. *Los Grandes*, Seaworthy and his associates, had gone ashore in a boat with two of the seamen.

And the next morning, Finnegan and Anastasia went ashore in the other boat, and the Devil also, and the titaness Marie, and Joe Cross the red-headed seaman. They had coffee at a compassionate little place, after which Joe and the iridescent Marie went to find a smooth beach. Finnegan and Anastasia got an amphora of rum, or a little less, and went up past the cigar factory to climb over the ruins and old walls. The Devil meanwhile went about the Devil's own business.

The old walls were luxuriant, overgrown by a perversity of grass and brush, full of lizards and small snakes and angry birds. Then the two climbers found a giant's chair up in the old walls, and from there they spied on the world. Anastasia commented on everyone.

"Art Emery is picking his nose on the fantail of the Brunhilde. It doesn't need it: he picked it yesterday. He is desolate. He used to be the Devil's catamount, and now the Devil rejects him. Harry Scott is scrubbing out his

T-shirts in that little tub but what he is trying to scrub out isn't on his T-shirts. Manuel is saying his prayers, and the cook De Polis is putting garlic in the stew, so both are gainfully employed. Prayer and garlic are the only two things that can change the nature of the world.

"Chris McAbney is filling his pipe as he waits for *Los Grandes*. He counts every grain and shred that goes in. He knows just how many little pieces of tobacco there ought to be in a can of crimp cut. Why don't Joe and Marie walk on the open beach instead of under the trees? How can you spy on people if they walk under the trees?"

"It narrows further down, and they will have to come into the open," Finnegan said. "Then you can spy all you wish, Anastasia."

"Where the Devil did the Devil go?"

"I don't know. He seemed lonesome. There's a story that he loves company, but he abuses it."

"Ten days ago I knew all the answers, Finnegan. I knew whose creature everyone was, how much blood was on everyone's hands, and where most of the bodies were buried. Now it has changed."

"What changed it?"

"The Devil changed it. There is something the matter with the Devil, Finnegan."

"That has always been the opinion."

"That isn't what I mean! He isn't like the old Devil he used to be. When you can't depend on the Devil, who can you depend on? And I don't even know where you come in, Finnegan. Everyone thinks you are Seaworthy's creature. I think you are the Devil's."

"I am nobody's creature, Anastasia. It all happened as casually as I told you."

"You may not know it yourself, Finn, but there is more than that to it. Do you understand that the Brunhilde is a plague ship, and everywhere it touches it infects."

"I think I understand that."

"It wasn't casual that *I* came along, Finnegan. I told you several sets of lies as to why I came. The truth is that I decided to deal myself a hand in this."

"Who are you, Anastasia? And aren't you awful little to be dealing yourself a hand?"

"I am your sister, which you do not understand. And I still deal me a hand."

"What is between you and Don Lewis?"

"Nothing. How could there be? We hardly ever speak."

"You are so careful to stay apart, there is something between you. Is Marie also a part of the plague?"

"Of course she is. And she can read me like a book; I am her patsy. I can't make a move she doesn't know. She seems so transparent, and she isn't. She's clear mad, you know. I mean it. She's crazy."

The giant's chair was a rock slab eight feet wide, dished and backed. It was all that was left of an old rock flooring and an old wall.

"I don't want us to be at cross purposes," Finnegan said. "I may have to play a hand too, and there are too many jokers and one-eyed jacks in this deck. It frightens me that I have seen you dead."

"Everyone to his own premonitions. I trust my own, and it will take more than a premonition to kill me. Listen, little brother, we are very close without ever talking about it. You call me an urchin and a tramp, but I know how much you're taken with me. But it will have to wait."

Papa Devil came up the old walls and appeared like a spook. He was a big man who could move without noise. With the Devil was a Descalced who also moved noiselessly. But he had natural advantages for that.

"What have you two been watching?" the Devil asked them with the voice that seemed to come out of the bowels of the green earth.

"We watch everyone," Anastasia said. "We have been watching Joe and Marie, but they keep going under the trees."

"Don't watch too many things. There is a sickness, it might even be a fatality, that comes to those who see too much. Don't stay here long. We leave almost at once."

Papa Devil went down again, over the rough path. The rocks and creepers stayed out of his way, not daring to interfere with him.

"He is a remarkable man," said the Descalced. "A priest sees every sort of evil in the course of his life, but this man goes beyond all that, in the aura of him."

"Are you sure he is a man?" Finnegan asked the barefoot priest.

"A man? Oh, I understand what you mean, but we must

assume that he is. We all have something of the unnatural and unmentionable in us. But he is remarkably evil, astute, satanic. Partly, of course, he was having fun with me because I am a religious; and I was having fun with him. The Devil is not so purple as he is painted, nor am I so naive as I seem. But withal, he is very evil."

"Withal, he is that," said Finnegan. They gave the Descalced the last drink. He blessed them for it with his eyes, and he walked down to the boat with them.

Chris McAbney did not sail with them from that place. Finnegan heard that he was dead.

2.

Finnegan swam a lot beneath the surface of the water wearing a face mask. At least one of the barroom panels would be an underwater picture, and he was studying the lights and color. That, and the sunlit swarms of peanut-sized fishes.

It was while swimming underwater that an episode came back to Finnegan like a grotesque dream, an episode of the vague night on which he had first met Saxon X. Seaworthy.

Freud was not acquainted with underwater swimming as a trigger for dream or suppressed incident recall; and nobody else has treated the subject properly. But there *is* a submarine parallel to the unconscious, and many divers have mentioned the effect on themselves.

Finnegan had begun to remember it that very morning when Seaworthy had had a long talk with him. It had set the basis for the recall.

"I had a dream last night," said Seaworthy, "and this was it:

"I was in India. India is often the site of my dreams, and it is the land of my unconscious. India is a night world, however bright it may be; it is the unconscious counterpart of the rest of the world. Did you know that there is a sect of Hindus who believe that India is itself Purgatory? And that they are already dead and expiating their sins? This has been taken by some as subtle attack on life under the British, but the sect is authentic.

58

"Anyhow, Finnegan, I was in India, and in a great and crowded city which I could not and cannot identify, but to which I have often been in my dreams. My dream was monotone, all in gray, with no real color in it at all. I had with me a corpse, and I was trying to get rid of it.

"This was a vivid dream, but there was a mystery about the face of the corpse. It sometimes had a very definite face, and then mercifully it would have no face at all."

"I like them better without faces," said Finnegan.

"So do I, but I know that it cannot be. That face will still confront me."

Saxon Seaworthy had had a curious look on him, the look of a man who will not scare in a situation where he has the right to be scared. He continued in his intricate voice that always surprised Finnegan, coming out of so dull-appearing and stony-faced a man.

"There is a certain embarrassment in being burdened with a corpse, Finnegan, even in a dream in India. I believe that the word embarrassed itself means to be burdened with. It is also very difficult to dispose of a corpse through irregular channels, any time, any where. There is a stickiness about corpses. You cannot let go of them.

"I had a small cart on which the body was loaded. One wheel was always coming off. This is a disability of those small Asian carts: the wheels are not wedged on properly. I was irritated with the poor construction, even though I knew I was dreaming.

"I also had a small shovel. I would start to dig a shallow grave in a little garden; and there would be such protest about it as if I were burying my own mother shamefully. The corpse was a male figure; it was not that of my mother.

"I would sometimes dump it into a gutter and start to run away with my clattering cart. But they would always catch me and make me load it up again. I pushed it several times through open windows, but persistent hands always pushed it out to me again. 'Take it along with you. It's your own fault,' they said. *'Ye tumhara hi kasur hai.'* The dream, of course, was in Hindi."

"The hands said that?"

"This was a dream, Finnegan. Subjects change in dreams, and grammar is unstable. I tried just leaving the corpse on the cart on the street and walking away whistling softly. I was brought back sternly this time and told 'If you don't get it out of here, people are going to start asking what you're doing with it in the first place.' After that it seemed that everyone looked askance at me and my corpse and drew away from us a little. And now I tried to recall where I had gotten the corpse, and I could not remember. What was I doing with it? And why was I responsible for it? Finnegan, did you ever try to get rid of an unaccountable corpse?"

"Not that I remember. Not in India. Not in a dream. What did you finally do?"

"I don't know. In the dream it seemed as though the corpse itself grappled with me when I had escaped all surveillance and was about to get it covered. 'Ah well, you can bury me,' it said, 'but who is going to bury you?' That is my dream, Finnegan. Do you know what it means?"

"No. I am not Joseph."

"I was hoping that you would know, Finnegan. For the dream is inextricably connected with the night on which I met you and at the end of which we ended up sitting on the sidewalk together. I wish that you would try to remember it for several reasons."

Seaworthy had a burrowing look. He meant that Finnegan had *better* remember it.

Finnegan had thought about it that morning with growing apprehension. He thought about it while he also considered the shoulders of Marie and the knees of Anastasia. He thought about it that afternoon as he swam underwater with a face mask.

He had read a little about dreams in both Gypsy Dream Books and in Freudian literature and had found about an equal sagacity in both. Now, a corpse may mean a lot of things. It could mean a wish for death, or a guilt of death, or any guilt. It could mean a violating or a corrupting. It could mean a terrible drunkenness. In all such cases the corpse would seem attached to one.

Finnegan got the answer while he was swimming. A dream object may be an euphemism for something more shocking than itself. But what, to a worried man, is more shocking than a corpse? And somewhere was the warning against overlooking the obvious.

The corpse was a corpse, that was all. It was literally itself. Saxon X. Seaworthy had been embarrassed by a corpse and had tried to dispose of it. And if India was his antipodal land, then it had probably happened in Western lands.

When?

It was inextricably connected with the night on which Finnegan and Seaworthy had met.

Finnegan gazed jowl to jowl with a little fish. Then he remembered about it and wished that he had not. There had been a corpse, and Finnegan had been involved.

3.

For, as a matter of fact, Finnegan *had* helped Saxon bury a body. It was odd that he had forgotten about it, and odder still that he could not now remember more.

He had been drinking to the point of oblivion—but no, that had been later, that had been after the burying. Finnegan had been drinking only a little, but his mood had been a drunken one before he started. He had felt then that he was going to have a bout with his old girl Amnesia. Seaworthy had already acquired the corpse when they met. The corpse, in fact, was not yet quite still. It had begun to move again, apparently long after Seaworthy had believed it finished. Seaworthy had quieted it with a shovel. He had broken the skull and spilled part of the brains.

It had been at night in a graveyard. Yes, it was in the graveyard that they met. Saxon had been startled, even displeased, at the encounter with Finnegan. He had been working at the grave before the corpse showed its last flicker of life, and he was working at the grave again, ineptly, when he saw Finnegan and turned ashen.

But Finnegan was at least neighborly. He would help any man in any situation.

"You call that the way to dig a grave?" Finnegan had asked. "You look like you don't know how to dig a grave. Let me dig now and you rest."

He remembered yet the quivering emotion of Seaworthy's face, and he could account not at all for his own conduct. He had been completely mindless, more than in a daze, in an emptiness. That poor old white-faced man needed help, Finnegan had reasoned unreasoningly. He had taken the shovel from him and dug.

Finnegan had dug it a little deeper, and had then broken through for a foot or so. It was an old digging, and there was air-space there below rotten wood splinters. Finnegan fumbled around with his hands in the crevices out of curiosity. His hands had not lost their deftness, even if his mind had done so. He appraised size and shape. He could have drawn every bone he handled. He could have made a good reconstruction of the thing there.

When Finnegan straightened up, Saxon Seaworthy was standing over him with the shovel raised and with an almost evil look on his face. Finnegan was scared of that look when he remembered it now, but he hadn't been so at the time. He realized that his innocence had saved him then; and that an unresolved incident of the event still kept him alive.

"It's deep enough," Finnegan had said. "Let's bury him."

"Yes. Hurry," Saxon Seaworthy had said.

And they completed the job swiftly.

"I wonder," Finnegan had said, "how they will get on?"

"Who?"

"The old one and the new one. The two men in the grave. We should have introduced them. They might be English, and they'll go a long time without speaking if they're not introduced."

"They—they have met before," Saxon had stammered, "and they are not English."

And now the face of that man he had helped bury came over Finnegan with real horror. He wished, as Saxon had, that the corpse might have no face at all. There was a cold current in the water, and Finnegan was at once very chilly. He left the water and climbed back on the Brunhilde.

Now the question was whether his friend Saxon had been as drunk as himself on that memorable night—he hadn't been, not till later, neither had Finnegan been—and whether he did not remember at all, or whether he remembered too well.

Had Saxon really had a dream? Or had he made up the dream to tell Finnegan, as an insistent hint that he would be called on to remember?

(Saxon Seaworthy had had the dream. Screaming dead men! but he had had that dream! He had had it for three nights running, but he didn't need to ask Finnegan what it meant.)

But he had asked Finnegan to remember, and now Finnegan had remembered. It might not be tactful, it might not be safe yet for Finnegan to tell that he had remembered.

Anastasia had said that she had once known where all the bodies were buried, but she hadn't meant it like that. She didn't know where that one was buried, even though she had worked only two hundred yards from it. No, it was not safe to know where or what was buried; and there was another aspect of it more frightening than merely burying a dead man.

The sequel to it had been hair-raising. Finnegan had been there, and he had missed it. But he didn't miss it now.

Finnegan went to the barroom now, and painted the face of the man they had buried, and the face of one other. Someone was going to be taken aback when he saw those two faces together.

4.

Another corpse, one that hadn't been seen, and should have been. The body of Dopey the seaman was not to be found, dead or alive. Somebody knew how to get rid of a corpse when there was no way at all to do it. And a man should have more blood in him than a bug, particularly a man with such a strong invisible residue as had Dopey the seaman. Finnegan sensed that dead but still hovering man every time he lay in his bunk.

And another short snatch read itself to Finnegan out of the envelope behind the overhead balk.

"I will rise high in this if I play it right, I will be rich, I will be power, I will rub peoples noses in it. I make people shake if I get into this I like that part. They will not laugh at Dopey then. Even now they laugh nervous at me. I spook lots of people. Why is bugle nose not dead yet as was suppost. There is not room for both. What if I am the one die trapped. I die here, I bet I die hard."

But apparently the seaman Dopey had died easy. Anyhow, there is always an incoherence about the writings of dead men.

Chapter Six

LULUWAY IS THE PLURAL OF DIAMOND

We speak now of the physical areas of dreams, particularly of sea-dreams. There are the ineffably sad dreams of seamen on the passage between Patrai and Taranto that are referred to in classical times. There are the howling horny dreams, obscenely murderous and of a towering sexuality, that have always possessed those going out of Trondheim fjord to the Faeroes. There is the terrible introspection akin to death that creeps into the dreams of those going from Port of Spain to the African Hump. Dreams do have a topography. Men do dream the same dreams when going through the same sectors.

How will it be when they go through the sectors of space?

—IAN MCIFREANN, *Psychologia Nugarum*

1.

They drifted down the Mexican coast and beyond. They stopped at Campeche, at Progreso, at Cozumel, at Ciudad Chetumal, at Belize, at Puerto Barrios, at La Ceiba, Trujillo, Cabo Gracias a Dios, Blue Fields, Limon, San Cristobal. They made from one hundred to two hundred miles a day. They went ashore at every port.

Sometimes Saxon Seaworthy took Finnegan along. Saxon was more friendly now. This day he was very friendly, and he talked.

"When a man has been very evil, Finnegan, he gets ideas. And I have been very evil. Never meant to be, really. It seems to be in my nature. Then I developed a taste for it, like a hunter after special game. When it's run its full, it gets a clamp on you. Do you believe in the Devil, Finnegan?"

"Oh yes. And he believes in me. There is no question of either of us not existing."

"You cannot kill the Devil, Finnegan. Is it possible that, if we both got as loaded as we were the night we met, we might both of us remember a little more? That was a well-orchestrated orgy. Did you ever kill a man, Finnegan?"

"I doubt it. I was on provisional patrol a few times, and we used to pot shot a couple hundred yards across a valley at our friends. But they never killed me, and I don't think I ever killed them."

"I think that I killed one man in particular, Finnegan. I am more sure that I killed him dead than that I am now alive. But he didn't stay dead.

"Finnegan, this has been puzzling me. A thing like that sticks in the back of your mind. Did I only imagine that I killed him? But there is a veracity that sticks like tar. Besides, I had a witness. If I have any sanity at all, I know that I killed him. Ah, but it does chill me every time I see him alive!"

Finnegan and Seaworthy got lit. Even themselves had hardly done it so thoroughly before. This was in San Cristobal. It was on either December 9th or 10th. They may have spent two days at it; it hurries things to try to do it properly in one.

They drank a great quantity of rum for a night and day, or possibly two nights and days. They exhausted the social possibilities of all the drinking places in that time, and were driven to the formation of a drinking club for themselves only.

They were lying in a garden or park. Saxon Seaworthy had bought this pretty plot of land from its owner for one thousand dollars American, and he had a deed to show for it.

Every hour or so a boy would come across the square to their garden to see how their rum was holding out. The boy was well paid for his trips. An official, who may not have been genuine, collected from them a special property tax on the land. Another official collected a tavern tax from them, as they were using the plot for a tavern. Afterwards, feeling that he had been taken advantage of,

Saxon refused to pay any more extraordinary taxes or assessments.

They did some deep talking. Saxon explained how it was possible for a man to fall into evil habits, and how it could be fun; but that it required ever-increasing participation for satisfaction.

Saxon explained that he himself was a consummate philosopher, and that he had the money in the bank to show for it. Never trust in the philosophy of a man without money, he said. A sound philosophy will always pay its way.

"No. Some day you will meet the confutation of your philosophy," Finnegan said.

"Yes, you are right," Seaworthy suddenly agreed. This was late in the afternoon of the second day. "The confutation of my philosophy has just appeared," Seaworthy said. "It is walking towards us from about a quarter of a mile away. It is coming up the road from the port towards us. I shrink a little, Finnegan, but I do not abandon my position."

"But that is only Papa Devil coming up the road towards us."

"Yes. Do you remember when you first saw his face, Finnegan?"

"There's three different recollections. One is when I went onto the ship with Anastasia for a drink and he ordered us off. One is of his bending over me; this may have been the night when he found me and brought me onto the ship before it sailed, but it seems as if I was seeing him for the first time. There was something wrong about his bending over me, as though I were in the wrong body and he were the Devil indeed. And he killed me then. I remember that clearly."

"He is, Finnegan, he is. He's the very Devil."

"I was terrified of him then, but I had no feeling of terror the night I was carried onto the ship. The other time, the third or the first time I saw him, is the memory of me bending over him. This is the version out of context. It has its hazy elements."

"Like a dream, Finnegan? Something like the dream I told you a couple of days ago? Something like the night we first met?"

"Yes, it is the same thing, Saxon. I have known it for a couple of days now."

"Then to the point, Finnegan, to the point! There could not be two faces like that?"

"Papa Devil's face is a great original, and there is something in all great originals that shocks us. Some things are not meant to happen twice."

"Finnegan, I am not crazy. Did you not help me bury that man Papadiabolous?"

"Yes. That is what happened."

"It couldn't have been a dream?"

"We could not both have dreamed it, Saxon."

"And we could not both be crazy on that point. Two people may be crazy, but they cannot be crazy on the same thing. To be crazy is to be singular. You were there! You do remember!"

"I do remember Papadiabolous dead. May I spend my life trying to forget it!"

"You will have a short life if you ever consider forgetting it. We *did* bury that man!"

"I buried Papa Devil. You couldn't bury a cat. You just don't know how to dig a grave, Saxon."

"And he was dead!"

"Papa Devil was dead. There are certain oozy details of gore and brain that should have insured that he stay dead."

"Ah, but he didn't, Finnegan. That's the whole pointless point of it; he didn't. What do you say to that?"

"That silence you hear is myself. I say nothing."

"But don't you think it odd that he should still be alive and coming up the road to take us back to the ship?"

"It *is* unusual. As you say, a thing like that sticks in the back of your mind. You killed him all right. I saw him dead, I saw him dead!"

"Yes, damned dead, Finnegan, damned dead. And he is here the second time. But I tell you, nobody drinks at my spring three times!"

Papadiabolous took them back to the ship and cleaned them up.

They went to Portobello and Mañana. They went to Cartagena and Santa Maria, Willemsted, Caracas, Cumana, Port of Spain. They were at Port of Spain eight or nine days. They were there Christmas and New Year's. It was on New Year's that Finnegan stopped drinking. He did not drink again till they were in Freetown, Sierra Leone on January 26. He had never been able to go all the way through January, but this time he was very near it.

2.

Now this was the situation at Port of Spain:

Finnegan knew, and Saxon X. Seaworthy did not know, that the Papadiabolous they had buried was not the same Papadiabolous who sailed on the Brunhilde with them. And yet he had the same face. He had the same everything. He convinced those who had been intimate with him for many years.

When Finnegan had painted Papadiabolous dead in the common grave in the Sindbad sequence, and shown him atop another dead man, it had attracted only amusement on board. Nobody except Saxon Seaworthy and Papa Devil understood the meaning. And everybody rather liked to see Papa Devil dead.

And when Finnegan painted another dead man with the real face of Papa Devil, it attracted no notice at all, other than for the startling strength of that face. Nobody could have recognized that face except Papa Devil himself, so only the Devil knew what Finnegan meant.

But some months later it would cause a wonder, when they saw that man dead on the dock, and then came back and saw his face in the cabin painting. Even then they did not know who he was, and Finnegan had escaped and was not there to tell them.

They were at Cayenne, at Belem, at São Luis, at Camocim. They were at Fortaleza and Natal. They were at Natal six days while they checked and stowed for the Atlantic crossing. They sailed from Natal on January 18th.

Finnegan believed that it was time to have a talk with the Devil. He felt his life to be in danger, though he had never prized it very highly. If Saxon Seaworthy had killed one man for unknown reasons, he might kill another man who knew about it. Finnegan believed that Seaworthy was keeping him alive as confirmation of his own sanity, as confirmation that the thing had actually happened. When he finally discovered that the man he had killed was really dead, he would no longer have any reason for keeping Finnegan alive.

But Papa Devil, the key to everything here, would be a hard man to get anything out of. He hadn't even blinked when Finnegan had painted him in his real appearance which was unknown to anyone else on the Brunhilde. Papa Devil should have been curious about how Finnegan knew his appearance, and he didn't seem to be.

Besides, Finnegan was still a little bit afraid of the Devil, even though he knew that part of that sinister face was a mask. A man as big as Papa Devil was, and one as often on the edge of anger, was a man to be a little afraid of. And every encounter with the Devil raised more mysteries than it followed.

"What is the Devil up to? What is his aim?" Finnegan said loudly, coming on the Devil suddenly during the Atlantic crossing. It was on a dark deck and Finnegan had come up behind the Devil silently, but he certainly hadn't slipped up on him.

"Ah, the first aim of the Devil is to convince people that he doesn't exist," the Devil said easily, "just as the first aim of all conspirators is to convince people that there are no conspiracies. It is by this tactic that he achieves his goals. Oh, you mean myself? I am up to nothing, Finnegan."

"Papa Devil, you can play smoother games than I can. I will have to talk to you directly. A week or so before we sailed there was a man who was killed and buried and who looked very like you."

"He must have been a handsome fellow, Finn boy. I didn't know that such a masterpiece could occur twice."

"Neither did I. That is the trouble, Papa. Such a masterpiece *has* occurred twice."

"Are you sure that he was dead and buried?"

"Yes. I handled him dead. And I buried him. There is at least one who believes that man was you."

"He must be a gullible sort."

"He is the least gullible man in the world. He also believes now that you cannot kill the Devil."

"That is for God and St. Michael to worry about, Finn, not for us. We haven't the equipment for it."

"He halfway believes that you *are* the Devil."

"I halfway am, Finnegan, but not in the literal sense. But I can understand the effect it might have on one to kill a man, and then to encounter him alive the next day; quite early the next day it was, before he had recovered from his bout. I try to enhance the effect in him as much as I am able. It should worry him a lot, and you a little. You must be putting in some sleepless nights, now that you are not drinking. That's the time to catch up on your thinking."

"Yes. I try to catch up. There is a mimicry here beyond all believing. How can you do it so well as to fool even those who knew him for many years?"

"Knew who, Finnegan?"

"The original Papadiabolous."

"But I *am* Papadiabolous, and there has never been any other. You surely don't think you have come on the answer, do you, Finnegan?"

"It is sheer art, and there is no more than an ounce of filler in your face. And the voice, the gait, the handling of the body, the habits, the knowledge of details, they must be more than perfect. You have never slipped once, it seems. Where had you observed him? Your real face isn't known to any of them on the Brunhilde, and some of them knew the original Papadiabolous for many years. How do you do it?"

"You speak in riddles, boy. There is no me but me."

"Your face is part mask, Papa Devil."

"Perhaps it is, Finnegan, and perhaps it has been so the many years. You are shopping for easy falsehoods, and the truth is more wonderful. Is it not wonderful, Finnegan, that I was dead and that now I live? That was a fine portrait that you painted of me dead, Finnegan. Quite good of me."

"Which one, Papa Devil, which one?"

"I saw but one. Did you paint two of me, Finnegan? Are there two of me?"

"Not only are there two of you; you make it seem that

there are two of me. Papa Devil, how did you kill Doppio di Pinne and leave no trace?"

"I kill a man, Finnegan? Why, I am like a lamb. Dopey the seaman was your double, your fetch, Finnegan. I suspect that you killed him, if he ever lived. Perhaps you are Dopey with only an ounce of filler added to the nose."

Well, Finnegan knew he wasn't, but how do you argue with the Devil?

They left Natal January 18th. They arrived at Freetown, Sierra Leone on January 26, quite a few years ago. It was a smoky old crossing. A ship should never go from Brazil to Africa, only from Africa to Brazil. It is much easier to drift West.

According to Papadiabolous, the westward drift had been accomplished by every people who ever lived on the east shore of the Atlantic. For, once caught in the current and the winds, it is hard for a small boat to get back to Africa or Europe. When they had given up, they would go west and southwest, straight on; and in from four hundred to five hundred and fifty hours they would be off the Brazil coast.

"But the returns were difficult,'" said Papa Devil as he talked to several of them. "They were almost impossible, like a return from the grave, which is difficult and nearly impossible. Only a few have made either return, and these have been regarded askance."

Saxon Seaworthy was uneasy when this discourse was given by Papadiabolous, but he said he believed that very few primitives had ever arrived alive on the Brazil coast, just as few arrived alive into the grave. And he gave it as his measured opinion that even fewer had returned from those latter shores, and that they returned at their peril. It could be a very dangerous trip back, he said.

Finnegan was interested in this duel between Seaworthy and the Devil, especially when Seaworthy gave his considered opinion that nobody was likely to make the return trip twice.

'... the terrible introspection akin to death that creeps into the dreams of those going to the African Hump ...'
Oh well, it wasn't as extreme as that, but the apprehension did creep into the dreams of Finnegan.

"I have never felt myself to be a person," he said as he sat and talked to himself across a table. "I have never been able to touch any human person in any way. I have never had a friend in the human flesh.

"Oh, there are those who are friendly enough to me in my normal life, Vincent and Casey and Hans and Henry, Show Boat and Dotty Yekouris and Marie Monaghan, Mary Schaeffer, Loy Larkin and Tom Shire and Freddy Castle, the Howlands, Absalom Stein and Melchisedech Duffy, Mr. X and Hillary Hilton and my sister Patty. Oh, they like me and perhaps they love me (some of them do), and I would love them if I knew how it was done. But there is a barrier between myself and the human kind.

"The only human I was ever able to touch was my own father. That was for only a short moment, and it was many years after he was dead. And my father also had this difficulty all his life. He was not able to make contact with the human kind. What do you think of that, Finnegan?"

Then Finnegan shifted his mind into the other Finnegan across the table, went over and looked out of his eyes and talked out of his mouth. He talked back across the table to the Finnegan he had just inhabited:

"Well, Finnegan, if I am not people, what am I? We know that I do not remember my own childhood except as a derivative thing, as though told me of someone else. The world began for me when I was walking down a street with Vincent Stranahan in Sydney Town back in the war years. It began that sudden morning, but it has also begun at other times. I am newborn out of the oblivions time after time, but is there anything, other than memory once removed, that links these separate existences of mine?

"Finnegan, I have passed, nearly, for a human person all the days of my life, except for the great unremembered gaps in that life. Here on the Brunhilde I sometimes catch a phrase out of the air 'the other human race', and I am not sure whom I catch it from. Well, is there another human race? What am I? There is, I know, an animal inside me, but it isn't a human animal in the regular sense. Perhaps it is the other sort of human animal. Say, I *do* look more like Dopey the seaman than I believed. I'll slip across the table and find out if the me here looks like Dopey too."

Finnegan skipped his mind over and looked out of the other Finnegan's eyes. Sure enough, the Finnegan he had just been in looked quite a bit like Dopey also.

Quite a few of those introspective ocean dreams, quite odd ones. There was one that involved Marie Courtois, and Finnegan was not sure whether they both were bodily present or how much of the dream was a waking one.

Marie said that she was Demeter, and that she was also her own daughter Persephone, that she lived in Hell in her one person, but that she returned to Earth every year in her own reincarnation.

"This return of the earthy ones is the only immortality there is, Finnegan," she told him. "All the rest is up in the air, and we are of the Earth. I will make you understand that there cannot be anything else."

"You are wrong, but the proof isn't here," Finnegan said. "We will all cross that bridge in our own time. And what good is it then to say I could have told you."

"Believe me, Finnegan, that bridge has only one shore."

"We would have to ask someone who has been over it, Marie."

"I *have* been over it. There is no other side."

"Your Demeter was only a corn goddess, Marie, and you are full of corn."

"We are all of us that, Finnegan, and you are one of us. And this old earthiness, which you still call evil, is a lot of fun. Until you have blood on your hands you cannot know how much fun it is."

"And you have?"

"Finnegan, the blood on my hands is what sings me to sleep at night."

They were on a jungle-crowded beach (for all that they should have been on the Brunhilde in mid-Atlantic) and Finnegan lay with his head in Marie's lap, and entirely encircled with her hair. She looped it clear around him and tied him in with knots.

She talked to him a mystic bit about kopolatry, and the *gremium matris*, which is the Earth itself, and which is the lap of Marie also; about the *pietà* form of the thirteenth station which, in the old Roman Way of the Cross, was located on Aventine hill where earlier was a representation of Demeter and Pontos in such a grouping. "Oh, it is earthy!" she said, "and it is so childish to seek for a chaste element in it."

Well, well, was there a seduction scene then?

Enjoy or abhor such things according to your inclination, as the sage says, but it is contemptible to seek such vicariously.

3.

Finnegan fell from grace on January 26, the day that they landed, and went back on the drink. This was in Freetown.

"This reminds me of a joke of my own making," he told Joseph. "One man said 'Did you ever try to sit on a girl's lap?' and the other one said 'Sure. That's how I fell from Grace.'"

"That's an interesting story," said Joseph. "I hadn't known that was the origin of the phrase."

Joseph was a Haussa boy, and Finnegan was getting drunk with him. Joseph himself had a very hard head and was not affected. Joseph was from further south, Nigeria or the Gold Coast. He was much traveled. He had been a caravan boy and a seaman. They were drinking *bam*, which is a palm wine.

"You are a low-lifer like me," Joseph said, "or you would be in the hotel bar drinking whisky or Holland gin with your shipmates, the golden goddess and the little sparrow. You are *Bature?*"

"Yes. Italian is my ancestry."

"You could almost be black. *Mi ke nan.* Surely you have been taken for black before. *Kava sunan ka?*"

"Kaka whatta? Oh, my name? I am Finnegan."

"What is your Christian name?"

"John."

"John, we will be friends. If you are tired of *bam*, we will go to my room where I have a bottle of gin. We will go into the garden and drink it. Then I will make you a proposition."

Joseph the Haussa boy had gone far. They were drinking the gin in the garden.

"I have the languages," Joseph told Finnegan. "My

English, while not perfect, is better than your own. Arabic I have long ago when I am a caravan boy, and Ful is like my own Haussa to me. Do you know that there are twenty-five million people who understand these two? French I have when I am with the caravans also. Afrikaans I know, but not proper Dutch. I will have to learn this; I need it in my business."

"What business?" Finnegan asked. "Why would anyone need Dutch? And why in peanut picker's heaven would anyone need proper Dutch?"

"It is difficult to find trustworthy partners, Finnegan. I myself do not cut too good a figure in Paris or Amsterdam or New York when I must market there. There are those who would take advantage of a black man, particularly one who walks awkwardly in shoes. I need someone like you, suave and worldly and honest, and who will not spoil a deal by haste or nervousness. It is sometimes years before we can realize on a consignment."

"You sound like a businessman, Joseph."

"We Haussa have been called the Jews of Africa. My father was a merchant, and I also am a merchant of a rare commodity."

"What is the commodity? What are you, Joseph?"

"I am a diamond smuggler. That is my trade and the way I make my living. That is my way of life."

"This would seem an odd stop-off place for diamonds, where they are neither produced, nor—if that is the word—consumed."

"But here they *are* produced. Not all African diamonds are South African. Sierra Leone is a big producer. Out of here are many pedlars, and in some ways I am the most unlikely. But I do well.

"I can still do the back-country boy, with the simple come-on story, and the raw stone in my little black hand. And I can do the dandy. But the big deals aren't here; they are where the foreign marketing is done; distance multiplies the value of this merchandise remarkably. You will work with me in this and we will prosper."

"Joseph, I know very little about the *lulus*."

"All this will come to you. And *luluway*, not *lulus*, is the plural of diamond. Each man must have his own technique. It is better to take no models, for all the master pedlars have made mistakes. Simply forget that you have the stuff with you and follow other apparent business. You will find in you a talent for this. You do not look like a diamond smuggler, Finnegan, but I am at a loss to say just what you do look like. By the way, why do you, a good man, travel with these evil ones?"

"Do I look like a good man, skunk drunk here, Joseph?"

"Yes, you are a good man."

"And are you sure that they are evil?"

"John, even the carrion birds would not touch them when they are dead. I know what they are."

Finnegan was with Joseph for several days. When he left him he had a very heavy leather sack full of rocks. For the next few years, until his death, Finnegan marketed from that sack, and from two others, and sent drafts to Freetown. Though he starved and went all the way down sometimes, this was a source of many of his amazing comebacks.

But in the meanwhile he was on the drink again, and could only break off from it once or twice a year, and then for only a few days at a time. And he was in peril, and traveling with wicked men on a plague ship.

They started up coast on the first day of February. They went to Bissau, Bathurst, Dakar, St. Louis. They went to Memrhar, Port Etienne, Villa Cisneros, Las Palmas. They went to the Grand Canary where they stayed two days.

Chapter Seven

HABIB, I HAVE FOUND SOMETHING

But I have dreamed a dreary dream Beyond the Isle of Sky; I saw a dead man win a fight, and I think that man was I.
—CHEVY CHASE

1.

"This is fantastic," Finnegan said to Don Lewis. They were on the Grand Canary, and Finnegan had a pack of newspapers in English, Spanish, Portuguese and French. "I always liked to be where things were happening, and I've had pretty good luck in my life thus far. But we've been missing everything! It isn't possible! Riots, massacres, treasons, mad-man movements, genocides, mass rapes, murders of entire groups. The world is aghast, and yet the world is delighted; it likes exciting things. Towns burned down! Declarations!

"But, Don, we barely missed every damned one of them. We were a little too early in every place. Here are two dozen points in two worlds that have gone crazy, and in every case the ruckus took place within several days of our leaving. It's uncanny."

"No, it's canny enough, Finnegan," Don Lewis said. "The fires that have started in these coastal places will burn till the whole little countries are consumed; and will spread to others. The world is on fire, Finnegan. We've been torching it with short fuses."

"Will it burn up, do you think, Don?"

"I don't know. It hasn't quite before. They have better technique every time they try it," said Don Barnaby. No, no! This was Don Lewis and not Don Barnaby! Finnegan later became confused on them, but the historian must not be confused on this point.

"Why do we—they—do it, Don? Don, you are looking bad these days."

"I think we—they—are jealous of people, Finnegan. Yes, I look bad; like a man who has not quite two weeks to live, Finnegan? It's sad about my going so young."

It was luxurious here on the Grand Canary. They had cleaned up and dressed. It was a night restaurant, grand in the old manner, and they were the grandest things in it.

Papa Devil lacked only a monocle to look like Count von Baummenbauch. Then Finnegan gasped. Papa Devil popped the monocle into his face. He was perfect, the great evil Count himself, the Devil masquerading as the Count in perfect form.

Anastasia needed nothing at all to look like a high Renaissance dream, Venetian surely (did you know that Naxos was once Venetian?), as she had been in one of her incarnations.

Marie Courtois looked like Lilith of the enchanted hair, but much more exciting. Lilith had not such shoulders, could not have stood out so golden in a crowd.

Finnegan was the very person of a Montenegran prince, noble of nose and burned almost black. And nobody could wear evening clothes like Finnegan.

Saxon X. Seaworthy could have been Merlin the wizard, if wizardry paid as well as the line he was in. There is something about high granite that not even travertine marble can touch. What a face Seaworthy did have when it came alive!

Joe Cross had his very youthful face now encircled with a red beard. What younger brother of a king was he anyhow?

Manuel the stowaway, clad by the bounty of Saxon Seaworthy in evening clothes, was a distinguished and weary old nobleman, one who habitually dined with cardinals and ministers of state.

Orestes Gonof, the forgotten captain of the Brunhilde, could have been a Phoenician sea captain come back to the Grand Canary after a three thousand year absence.

Don Lewis, who already had the mark of death on him, was attractive in his role. He had a fevered handsomeness, and he would be the featured person in the next act of the masque.

All of them were burned much blacker than their usual color, and they had a sparkle on them as they talked under the lights.

It happened that there were personages in the dining room that night who would ordinarily be stared at. But it was the personages instead who stared enraptured at the party of Seaworthy and the Devil, and whispered about him. For that was Saxon X. Seaworthy, the mysterious millionaire (though some of the personages were as wealthy), and that was the even more mysterious Papadiabolous. And these were likely some sort of exiled royalty with them, for Seaworthy, among other things, had dealt in exiled royalty. Whatever it was, some cabinet head in some state would surely sleep less easily that night because of them.

And they *were* an exiled royalty, exiled for thousands of years, and returning and returning again and again. They were timeless, and they were alive and vigorous.

So the personages gazed at the party from across the room. And the waiter, who was a Guanche from before the time of Spain, brought the brandy. They drank till it was time for the dining room to close. Then they went to their rooms in the hotel on the island that was once a volcano.

After this, things went rapidly. They went to Arrecife on Lanzarote, and to Ifni; to Agadir, Magadar, Safti, Mazagan, Casablanca, Rabat. They went to Tangier where they stayed for three days. This was Tuesday, Wednesday, and Thursday of the second week of lent.

2.

In Tangier something happened that had been hanging like a storm, and it broke on the third day there. Doomsday morning was sullen, and it became an angry day full of angry people.

Anastasia was sulky and scared. She would not go walking with Finnegan, even to the casbah. "Oh, don't be so damned childish," she flared, and then she said "dear," as an afterthought. Well, of course it was childish, but all travel and all new things are childish. She had been crying. There was no getting at what was in her.

Finnegan met Joe Cross in the street and asked him to come along and see if they could find anything exciting in the town.

"Don't bother me, boy, don't get in my way," Joe growled. "Stay out of the way or I'll show you something exciting. It could be you."

This was unexpected. Joe was always friendly. Joe had bulges. Joe was armed today.

Don Lewis had not been seen by anyone since early the day before. Somebody said that he had jumped ship. And yet there he was now, plain enough, standing in a little lane and seeming to seek a shadow behind a group of locals.

"Are you all right, Don?" Finnegan asked him, for there did seem to be something different about Don today.

"You don't even know me, Finnegan!" Don croaked. "My God, you don't know me. How could you know it was me? Don't be near me. Don't even follow me. Just go away somewhere. How do I know you're not the one?"

"I'm worried about you, Don."

"Not as much as I am. But it can be you as well as any of them. I'm telling you to stand off!"

Don was robed and hooded in what he must have believed was some native style, and his face was hidden. But how does a man believe he can masquerade from those who know him? Don Lewis also had a bulge on him that even the robe couldn't hide. Everyone was armed and unfriendly to Finnegan.

Either Finnegan had picked up a new stench unknown to himself, or there was something odd afoot. Finnegan *did* have the stenches that are common to casual travel, but he didn't have any new ones.

And even the golden giantess was aloof.

"Darling, I would rather frolic with you than anyone else in the world," Marie said. "You know that. Ask me again. Ask me every day, but not today. I have various offices to visit and a tremendous amount of paper work to accomplish. That is the penalty of being a secretary."

Now Finnegan knew that the strangely talented Marie Courtois could accomplish all paper work with amazing speed, and she ate up agenda like apricots. What offices in strange ports were visited were visited by Seaworthy and his queer cronies. Work was unlikely to stand in the way of pleasure with Marie.

And she couldn't be doing paper work strolling in the street there, but at least she had no bulges other than those normal to her.

Papa Devil was standing on a street corner and he glanced icily at Finnegan.

"My God, Finnegan, I'd forgotten about you," he blurted. "It had better *not* be you! How can I watch everyone at once? I say it is *not* going to happen to him!"

"Why do you have to watch anyone, Papa Devil? Relax a little. Come shoot a game of Kelly pool with me. I know a place."

But Papa Devil exploded with a profanity known only by the Devil and used by him only in moments of stress. Papa of the evil liver and disposition was in no mood to talk to Finnegan or to anybody.

Seaworthy had taken hotel rooms for them these days. He had more than usual business in Tangier.

It was a hunt today. The horns were blowing already if you had ears for them. A death hunt, and Finnegan didn't even know the predators from the prey.

Finnegan tried to keep track of his mates, but they all scattered like a flock of blackbirds, and in all directions: Don and Joe and Marie and Papa Devil and Manuel and Orestes the captain and Art and Harry. The Devil himself was loose in the streets, and it was the long last day of life for someone.

So Finnegan wandered that day through the rich town and the poor town, wondering how he could keep a friend from getting killed, not knowing for sure which friend it was, not sure what was going to happen, not knowing how he knew that something was to happen.

He ate almonds and burned sheep and drank lemonade and Spanish wine. He talked to people in Spanish and French. He also talked to people in Arabic, but they looked at him in incomprehension, especially the Arabs. Hell, Finnegan had been through a book on colloquial Arabic on the trans-Atlantic voyage. It was put together by a man named O'Leary. Would an Irishman do a man wrong in this? But the Arabs did not recognize their own language from the Finnegan mouth.

Finn played the finger-count game with a little Arab boy. Finnegan had always thought the game was Italian, but the boy said that they also had always had it. Finnegan and the boy pledged friendship for life, after which the boy organized a valiant body of runners to keep Finnegan informed. The little boys understood Finnegan better than did the big people; they were smarter.

Finn bought small pieces of jewelry for Anastasia, and a sort of white shawl or stole for himself. He wound it around his head for protection from the sun, and let it hang down.

He picked up the various spoors of his shipmates, and noticed that some of them were following others. Three who took one general direction were Don Lewis, still robed in his inexplicable disguise as any sensor could sense, and Marie, and Papa Devil; though they did not go at the same time nor from the same places.

"I should be a tracker," Finnegan said. "I would be good at it. I wonder if there is any money in the tracker business today."

Finnegan wandered out where the weeds were denser and the shanties more sparse, hoping he would arrive at the right place by the right time, not knowing if there was a right time.

Why should Papa Devil have to watch everyone, and who would watch Papa? If Papa didn't know what was happening, who would know? Papa Devil knew everything. Finnegan had to stop something, and didn't even know where to start with it.

Then, with black apprehension, he knew that he was missing it. Too late, he ran furiously where he was impelled.

3.

Don Lewis was a coward. He had twice proclaimed himself to be that. However, he was playing a rather loose game for a coward, and he had been playing it for months and perhaps years.

He had begun to assemble the nucleus of a resistance on the Brunhilde itself, and he had established ingenious communication to circumvent the directors of the ship. He had brought about the appearance of Joe Cross, and Manuel, and Anastasia, and done it deftly so that none knew they were even a loose group. And it was Don's communication that had brought about the resurrection of the Devil, after he was murdered; but Don was totally in the dark about a critical part of that happening. And Don had brought about the appearance of Finnegan on the scene, which Finnegan now dimly suspected. And Don had also tilted the balance so that it was Finnegan who lived and Dopey the seaman who died.

Don had misled the powers of the Brunhilde for a while. At Campeche or at Paraiso, one of the seamen had been killed and left behind, due to Don's careful shifting on the suspicion from himself to that one. He'd had them killing their own.

Now he had slipped, still not knowing how. They were onto him, and it would be final. He had come to the long last day of his life. He was loose in Tangier like a rat in a burrow, and the snakes were in after him at every entrance. He must find sanctuary.

Don went to the consulate of his own country. He wanted to claim protection from the stalking killers. But he saw Saxon Seaworthy there, standing inside the building and talking to one of the officials. Don knew, as well as if he had heard it, that Seaworthy was telling the official that there was this seaman of his, and that he was a looney. And Seaworthy would be believed. There was a prime snake at this entrance of the burrow.

In rich town or poor town, in wide streets or narrow, where can one best find safety? Would they hesitate to kill him in a crowd, or would they kill him the more readily in the confusion of the crowd? Some of the men of the Brunhilde were not given to hesitating at all.

Art or Harry would kill him if they were told to kill. Chris McAbney would have done it; but Chris, of course, had long since been done for. Yet there was something of that unpleasant dead man that followed Don Lewis now. Must it be a hand of flesh that kills?

Captain Gonof himself might do it as his proper job, or even one of *Los Grandes*. The Devil might do it. Was he even sure of Joe Cross, now that Joe had become close to Marie? Or Finnegan? But who was Finnegan really? Finnegan himself did not know that. What did *anyone* know about Finnegan; what had he to recommend him, other than that Anastasia trusted him? And that he had been recommended by another man as shadowy as himself? Finnegan may have been Seaworthy's man, and killing may have been his specialty.

And who the devil *was* the Devil now? Papadiabolous had once given Don Lewis the sign, known only to a man Don had contacted distantly. How had Papa known to give the sign? How had he intercepted? Anastasia had told Don that the Devil might not be the same Devil. How could he not be the same?

Don Lewis bolted in panic when he discovered that the narrow street he had been walking during his introspection was a dead end. He wouldn't be caught in a dead end; he'd rather be caught in the absolute open. He retraced his way, running, knocking into people. He came to a stop in an open square.

"You are nervous?" a European man asked him. "You are in trouble?" The man spoke in Spanish, but sounded French.

"I am in deep trouble. It is for my life. I have to hide." Don also spoke in Spanish, and sounded like an American trying to sound like an Arab.

"There is such a place where you might go," the man said. "Listen carefully." Then the man told Don that there was a man, at a certain junction of a certain street, who would hide anyone for money. "You have money?" the man asked.

"Yes. I have money. I will try anything. Thank you."

Don found the street. He found the man who would hide a man for money.

"You have come," said that man. "They said that it was better to overestimate than to underestimate you. But they didn't think you would know to come here."

"You know who I am?" Don breathed heavily. "You know what I want?"

"It is my business to know. Naturally they contacted me. I am the only one in this town who can hide a man, and nobody can hide from me."

"Are you can hide me for money?"

"That is my business. I can hide you even from them, for enough money. How much do you have?"

85

"Five hundred dollars American."

The face of the man twisted as if in a spasm. Don thought that he was sick or stricken. Then he discovered that the man was laughing at him.

"Five h-h-h-hundred," the man giggled. "Oh, it is such light moments as this that I live for! Oh, you are the rich one!"

"I don't understand," Don gaped, shattered by his own apprehensions.

"Five hundred dollars wouldn't be coffee money for me. I wouldn't sell my own sister or betray my mother for so small a sum. Five hundred dollars! That wouldn't keep a nervous man in toothpicks one morning. Those who hunt you would be shocked to know that you place so small a value on your own life."

"That's all I have!"

"Shall I phone for them to come for you here? I have a room where they can take care of you with a minimum of fuss. You can die clean. It will be better for everyone that way. It's much better than dying with your face in the dust."

Don bolted from that establishment. There was likewise a snake at that entrance of the burrow. Seaworthy, of course, would know about the man who could hide anyone and who could not be hid from. Now Seaworthy would know, likely he had already known, that his prey was robed and hooded now.

Don's mind was working furiously and he missed no detail. He worked to the shabby fringes of the city. He knew that he had given Art and Harry the slip, and he believed himself more than competent to deal with either. Joe Cross seemed to be staying between the ship and the hotel as though to watch both, and Don had no intention of approaching either. And Don had lost Captain Gonof; the captain had not seemed to be following seriously.

Papa Devil was following, but he was following uncertainly; Don believed that he would be able to sense his nearness. And he had tricked that damned Finnegan onto a false trail for the moment.

Los Grandes, Seaworthy and Wirt and Gerecke, were not likely to do it themselves, but they might have local men do it. It was a chance to be taken. Don knew even where were Manuel and De Polis, and every man of the Brunhilde. Momentarily he was clear of every man of them. He hoped to reach one of the near farmsteads unobserved and to hide until darkness. He slunk through a weed-grown shanty town. Every man was accounted for, and he still might have a live chance.

Then one came down on him like a shimmering cloud to kill him.

"Not you!" Don cried in unbelieving terror as he died, "no, no, not you!"

4.

"Habib," said a little boy, one of the runners, "I have found something."

"Habib, what have you found?" asked Finnegan, choking on his anger, afraid of what it was.

"Go to the bottom of the *tell* and look," the little boy said. Then he ran away.

Finnegan went to the bottom of the *tell*. He had already been heading there. He knew, with swelling frustration and horror, what he would find.

At the bottom of the *tell*, in a weed patch, he found Don Lewis dead. He was stripped of robe and hood, and all his pockets had been turned inside out.

"They needn't have done that," said Finnegan miserably. "Whatever he carried, he carried in his head and not his pockets. Don, I never knew you. We came so close, and we never touched!"

There was no blood on Don except a trickle at the mouth. He had been throttled and his neck was broken. Hell, his neck had been wrung like a bird's!

Anyone from the ship might have killed Don, but who would have the amazing strength to wring his neck like that? Papa Devil could have done it. Papa was a giant. But no other man of the Brunhilde could have done it. So the game became very narrow.

Nobody was there except a curious goat, the only eye-witness. The nearest shanty was fifty yards away; there were only weeds, brush, and waste. But Finnegan did not leave Don Lewis where he was. He looked for a cleaner place. He carried Don a hundred yards to where he found soft sand under the creepers, and he scooped out a grave for him there.

This was clean sand here, and the creepers were from aromatic bushes, not from weeds. It was soft, and Finnegan scooped and delved diligently, having only his hands and a short hand-knife. But he had it about deep enough.

"Dig it deeper!" Papa Devil exploded like a crack of thunder, his voice rumbling with hate. "Deeper, I say. It will have to hold you both."

"Oh, go to Hell!" Finnegan told Papa Devil, himself shaking with a conflict of emotions.

Finnegan was doubly upset. He hadn't suspected that Papa Devil was nearly so close. He had thought that the steps following him from the bottom of the *tell* were those of the curious goat.

Not only was a friend murdered, but the Devil had already come to claim both the friend and himself. Finnegan placed the body of Don Lewis in the shallow grave in the sand.

"Go to Hell!" Finnegan told the Devil again. "Be off. I'm cloudy in my mind. I can't wake from it with you standing there."

"I wasn't sure you would be cool when you came to your end," said Papa Devil thickly out of a distorted face. "Many are not cool. You seem to have a talent for digging graves and burying people, Finnegan. Once you buried me. Now I will bury you."

But Finnegan was too furious to be scared yet. He had, moreover, a prior duty to perform. He ministered to the body of Don Lewis, or Timothy Lorrigan, or whomever the dead man was. He made him comfortable there, and prayed quickly that the perpetual light should shine on him.

"I wonder if *he* will be puzzled when the body isn't found where it was supposed to be," said Papa Devil, still talking tightly, "and I wonder if anyone will miss you at all, Finnegan?"

"You're a fool, Papa, a fool," Finnegan said with contempt. "I couldn't have done it. But you could have. Look out. I wake up from it now."

And Papa Devil had become a little unsure. "Yes, I see

now that you couldn't have killed him like that, Finnegan. You're not the man for it."

"And you are, Papa Devil. I believe you did it. But if not, or if I am able to call you to account here, then he *will* be puzzled. He will think that another of his dead did not stay dead."

Finnegan had done all he could do for Don Lewis except the last thing.

"I will leave it open," he announced evenly. "It is going to hold two all right. Either you go in the grave, Papa, or I do. One of us dies right now!"

Finnegan was out of the grave like a shrike, his handknife dangerously in his hand.

And encountered empty air!

Papa Devil was nowhere to be seen. Only the curious goat was there. It was unsettling the way Papadiabolous appeared and disappeared. Finnegan knew that Papa Devil did not turn from goat to man and back again, but that was the seeming of it.

Still trembling, Finnegan covered Don Lewis with sand, burying him properly and alone. Then, as a little clarity came to Finnegan, he knew that Papa Devil was not the killer.

And he knew who was.

5.

Finnegan found Marie Courtois in her hotel room. He could hear her ecstatic breathing inside, but she would not answer his knock. She was cooing and making strange noises.

When Finnegan broke in she did not see him. Lying across the bed on her back, she was smiling in quiet rapture, eyes half-closed and focused distantly. A bright silver slaver like the trail of a snail ran down her chin. She was in a transport of delight and gave little squeals of demented joy. She was clear crazy.

Finnegan could not rouse her with blows or slaps or choking. He knelt on her, he stood on her to break her catalepsy. And it broke slowly.

Marie came half awake, stretching like a big cat, still

only half aware of who Finnegan was. He struck her savagely, but she manacled him easily with her two hands.

"It was wonderful, Finn darling. I could almost have eaten him also. In a way it was to be intimate with him, who wouldn't otherwise be so with me. I have even forgotten his name, and forever, but the thing itself I will not forget. Nobody should know about it, and yet I want the whole world to know. Oh, you'll never understand it if you haven't done it! This will sing me to sleep tonight."

No man of the Brunhilde except Papa Devil had the strength to kill a man as Don Lewis had been killed. But a woman, Marie Courtois, if she were indeed a woman, had such strength when taken by the earthy passion. And the titaness was completely insane.

She was still in transport, but now her eyes had the alertness of a tigress. She was a great cat in the room and watching Finnegan's every move. Finnegan was sick with revulsion. Momentarily unarmed, he was powerless to kill her.

He remembered Joe Cross prowling and puzzling in the streets outside. Now he was sure of Joe. He went out and found Joe and told him about it.

Joe had a gun, and they started back in to kill Marie. But Papadiabolous, once more appearing suddenly, disarmed Joe, and said that it wasn't the time for that yet.

Finnegan began to see the line-up, and to understand for the first time that Papa wasn't a Devil, and that most of the rest were.

Saxon Seaworthy *was* puzzled when the body wasn't found where Marie had reported it was, where it was supposed to be; and he *did* wonder whether another of his dead had not stayed dead. There had been some embarrassment when he reported that one of his seamen had been murdered by native toughs for his money, and the seaman was not where he was reported to be, was not anywhere at all. The little policemen wanted to know who had started such a story and why. But soon the big policemen disembarrassed the little policemen of their curiosity, for Seaworthy was highly connected.

That evening there were flares and flashlights around the spot where Don Lewis had died, but he was not found there. And Finnegan who could do the Don Lewis voice, who could do almost any voice, taunted Saxon Seaworthy out of the dark in the voice of Don Lewis. Ah, there would be tension in that man Seaworthy! Finnegan also did the Chris McAbney voice a little later. There was black fun in it.

They left Tangier in the morning.

Marie Courtois was now out of favor with almost everyone. She was hated by one group because they knew she was the murderess of Don Lewis. She was distrusted by the other group because they were afraid she had botched a job and had not killed after all. And it had been a job that Marie had been asking for for a long time.

6.

After this, it was sheer travel along the North African littoral, and the Mediterranean, and Sicily, and Greece. These scenes of the last three weeks before the catastrophe were the scenes that Finnegan painted for the rest of his rather short life, whenever he was in the condition or mood to work at his trade: sky blue splendor, as seen through the eyes of one who was member of both the human races, and the aspect of death behind that beauty.

At Palermo Finnegan was in his glory and talked Italian with every idler who would join him, until he found that Papadiabolous could do the Sicilian better than he. At Palermo also Finnegan got his mail for the first time since leaving the States. No matter how he got it, he got it: letters from his other life, from friends in New Orleans and St. Louis and Chicago; also one from Mr. X from nowhere at all. But it was a thing peculiar here: Finnegan now doubted that it was himself who had lived that other life; these cherished friends were as those known at second hand, known to somebody else and the knowledge merely transferred to him. It seemed not the Finnegan here present who had been in that other life; it was some other Finnegan in some other context.

Then there was Messina, whence they jumped to Zakinthos, a Greek thing and thus within the sphere of Anastasia. It was here that Finnegan first began to feel that he was on alien ground and the rest were at home.

Then in a sudden change, Finnegan felt that he was indeed of the oldest and most other people of them all. This was the region where the duality was strongest.

For Saxon X. Seaworthy himself was Greek, though nobody looked less so. Papa Devil was at home here; for, though the Devil himself is of unknown nationality and is a true cosmopolitan, yet Cosmopolis itself is the Greek idea.

Orestes Gonof, at the first approach of a Greek island, raised his head like a colt that smells rain and revealed his origin.

After a few days they came to Naxos, the home of Ariadne and the white wine. And also the home of Anastasia Demetriades who claimed descent from the fishtail people.

It was March 14th, Passion Sunday.

Chapter Eight

ANASTASIA DEMETRIADES

*The Isles of Greece, the Isles of Greece,
Where Anastasia rose and shone,
Where others found another peace,
And I had found a peace mine own,
And if it lasted but a day
Then how much longer should it stay?*

*Was here the girl with purple eyes
And here the touch of Grecian fire;
And bound a day the Bel of lies
Who scuttled Nineveh and Tyre.
Eternal summer's not begun,
And we sit waiting for the sun.*

Was here we walked in Paradis
*Where we'll yet walk a later while,
For I had found the Isle of Bliss
That almost was on Naxos Isle.
And all my friends who here were led
Were with me, if they were not dead.*

—*Unwritten poems of Finnegan*

1.

Now, as Finnegan had been a sinner since arriving at Freetown, and as it was already Passion Sunday, he wanted to make his Easter Duty and change his ways. As this was Orthodox land, it would be hard to find a priest to hear his confession before Mass, as it would require one who understood English or Italian. Finnegan's Romaic, in spite of close association with Anastasia since early November, would not suffice for the shriving, nor would any sort of pidgeon; for Finnegan had intricate sins which required full expression.

But a young Capuchin priest was spotted at the first sortee. He was a dago! He had to be. But he said he was Greek; he must have been confused about himself. He spoke the Italian well enough, but he chided Finnegan for his ignorance.

"That a young man named Solli should not know better Greek, that is too bad. Though the fault is History's and not your own, yet it is a fault. Do you know that it is only by an unfortunate accident that the Italians speak Italian? They should talk Greek, like men in their full heritage.

"Did you know that there was once a Naxos on Sicily? It was the first of all Greek colonies in what now pertains to Italy, and was in the seventh century before Christ. The colonists were from this very island, and it was for our own place that the new Naxos was named. Who could guess then that it would go wrong?

"Then, accidentally, that Rome thing got out of hand, and moved down over all the peninsula and Sicily as well. It was there, as you tell me, that your own people came from; for the Naxos of Sicily was only sixty miles from your Messina."

They went in then for the Capuchin to hear Finnegan's confession, in spite of his being a barbarian of insufficient Greek.

"Bless me, father," Finnegan said. "I have been on the drink for some weeks and have lived as a bare sinner. Yet it seems that it is not myself who does these things, but another person inside me."

"It is yourself who does them," the priest said. "It is a common transference to blame them on another."

"I know that, but this is something else. My old memories are now once removed, as though they belonged to someone else. I have a new set of memories now: that I am of the Devil's kindred, that I belong on a murky crusade, that I must tear down and subvert and inflame. I am of a different blood than I had believed. There is an old animal in me, and it begins to take me over. I doubt if I am human in the accepted sense. I'm of another recension."

"This is a much rarer state than the other, but it is not unheard of. And I do not believe it is imaginary. There *is* another kindred. I have been convinced of this for some time. Well, we must assume that salvation is for that other kindred as well, but nothing will ever be easy for you. I absolve you."

"You can absolve me, but can you absolve the animal inside me?"

"I absolve your person here present, in all its aspects."

After confession and after Mass in the very small church, Finnegan met Anastasia, and they had breakfast with Papadiabolous the Devil at a breakwater cafe. Papa was cryptic today, and it seemed as though he and Anastasia had a secret. This was peculiar, for the only one of the Brunhilde that Anastasia ever shared secrets with was Finnegan.

"There has been a bird on the main stack of the Brunhilde for days," Finnegan said. "He sticks there and will not leave."

"Yes, a bird, a gannet," Papa Devil said.

"Manuel says that it means someone else will die," said Finnegan.

"Manuel knows that someone else will die," Papa said, "and it wasn't a bird who told him."

"Will you answer me some questions, either you or Anastasia, Papa?"

"A few. But everything will not be cleared up for you."

"Did Don Lewis know who you are, Papa? I don't know, but did he know?"

"No. He didn't know, and there was no point in telling him. Though he was the one who contacted me at a distance, yet he didn't know me when I arrived; he didn't know that anyone had arrived. I stepped into an old pair of shoes when I came."

"I am a grown man," Finnegan said, "and old for my age. May I not be told the plot?"

"Why, Finnegan, it's simply the old game of monsters and men, of *Policia y Ladrones,* of the Beneficient and the Maleficient."

"You mean cops and robbers?"

"An apt phrase. I could never turn one. But the cops and the robbers are only partly of the same species. It is really a game of counter-agents and counter-counter-agents. There are two groups of a different basic, and the dialogue will have to be talked out in blood. We come to the narrow way now. I have not played the Devil for a game. Anastasia has only recently known that I am not the old Devil. For a long time I was not sure that you knew, Finnegan, even though you drew the face that I will wear tonight, and perhaps will die in.

"That was a good old ship we were on, though she kept bad company. I do not believe that any of us three will ever board her again. However we leave here, it will be by another boat, my own, or Charon's."

"I'm not as afraid as I was at Tangier," Anastasia said. "From what I overheard there, I thought that I was the one to be killed. If I go now, I hope that the Marie goes too, but not at the same time. I'd like to have a few minutes start on her. I'd be afraid of her in the narrow way; I understand it is very narrow just a few seconds after one dies, and she would be waiting for me there. That's the only thing I'm afraid of."

"Papa Devil, who was Dopey the seaman?" Finnegan demanded.

"Why, he was your own fetch, your own double, Finnegan, just as I was the close double of another."

"People do not have doubles literally, not ghostly ones who disappear and are absorbed into one."

"Well, maybe non-people have them, Finnegan, and we all three here belong to the Non-people. I'm not sure how close his duality with you was. But Dopey was also of the strange blood, he was a seaman who was also a sometime killer, and Seaworthy had sent for him to kill the man named Papadiabolous. When you appeared, Seaworthy mistook you for Dopey, and you do look remarkably alike. There is quite a bit of confusion concerning the night that you and Seaworthy buried the first me, and if you cannot clear it up, I cannot. You were there and I wasn't."

"Papa, how did you kill Dopey and leave no body?"

"I'm not sure which of us killed Dopey, Finnegan. The idea that you rejected may be the true one, that he was your ghostly fetch, and that he disappeared and was absorbed into you. Sometime, Finnegan, if you happen to think of it, and if you find that you are alive at the time, you may want to take a hand in this yourself. I hope that you will be alive, but there is a mutually exclusive affair here. Not all of us who came here on the Brunhilde can be alive at this time tomorrow. Finnegan, do you know what a tiger looks like turned inside out?"

"Yes, he would be a six-foot-four, three hundred pound hunk of bologna encased in the membrane of his own duodenum. In fact, he would look a lot like you, Papa."

"I'm glad you think so, for I'm talking about myself."

"But the converse isn't true, Papa. When you turn a piece of bologna inside out, it doesn't become a tiger."

"I hope you're wrong. I was a tiger once, and I intend to be again. I will disappear after dark tonight and try to regrow my lost stripes. And when I come back as a tiger I hope that they will not know me.

"Finnegan, there is a little boat which we call Shouakh, and it is spelled S-e-a-b-a-c-h. Isn't that a funny way to spell it, Finnegan? And you use an Irish nickname, but you wouldn't know that."

"I know that it means a hawk, but what is the hawk?"

"Oh, it's my little boat. It doesn't go very fast; but, like the hawk, it is there suddenly. I wish that I could promise you a ride on the Hawk, as a smaller man gave you a ride on a bigger boat. We may all ride on her tomorrow, in the event that all goes well with us. But it is very small; it doesn't even have a bar."

"Tomorrow seems pretty uncertain," Finnegan said. "I'll be surprised if the sun even rises."

"There's the further difficulty that it may turn into a double ambush," Papa Devil said. "My hawk may be tangled by a Retiarius waiting for her. Our antagonist is very clever, and he seems to be following into our trap too easily. It's a risk that might kill us all."

"You are cheerful this morning, Papa Devil," Anastasia said.

"In rare good humor, the mark of a fool. I hope you two children have a happy day of it. It is possibly your last day on Earth, and it will be nice to have a happy one to look back upon. I hear you are to have a sort of picnic.

"If I never see you again, Finnegan, and I doubt that I shall, I will be sorry that we hadn't gotten better acquainted. My own personality is a sharper one than that of Papa Devil, and it's a loss that you couldn't have known it. You are the only one who learned without being told that I wasn't really Papadiabolous. And perhaps I am the only one who divines that there is more to you than Finn the

Gin. You say that you have never been able to touch any human person. But we are both partly human, and we could have touched. I wish I were going with you today; I haven't had a carefree day in years."

"We wish you were going too, Papa," Anastasia said, "but with you, three would be a multitude."

2.

Finnegan and Anastasia had rented a donkey, loaded it with two paniers, and gone to visit Anastasia's grandmother, the matriarch of the Demetriades. This was a winding road, uphill for four miles.

Anastasia rode the donkey a while. Then Finnegan knocked her off it, stood on her for mounting block while she was on hands and knees in the dust, and rode the donkey in her place. She pulled him off, rolled him in the road, and trampled on him. Anastasia rode Finnegan a while. Then Finnegan rode Anastasia. She was so little that his feet dangled in the dust while he rode on her back. Then they ran up the hill and whistled to the donkey, and he followed them like a dog.

They were the three happiest people in the world. People are often happiest when they are spooked or under a cloud, just before it breaks open. It was mid-March and the sun had been climbing for several hours. They ran quite a ways and then stopped at a farm house.

"Thispo poly," Anastasia told the lady there, and they and the donkey were given a drink at the well.

"Kathisate," said the lady, but they had no time, and went on up the road.

"Who of your family is left?" Finnegan asked.

"I don't know. My grandmother, at least, I think, I feel. Maybe others. Surely there will be someone here."

"Will they understand about you and me, that it is all right with us?"

"Oh yes. You are my brother now. We could give Plato lessons, you and I. Plato wasn't very platonic himself. It takes people like us to develop his ideas for him."

"How do we explain to people about the donkey?"

"He *does* make us look like an old married couple. We

could pass off a child with some story or other, but how do you explain a donkey? We'll just have to pretend that we don't know him. Sorry, Papapaleologus, we love you, but we can't let on that we know you. Stop walking between us. You stay three steps behind."

The donkey was named Papapaleologus, being a lineal descendant of the last Roman Emperors of the East.

"I think I'll tell Papapaleologus the story about the donkey who married the lady zebra," Finnegan said.

"I have heard it," the donkey signalled. He did this by letting both ears drop wearily.

Naxos is twelve miles square and has a mountain in the middle of it. There are figs and olives and lemons and grapes. And honey. They make a white wine there. And they mine emery. The farm of the Demetriades was up the mountain road.

Hardly anyone still lived on the mountain except the grandmothers. But even Finnegan knew the grandmother herself when they came up to her. She was black-haired and black-eyed.

"I am Anastasia Granddaughter," Anastasia said, but at first the grandmother pretended not to know her.

"I have so many granddaughters, and such a lot of them went to France and to America. Anyone can come along nowadays and say she is my granddaughter, and who is to know the difference? There must be a dozen a week."

"But I used to live with you in the summer. I used to play on that rock pile."

"So they all say. There were so many, Irene and Helen and Mary."

"But only one Anastasia. You know me! You know me. We play a game in this."

And of course Anastasia Grandmother had known her immediately. Anastasia *Gyiagyia* (grandmother) spoke Romaic only, which Papapaleologus the donkey understood perfectly, and Anastasia *Engone* (granddaughter) almost all, and Finnegan whom Anastasia had taken for her brother only about half. There was, however, perfect understanding among the four of them, and no need for translating.

The house had once been larger, and not all of it was now used. Some of the old rooms were fire-damaged and had been boarded off. There had been some hardship here and Anastasia Grandmother was the only one left.

But it hadn't darkened her mood. She was vital and pretty, she had been prettier than Anastasia Granddaughter, though fairly destitute. She would have been able to feed a small family of visiting mice, but that was all. She wouldn't have been able to feed a large family of visiting mice.

Finnegan unloaded the paniers that Papapaleologus had carried up the hill; and spread out bread, oil, honey, eggs, coffee, cheese, wine, pickles, sugar, rice, tea, milk, flour, salt, chocolate, and tobacco. Then Finnegan and Anastasia went to a neighbor and bought a kid.

Finnegan was a town boy and he had never killed a kid. They put it on a flat rock, and Anastasia showed him how. They skinned the kid, split it out, cleaned it, cut it up, and left it in charge of Anastasia Grandmother. Then they went further up the mountain, in company of the donkey, while Anastasia Grandmother made the dinner. They stopped and bought a skin bottle of wine at one of the farms. Then they climbed to the top of the mountain.

"From here you can see all of the island, and half a dozen other islands," said Anastasia, "and the smallest of them over there is where I was born. You can watch all the seaways from here. For a reason which I will not tell you, but which you have guessed a little, I may spend some hours up here tonight. We can leave the skin bottle up here in the fork of the bush; then we'll have something to pass the time if you want to keep me company. There will be a moon all the early night, and then it will be down a few hours before dawn. Then I must watch."

"For what, my eccentric little sister?"

"A boat that should come to the island in the very dark hours, and I must signal it, if there is not another signal from below first. It isn't hard to do, but it scares me. I will signal out of this very narrow glen here, and my signal can only be seen in a narrow sector."

They went back down to Anastasia Grandmother's for the dinner. They ate and drank outdoors at a little table.

Eating and drinking are ordinary things; everybody does them. Yet this was somehow remarkable: to be eating outside of a little farm house on the side of a blue mountain on a Greek Island. There was a blue haze in the air that was not a cloud, but only something to filter the sun.

"The sky is different over the different lands and islands," said Finnegan. "It depends on whether they burn brush or faggots or pine or hard wood or turf or coal or gas or dung. Each of these raises a different haze. You may not have noticed it, Anastasia *Engone,* but all this fall and winter and spring, when we were going up and down the coasts, we could always tell what they burned on the shores. It's been centuries since anyone has seen the sky as it really is, even here. But soon it will be all electric heat, or solar, or atomic. Then the color of the sky will be the one we have not seen since that morning when Prometheus came down. Do you remember that morning?"

"Sure. Gee, it was cold," said Anastasia Granddaughter.

"You could not remember. You were too little," said Anastasia Grandmother.

They stayed and talked with Anastasia Grandmother till evening.

"You are one of the violent ones, those of the other blood," Anastasia Grandmother said to Finnegan.

"I don't know what it is. It may be that I am."

"I am of it," said Anastasia Grandmother. "And my granddaughter here is of it a little."

Chapter Nine

DIANA ARTEMIS

> There are creatures who are of unredeemable species and are denied the gift of eternal life. In place of this, they are given very long sublunar life. Some of these live for thousands of years, as flesh, as ghost returning irregularly as flesh, and as continuing legend. Most are evil. Some are indifferent or even helpful, but in no case are they to be trusted. They are on shores and mountains and islands. Some of them are on our own island.
> —SAINT BRENDON, *Trachtas*

1.

Finnegan and Anastasia went back up the mountain. Finnegan had acquired a bottle of gin in addition to another skinful of wine. He had a premonition, and gin has always been a sovereign against premonitions. Finnegan had his sea jacket.

Anastasia had a blanket and shawl from her grandmother's, and a magic lantern from somewhere. The magic lantern was not a projector. It was an assembly of reflecting mirrors and a lantern. It was in a sort of binnacle case from some old boat.

They found a flat clean rock and sat down for the vigil that was still puzzling to Finnegan. Anastasia seemed anxious and worried.

"Your boat, it isn't coming from the mainland?" Finnegan asked.

"Who said something about a boat?"

"You said something about a boat. Papa Devil said quite a bit about a boat. Why else are we here? What else is it then, a sea gull, or a sea plane? Where will the Hawk come from?"

"The hawk just appears suddenly. The hawks have their

nests in the sky, just out of sight. Everybody knows that. Then they swoop down."

"I could watch one sector if you would tell me what to watch for. Is it coming from Rhodes, or Crete, or Anatolia, or Egypt, or Lebanon?"

"No. I have to watch for myself, Finn. I don't want you to get involved. Of course, we will probably get you killed, but we don't want to get you involved. Or this might not be the night. But this *has* to be the night."

There were quite a lot of cow bells and sheep bells. There were bells around the landings and on some of the little boats. Some of the buoys out on the shipways had bells that clanged as they rolled with the rollers. And there were dinner bells in many of the farm yards with a rope pull from the kitchen window.

"The bells are the only things left here from the bronze age," Finnegan said, "the only things that cannot be made better than out of bronze. Here it is perfect, for the whole island is a rock and it vibrates with them."

The moon was already high in the sky when the sun went down. It was March and it would get chilly. Now the moon suddenly lit up, like a light controlled by an astronomical switch to come on at a certain time of dusk.

"You have to see it here to understand how the old Greeks were so mistaken about the sun and the moon when they were mistaken about very little else," Finnegan said. "They estimated their size, some as big as a wash basin, some as big as a wagon wheel, some as big as a barn or a ship, but none of them believed them really huge. They appear so close, the moon particularly, here.

"Galen estimated the moon's size from a Goat-Sucker that he saw fly behind it and emerge from the other side. This took the time of twelve wing beats, and indicated a large moon, as big as a large ship. He thought that it would take a very high tower to reach it, since catapults had never been able to do so. There is the further difficulty that the moon may be nearer at night, for it is only at night that birds have actually been seen to fly behind it."

"If any bird is able to fly behind it, it is this same Goat-Sucker," Anastasia said, "I saw one do it just then. If he didn't go behind it, where did he go? And there he appears again! He was behind it after all."

There was a chorus of cicadas about them and below.

And Papapaleologus the donkey was chomping grass in the narrow glen beneath their feet. The moon lacked a week of being full, but the night was very bright. Here on top was nothing but rocks and gnarled old branches and stump trees. That is the way the top of the world always looks. But by Greek moon it was even stranger. Moonlight is different in Greece. As you know, it was the Greeks who invented the moon.

Anastasia sat on the blanket and could see the sea on all sides of the island. Finnegan lay with his head on her lap. Her legs were the color of moonlight and her head was like that of Diana.

Not the Diana of Nemi or Ephesus over whom the silversmith Demetrios and St. Paul quarreled. St. Paul was right to oppose Demetrios in this. Demetrios always made the heads of his Dianas too large and pasty, and the silver color did not become them.

But that other Diana, Diana Artemis the bringer of light; she whose little statue Pausanius saw at Messene in the sanctuary of Asclepius, she who was painted marble of a natural expression. Or the little Diana Artemis of cypress wood that stood on the stoa of the temple at Delos so many years ago. That is what Anastasia's head was like.

Finnegan's head was that of a gargoyle, but no matter. They also are noble, or at least they are fitting on a night like this.

Finnegan strung verses together as he lay with his head in her lap. And because he identified fourteen bells, eight from the land and six from the sea, he made it a sonnet; which word means a little bell as well as a little song:

I've seen the ending darkly through a glass,
The last I tipped, the last time I was fried,
And that old sacred snake that never died
Has bit the world and left it in its grass.
I rue to see its final agony;
The world was mighty rum and mighty queer.
Now only Anastasia is here
And Papapaleologus and me.

We three have flown the world and left it there,
And mourn its end, and us, and what shall be;

And may God help us when the moon shall drop!
And now there come night thoughts to raise our hair,
And now there is a Hawk upon the Sea,
And Oreads upon the mountain top.

"Have you a piece of paper and a pencil in your pocket?" Finnegan asked Anastasia.
"I have. And why do you want them?"
"I made a sonnet. I want to write it down before I forget it."
"It's too dark. Go to sleep."
"But I always make them at night, and I never get to write them down. In the morning I forget them. What if Laura hadn't given Petrarch a piece of paper and a pencil when he wanted them?"
"You go to sleep."
"It's real good and you're in it."
"I'm sure it is. Go to sleep."

2.

Six men in a little boat were coming out of Anatolia. They were coming towards the blind side of Naxos, the side opposite the harbor. The boat looked as though it had been cobbled together by drunken Irish carpenters out of Hogan's alley; and parts of it had been. Its sail was too big for it, and its donkey engine too small. Yet it could take the wind and move. The name on it was the Seabach, but it was to be found in no registry. It hadn't a proper log, or a business-like listing of the crewmen.

The log consisted of random notations, cryptic jottings in some kind of number code, and private notes of amounts of winnings and losings at cards. The roster did not give the crewmen by name, but it did give an incisive description of each, though in an unusual form that is sometimes called doggerel:

Was one a Bloke, and one a Black,
And one a Buck, and one a Smasher,
And one a Clerk, and one a Hack,
And one a bleeding Haberdasher.

Seven men that would indicate; but there were only six men on the craft. The seventh man, the leading man of them all, the Smasher, had been on distant leave from them. Now he awaited them very near.

The buck of a man was only a boy. He would stay on the craft till the end and use it as a ram. The black man wore a little pearl-gray derby hat that was too small for him; he was a clown in his moments. The bloke wore a digger hat, filthy with old grease. The clerk and the hack were the navigator and the engineer, and the haberdasher was acting captain and pilot. But they were all men of some talent or they would not have been there; and they would gamble on the short end of the stick.

It did not seem a disciplined group, but it had a solid unity. They all wore olive shirts that were a sort of uniform. They had Enfield rifles of old British issue, but they had nothing else in common.

The Seabach coasted into the blind side of Naxos after dark, signaled but once with its light, and thereafter gave no signal at all. Later, there might or might not be a signal to them from a narrow glen in the mountain, and they might or might not heed it. Likely they would go ahead with what they intended to do regardless of any signal.

They were, in fact, doing it shortly after midnight. Five of the men came ashore around the shoulder of the island, and the sixth man took the boat off again. The five men followed a path, and a road, and another path, the information of them having come to them partly from maps too small and undetailed, and partly from the childhood memories of a girl. Nevertheless, they followed these ways in the dark.

The one man on the boat, the young buck of a man, would take the thing around by himself, and at the proper moment he himself alone would launch an attack from the sea, coming in with gun and spotlight to take attention away from the men raiding from the shore side. It was a loose plan that had been worked out by a loose sort of man who hadn't much to work with.

Meanwhile, on the Brunhilde, an old Retiarius waited, his nets ready. He had his own love for a fight and his own tactics. He could smell a trap half-way around a world, and his nets were adaptable. With the old netman were his two cronies, Gerecke and Wirt. They may have been set down as nonentities, but they weren't; they were cockeyed old foxes who had been in battles before. There were some who had wondered what they were good for. Now they were like to find out.

And sometime in the middle of the night, a big man slipped off the Brunhilde to try his hand once more at being a tiger, to regrow his lost stripes.

3.

Finnegan dreamed a while on the mountain, and the Oreads came. They were three girls who emerged from the bushes and signaled to him. And he went and talked to them.

"We are three Oreads," they said, "and our names, as you may have guessed, are Anemotrephes and Akroreia and Oreibates. Anastasia is our sister. She will be with us after tonight. But you will never be able to see her again unless you are on the right mountain at the right time. Or rather, you will not see her until long after, when the world is remade and we will all be resolved together. But that is not for us now."

"It will never be for you," Finnegan told them. "Oreibates has the mark of the polypus on her wrist, and I believe the other two also have it dimly. I didn't know that Oreads were of that kindred, but I should have guessed."

"Oh, we have no such marks," they told him. "We are Oreads and no other thing, and we try to explain the night's business to you. Anastasia has taken you for her brother, so you are our brother also. But after it has happened to her, do you not stay here. Go as far and as fast as you can. This isn't the time for you yet."

"You're talking in your sleep," Anastasia said. "Who are you talking to?"

"Anemotrephes and Akroreia and Oreibates," Finnegan told her, half awakening.

"I didn't know that you knew them."

"They said they were your sisters."

"I've often suspected that they are. Why should we let millennia separate sisters? But regular people can't talk to them. You must belong to the other people, Finnegan. I was pretty sure that you did."

Finnegan saw that, though it was several miles down the mountain by the road, yet one could go down rapidly if he went down sheer. It was hardly four hundred feet down the face of the cliff, and was bushed and brambled all the way. A careful man might pick his way down there in the daytime, or a foolhardy man at night. Finnegan liked to know all the doors that led out of a place, whether it was a room or a mountain.

But he dreamed again almost immediately while the sea boomed around the island. The Oreads were still there but he could not come up to them. He had thought that they were already on the top of the mountain, but this was not so. They were only on the top of a little mountain; there was a bridge that he had not noticed before and it led to the bottom of a brand new mountain.

This was different from most mountains in that it had a light inside it and was translucent like ice. And yet it was a mountain in its essence.

There was a sparkle on everything. Finnegan climbed very high after the Oreads. He liked to watch their beautiful ankles and knees as they climbed. The rocks were like fox-fire, and the trees like jewels. They climbed so high that the first mountain shrank to a very small rock with moss on it down under the moon. But he couldn't catch the Oreads.

"You can't come with us," they told him. "You don't belong up here yet. Even people can't come up here. Certainly a teras or a drakon cannot come here."

"I'm a person. I'm not a teras or drakon," Finnegan insisted. "I want to climb to the top of the mountain."

"Even we haven't done that, and we live here. We climb forever, but we never reach the top. And if we cannot, then a teras cannot."

He followed them yet, and their heels sparkled like gems above him.

"You be as much teras as I," he called up to them.

"No, we are not," Anemotrephes insisted. "How did you know that we are?" Akroreia asked sadly. "It is our destitution and destruction," Oreibates keened, "but we try to climb up to the light. You have to go. You know too much."

Then they pushed Finnegan off the mountain. He fell a very long way down: three leagues, a parasang, a stadia and a half. He turned over and over as he fell through the air. But he was unhurt in the landing, and came to rest with his head on the knees of Anastasia which were very like those of her sisters the Oreads. This he hadn't noticed before.

"Who were you dreaming about that time?" Anastasia asked him.

"The same three girls. They pushed me off the mountain."

"I knew they would. You didn't have any business up there. How do you know my sisters so well?"

"I never met the girls before tonight. They said I was a teras, a drakon."

"You are, Finnegan. So am I. So are they a little. But we try to make amends. Whatever would happen to people if some of us didn't help them?"

The moon went down, and there was nothing but star light and a few lanterns by the landing.

"How will you see the boat, or the hawk, when it comes?" Finnegan said. "Will it show a light?"

"No. I think it has already come. No, it won't show a light till it begins."

Finnegan didn't doze off. He entered a sleep vigorously as though shouldering his way through a door. There was an old teras sitting on the ground in a cave, or at the foot of a cliff. The teras had a face made out of gloomy granite.

"If we were first, how did they get ahead of us?" Finnegan asked the teras.

"I don't know, boy, I don't know," the old teras muttered dumbly.

"And which are the aliens, ourselves, or them?" Finnegan also was sitting on the ground.

"It is always the others who are the aliens, boy."

"I feel other. Why do we destroy them?"

"I don't know, boy, I don't know."

"And why do some of us revolt against the revolt?"

"Treachery, treachery, or perhaps it has another name if you say it in another tone."

"Which one of us was sitting here on the sidewalk first?"

"I don't know what is sidewalk, boy. I sit here a long time, and you as long as you wish."

The next time that Finnegan awakened he was alone on the blanket. He had a steep feeling of bereavement, of everlasting loss, unquenchable gloom. Anastasia was gone. The false dawn had started to glow in the East but it would be an hour and a half before the sun was up.

As he started down the mountain, the sheer way down the brambled face, he heard the first of the distant shots.

Chapter Ten

DOWN WITH THE DEAD MEN

The children were playing 'Other Kind of People', and I asked them what it meant. "We play we're the Other Kind of People, and nobody can tell we're not regular people," they said. "They can't even guess it." "I don't understand it," I told them. "Oh, did you never play 'Other Kind of People' when you were small?" Helena asked. "Children everywhere have always played it."
—CLEMENT GOLDBEATER, *Enniscorthy Chronicle*

1.

Even the headlong way was a long way down the mountain in the dark. There was shooting of rifles and BARs, of fifty caliber machine guns; and a rich ripe note heavy enough to be a forty-five millimeter at devastatingly close range. The rifle shots kept it up a while, then died one by one under fire of automatics and machine guns.

It was maddening to listen to such a conversation of ordinance and not know what was really going on. Finnegan was still high on the hill after the shooting had been stopped and been followed by shrill whistling. Gunshot almost anywhere in the world will be followed by whistles of police and officials.

There were brambles and trees and fences, but Finnegan burst through them in an angry rush, tumbling downward. The whole world would be killed before he got there.

"You make more noise than a cow. Stop it!" It was a young boy talking to Finnegan, and then following him as he talked, a boy like someone Finnegan knew.

"What's noise? I'm in a hurry," Finnegan gasped. "Show me a faster way down."

"Don't hurry. If they're waiting to hang you, let them wait a little longer."

"Let them hang me. Show me the path down."

"No. I came to cut you off. She left word: If it goes wrong, go cut him off. If I were you I would lie flat inside that clutter of rocks for an hour at least. And if nothing happened then, I would crawl as quietly as I could to the deepest thicket I could find. I would lie there for three days and nights without breathing."

"Boy, there is trouble at the landing. They will need me."

"They don't need you for anything, brother. The trouble is all over with them at the landing. They are hunting for you now to kill you."

"Me? Not me. Nobody wants to kill me."

"Yes, they hunt for you and for two others. Your friends from the ship hunt for you to kill you. Yes, you, the comical Italian with the Irish name."

"Well, I have to find out what happened."

"I told you. It is all over with them."

"I have to go down."

"Go quieter then. Go much quieter."

They came within about two hundred yards of the Brunhilde as she lay at the little dock. She seemed quiet and asleep, with only one pale gang light, and one cabin light burning, as was usual at night. But an old retiarius still waited there in the dark for whatever else his net could take.

Was the shooting over with? Finnegan seemed to hear a whistling of shots again, but the boy heard them not. Finnegan seemed to be shot in the wrist; it starred like cracked glass, it bled under the skin, it turned into the mark.

"It's on me openly now," Finnegan said, "but I won't accept it. Be damned with it. This marked man will tear it out of him."

"What, brother?" asked the boy. "You are wounded? No, I see it is an old wound or mark you have there. The ship isn't asleep, brother. You go nearer to her and you're finished. They have BARs. They can blow your head off with a BAR. Or maybe they'd let you come aboard first and then give it to you."

"Who was shooting at who? What happened?"

"Everybody was shooting at everybody, but there weren't many shots wasted. The dead are in the little street to the right, and the officials are with them. But you will get no help there. You yourself are being hunted as one of the murderers. You, and the big man who also disappeared, and the South American. You can't help the dead people now."

"I come too late. I come too late. There is one I must find out about. If she is dead, I might as well be."

"She is dead, brother, and I also feel strongly about it. She is my cousin, and I didn't even see her alive after she came. But you might try to stay alive if you can."

They went on down and around to the street, not taking the direct way.

"Another man is dead on the smaller boat, the one with the lights," the boy said. "They haven't taken him off yet, and she is sinking. That smaller boat came in shooting with only the one man on it. And they blasted it. Did you know they had a gun like that on your ship?"

"Yes. I guess I knew where it was, though it was always covered."

They went around through a lane and approached the street where the dead people were. Finnegan met Manuel there. He was crying.

"I cannot find Papadiabolous anywhere," Manuel said. "Now this has gone wrong and everybody is dead, and they hunt us to kill us also. Papadiabolous is the only one who could have pulled it off, and where is he?"

"Papa is here present," Finnegan said. For, when Finnegan saw one of the dead men spread out there, he knew that Papa Devil was dead this time for certain and would no more come back to life. This was the same face that Finnegan had reconstructed in his mind as the face of Papa Devil, the face he had painted on one of the dead men in the barroom painting on the Brunhilde.

Papa was very dead. He had been shot many times and had been bludgeoned. His pockets had all been turned inside out or cut out completely. His olive shirt, such as he had never worn before, was shredded, and even his shoes were removed. He was a tremendous man. The tiger had regrown his lost stripes, if only for a little while before he died.

There were six other dead men in the street, of whom five were strangers to Finnegan, and the sixth was the seaman Joe Cross. The five strangers wore olive-colored shirts that were almost a uniform. They were spread out on the wet cobbles, and lanterns were set to form a square about them.

There was a Negro man who had worn a little gray derby hat into battle and who had died laughing. There was the haberdasher still dapper in death. There was the bloke stretched out and his digger hat beside him disgraced with blood. The clerk had his horn rims, one lens catching the light of the lanterns, the other starred and with a shot-hole in the center. The hack was dead with a badly mauled cigar still in his mouth. They were still a mighty casual bunch and it seemed as if they had minded dying less than most would.

The officials told Finnegan and Manuel and the crowd to be off.

A lady took Finnegan to a near house. There he saw Anastasia his dead sister. She still had the smile of a happy pixie and her eyes were only half closed. They had put her on a sofa there. She had been shot once only. She had been wet.

"She fell off the breakwater when she was shot," someone said. "She was dead when we pulled her out."

An orthodox priest was there. "I gave her the last rites," he said. "Then I wondered if she had become a Roman. She had a Roman rosary. Do you know?"

"No. She was not a Roman. I gave her the rosary," Finnegan said.

This was all too matter-of-fact.

"You had better go and hide," the priest told him. "They plan to find you and kill you also. You and the big man they are looking for. It is dangerous for you to be down here."

The priest told Finnegan several other things that he did not quite understand with his insufficient Greek.

Finnegan slipped away with Manuel up the hill. Finn had all this time carried a gin bottle in his hand, the same that he had taken up on the mountain as a sovereign against premonitions. He had carried it through the rough climb down the mountain, through the alley off the street of the dead men, into the house where his sister was dead, and up onto the mountain again.

"I must be depraved," he said.

But he didn't throw it away.

2.

Finnegan and Manuel slipped up onto the mountain a little before sun-up. They lay up in a thicket all day. Sometimes they saw their own shipmates searching for them, or more likely for Papadiabolous.

"They are all very evil," said Manuel. "What had restrained them, as much as they were restrained, was Papa Devil. He frightened them because he had returned from the dead. But he had formerly been one of them also, and only myself and the beautiful Anastasia knew that he had changed, that he planned to trap them.

"They were all in it, Finnegan, though Joe Cross tried to play two sides as Don Lewis had done. He didn't want Anastasia killed, and he was murdered when he tried to prevent it. He wasn't killed in the street like the rest of them. He was killed on the ship and was dragged out there.

"And Marie Courtois, who I thought was not all bad, she insisted that Anastasia be killed, she was the one. Myself and you are also under sentence of death for having been too friendly with Anastasia and Papa Devil."

But Finnegan did not say anything. He thought how odd it is that people will not recognize a man just because he is wearing a different face. The men on the Brunhilde still didn't know that they had killed Papadiabolous.

"Have you no tears?" Manuel asked. "I thought you would be very sorry that Anastasia was dead."

"I am very sorry. I have cried about this many times in the past," Finnegan said. "Several months ago, it was given to me to know that this would happen. And today (that is, yesterday and the night) I spent with her the most beautiful and peaceful day of my life. She had become my sister and she is dead. She also told me, as did another once, that we would be together again. It is good to be sure of this."

"Yes. It is a good thing we are sure," Manuel said. "So much else had gone wrong."

"And now I am not sure of it," Finnegan said. "I'm of a people who have not that promise."

They lay up on the mountain till evening and watched the men hunting for them.

"Do you know what it was all about?" Finnegan asked. "The details?"

"Some of them. The men from the little launch and the big stranger were also of a group. This is what Papadiabolous was in contact with. They are an international bunch, impatient with their governments' ways of handling these things. They try to trap the gangs and to smash them. They are also illegal, of course, very illegal. I do not know if theirs is the right way or not.

"Anastasia also had three fingers in the soup. This is the island where she was born. I think that she talked Seaworthy into coming here; it isn't one of their regular stops. But it was a double trap, as it happened. You have heard the expression 'smarter than the Devil'; Seaworthy has proved to be so here.

"Now we are lost in a strange land. We cannot go back to the ship or they will kill us. And worse, they are tracking down Papadiabolous who is worth more than both of us together. If only there were a way of getting him away safely I would gladly sacrifice my life for it, and yours also."

"You are generous with both of us, but it is too late for that, Manuel. Everything is too late."

"They have found him already?"

"They do not know it; they will probably look for him for years. But the original Papa Devil really did die last year, and his surrogate died this morning. They—he—will not be back, either in himself or in anybody else."

"You know this? Can you tell me about it?"

"He is dead now and finally. So what do we do?"

"Finnegan, there are very evil creatures in the world and it should be made known. I believe they are of another species, and they are evil beyond recall."

"I hope not, Manuel, I hope not."

"What I will do, I will go to Rome and tell the Pope that there are evil men about in the world. Can you swim, Finnegan?"

"Yes."

"I know you can swim as anyone swims, and better. I have seen you swim around the ship. But can you swim to Paros?"

"I think so. How far is it?"

"Seven miles I guess. It is only a guess."

"It looks nearer from here on top of the mountain, but everything looks nearer from the top of the mountain. Seven miles, and the sea is not too choppy. Yes, I can swim it."

After dark they went down to a rocky stretch of shore. There were floats from an old fish net there. They put their clothes and shoes in leather sacks and roped them to floats to trail behind them. Finnegan still had a rather heavy bag of stones that he could not have taken without using a float.

They swam over to Paros.

They lay on the shore there for several hours as they were very tired. Later they dressed and hid themselves until dawn. They would have to be sure that the Brunhilde had not crossed over.

After they had reconnoitered, they walked into the town of Paros for breakfast.

They both of them emptied their pockets and put all their money on the table. Between them they had seven hundred and twenty dollars. This was more than they were supposed to have. Finnegan had an unaccountable roll. Though he was careless of money, he did not remember this at all. It was possible that Anastasia had put it into his jacket pocket before she left him sleeping on the mountain.

They split the money evenly. They said goodbye. Manuel went to Rome to tell the Pope that there were evil men loose in the world.

And Finnegan, for three days, sat at the little table in the inn like a man in a dream.

3.

On the evening of the third day, Mr. X came in and sat down across from Finnegan. If you have a wide acquaintanceship, you may already know X. Otherwise, latch onto him tightly. He is elusive. He was an acquaintance of Finnegan in both his lives.

"I thought you were dead," Finnegan said accusingly.

"No, I am not dead. I have never been dead."

"X, I have had knowledge during the last several months of one man who was dead and buried, and who didn't stay dead."

"That case has puzzled me also, Finnegan. I have followed it closely. Closely at a distance, that is. That is a paradox."

"I tell you, X, that I become a little impatient with people who are supposed to be dead and who keep reappearing. It loses its humor after a while."

"My own case I can explain. The other I cannot," said X. "Let us pool our knowledge and clear up these mysteries. Why did you think me dead, Finnegan?"

"One of the kids in New Orleans forwarded a clipping to me that seemed to say so. This had been sent to me, and it seemed to describe you dead. Yet I have received letters from you since that time. I thought it a little odd when I got them. Something that only you could do."

"That was all in the nature of a tall story, Finnegan. I sent the clipping to the kids. I also printed it. It was a contemptible trick, something that only I would do. I have a flair for the dramatic and I cannot always control myself. It was a well-written little notice, however, and I spent a lot of time on it. It told of the unidentified mysterious dead man, and it gave little details known only to my close friends that would identify me indubitably. Nothing but an impractical joke.

"Now, Finnegan, how can you explain the other? I have it on good authority that your recent patron believed that Papadiabolous had been killed. He was sure of it. Yet Papa came back to life and sailed with you. Was Mr. Seaworthy in his cups and only think that the man was killed? He does not usually make mistakes."

"No. Papadiabolous was dead all right. I helped bury him."

"You interest me. I did not know that part."

"That is where I met Seaworthy. We buried Papa Devil without a coffin, on top of another man, in an old grave. For further effect we will say that it was at midnight, for it must have been close to that hour. It's a scene that would have delighted you, X; I'm sorry that you missed it."

"It may be that I will not always have missed it. When I tell this in years to come I will, of course, make myself an eye-witness. I must have been very near the scene. I was in town and hot on the case, but I followed a wrong trail. I did not think that Seaworthy would do the job himself. I followed the hired killer, who looked remarkably like you; at first I thought he was you. He waited for Seaworthy, and Seaworthy failed the meeting. Old Saxon is devious."

"It was an accident that time, I believe. He took me for the killer. We found Papadiabolous. There is some confusion in my mind then, as though a blind had been pulled down over it. But Papadiabolous was dead; there is no question about that. And we buried him."

"Deaths are easy to explain, Finnegan. Resurrections are not. I can only hazard the guess that another took the place of Papadiabolous, and so perfectly that he fooled even the old associates. And yet this is impossible. Doubles do not grow on trees, not even on graveyard yew trees. Seaworthy was the only one who knew that he was going to kill Papadiabolous; the hired killer didn't know who the prey was. And Papa Devil surely didn't know he was going to be killed. Do you know who took the place of Papa Devil and how he did it so perfectly and so timely?"

"No. But he did it. He still has them fooled. They killed him and didn't know it was he they had killed. He scored a point there, but not the main point."

"And you do not know who he is . . . was?"

"I don't know his name, X. But this is he—"

Finnegan sketched him. It took a few minutes. It was that face that had hid so long behind another face.

"This is the same big man who was killed the other night or morning on the landing at Naxos?" X asked.

"The same man. I haven't done his face well. I didn't know his face well."

"It's well enough for me to know it. Do the Devils on the Brunhilde know that he was the one masquerading all these months?"

"No. It is incredible, but Manuel says that they didn't recognize him. They are still looking for Papa Devil now. They believe that the big man came on the little launch and they don't tie him in at all. I think this has them worried, and it will keep them worried."

"Yes, I know him, Finnegan. He is an Irish cop. I wish he were still alive. His name is either Noonan or Flaherty. It has been both. We have lost a valuable ally. He was not hampered by legal methods.

"He was a fantastic man, an amazing mimic. He could walk behind any man down a street, and manage at that moment to appear just like that man. But even that isn't enough to explain it. There is a lot here I don't know and will have to find out."

"X, I had come to like the Papadiabolous that I knew. Irish cop nothing! He will always be the Devil to me."

"The first death of Papadiabolous must have delighted him, Finnegan. They were enemies to the grave; and, as it now appears, beyond. Noonan had a hatred for the gang and had followed them before. Our Irish cop used many other names; he got around the world, and he had entree to most of the police stations of the globe. It's a shame that he got it.

"But he had been shot at so much that he had to be hit sometime. They don't know it, but they've killed a fish as big as Papa Devil."

"What was the original Papa Devil? Wasn't he the main one of them?"

"Yes. He was one of the alien conspirators; the biggest one, you might say. It was just a little internecine warfare. The whole clique is a catastrophe looking for a world to happen to. They have funds for whatever they may decide; they are given a remarkably free hand. They are almost the only free-roving group of their kind having complete sanction from the center. Seaworthy is the executive officer. You might have learned a little more while you traveled with them, if you hadn't been like a puppy born with his eyes closed. Now, with the Papadiabolous, True and False, dead, it becomes the rule of four men: Saxon X. Seaworthy, William Gerecke, Peter Wirt, and Orestes Gonof."

"I thought that Captain Gonof was a nonentity."

"No. He is one of the shrewdest and most evil of them all, Finnegan. Like Orestes of old, he would slay his own mother, which is Hellas, which is the world. And Gonof—do you know what Gonof means?"

"A thief. And it isn't Greek."

"You surprise me. Do you know what grave Papadiabolous is buried in, the name on it?"

"No. I don't know the name on the stone, but Saxon said that the men had met before. Another day, when I have the leisure, I will go back. I can locate it."

"The chances are, whenever you go there, in whatever year it is, you will find me standing by. There is a puzzle here that must have an answer. Even now I am suddenly taken by a theory and many facts are tumbling from the labyrinth of my memory."

"X, I was completely taken with Anastasia and I do not know it till she's dead. There's nothing left for me now. I'm dead too. Did you think I would die that easy?"

"I died like that too. We go on with it, and lead another life on a lesser level. I have a room in town here, Finnegan. Would you like to go to it and clean up and sleep? You have had no sleep for three days and nights, they tell me, except for little catnaps at this table. I worry about you."

"No. I think that I will just sit here for a while."

"You're filthy, you know. But when did you get the sign of the octopus on your wrist?"

"At the time of the shooting. I thought I was shot or scotched. But now the mark takes this shape. Am I also of that flesh, and how will I fight against it?"

"Is there an alien flesh, Finnegan? I myself haven't decided yet. There is, at any rate, a race that cuts across the races. Come, Finnegan. You've not even rinsed the salt out of your hair. It will make sores. And you smell too. You must come and clean up."

"No. I will just sit here for a few days. Then I will get a ship and go to another country. And someday my feelings will be less immediate."

"There is something else, Finnegan, and I say it with a little shame. I am not able to pay for my room. I took it really to be here to protect you if they ever came here to kill you in your present state of lassitude."

"All right. We will go to your room."

Finnegan sat in a chair by the window in the room of Mr. X and drank all night. From time to time X spoke to him from the bed.

"Anastasia Demetriades was buried this afternoon, Finnegan. Did you know that?"

"Yes. I knew that. I naturally know such things when they happen. And she had a rich funeral, but how did that come about? Did one of the Devils arrange it?"

"I think so, Finnegan. Seaworthy had a real affection for her. Not enough affection to save her life when it was apparent that she was part of a trap, but enough to bury her lavishly."

"I also know that Marie Courtois is dying on the Brunhilde," said Finnegan, "and she finds a certain pleasure in it. She was shot by Joe Cross, after she had shot Anastasia with an accurate hit at a distance, and Joe Cross was in turn shot. They were like dominoes knocking each other off. She's enjoyed dying these last days, but she'd rather have gone quickly and caught Anastasia on the narrow way just after she killed her.

"Even so, Marie is glad to die. She believes she will have a favored place. She also believes that the bridge itself has only one shore, X. Her eyes are distant now, and a slaver runs down her chin like a snail's trail. Persephone has been in Hell before. She often goes there. I see it all, but I don't know the reason for it. Whatever I do now, it is what I do after I am dead.

"X, I will clip that old granite-faced fox yet, and all of them. He has taken the thing I love best. He loves a meaner thing, but I'll take it, nevertheless. I will kill him then, after I have deprived him. Or he will kill me. I will devote my shadow life that is left to this hunt."

In the morning Finnegan paid for the room and gave X a hundred dollars to travel on. Then he went back to the inn and sat there for some days. Afterwards, he went to another country where his feelings became less immediate.

This was the first death of Finnegan.

He was later to die another death on another sort of island, a physical death that was final, in its way. But this first death had its own finality, even though it was followed by a sort of shadow life.

Chapter Eleven

36,000 PIECES OF PAPER

Some believe that the Tityroi are not of our world, that they are of an other world beyond the moon. Yet I believe that they are born of women of this world. Daemons, who may be of worlds beyond the moon, beget Tityroi or Satyroi on world women. Their children are hardly to be told from mankind, though they have ravening passions for the destruction of mankind, and have always a seeming of ape or goat or wolf or panther or other animal. They are the Satyrs. Those of the first generation, those begotten by the Daemons directly, are fertile and generate offspring. But those of the second generation, the offspring of Tityroi on Earth women, are not fertile, do not generate offspring, though they are in appearance and passion similar to the first generation. For this reason, the race must be renewed, and in every century the Daemons must come back to women of the world. In our own time, a Daemon begot children on thirteen women in Calchedon in Bithyni in a single night.

—GALEN, *Techne Iatrike*

1.

And remember, passerby, that Galen himself studied medicine under a man named Satyrus. Whence had the teacher his name? Whence had Galen his information?

This was after Finnegan had died that first time; but there are compensations to having already died. There is a relaxation of the restrictions and a certain gained freedom. There is a feeling that one is no longer bound by the conventions.

The mainstream of life is bound by conventions, but they are neither those of God nor of the gods. They are the accidental conventions of two meddlesome men, and they control by an abiding accident. They are the Unities of Aristotle, and the Heroics of Plutarch. But in the shadow life one is not bound by the unities nor obliged to abide by the heroic.

Several years had gone by since Finnegan had been on the Brunhilde, and we cannot say how many. Certain persons had gotten older. And others, apparently, had not. If there be another recension, it is said that the members of it do not age as rapidly as do people. They do not age, but they deepen.

Finnegan had been up and down in his fortunes. He had been back in his own country, and out of it, and into it again. Then one day he picked up the spoor of that old fox Seaworthy, and remembered his promise to rob him and then to kill him.

Finnegan had first met Seaworthy and the Devil in an island city. Now he was in another island city: bigger city, smaller island. It was nighttime, and Finnegan had gone feral.

He did not, as Papa Devil had done briefly, regrow his lost stripes and become a tiger. Finnegan was a smaller and other breed of cat; or ape, perhaps; or climbing grotesquerie.

There was in that city a small hotel of curious gothic style. It ran up to parapets and to those stone knobs that are called merlons. At this moment there was a living gargoyle sitting on one of those merlons and it seemed perfectly natural there. Such places are their dens, their nests.

The gargoyle was carved of dark brown stone that seemed blue in the dark and the ambient half-light. It had climbed up the outside of the building for six stories to come to roost there. Those things can climb; and the little hotel of gothic style was covered with ornamentation that made the climbing easier. The name of the living gargoyle was John Solli and his monicker was Finnegan.

You did not know that Finnegan had once been a steeplejack? Many do not know that. You did not know that lately he had been involved in several upper-story burglaries and that he was good at it? These had not been for profit, but to obtain evidence of several sorts.

For two or three days and nights now, there had been a

legend in that city (they love legends there) of an ape or monstrous man that climbed up the outsides of buildings at night and roosted on the pinnacles. It was even said that this was one of the stone gargoyles from an ornamental building come to life. It wasn't, though. It was Finnegan.

On an ornamentation of stone six stories up, he perched above the dark street. Through a blade-thin slit between drapes of a sixth floor window, Finnegan looked inside at a coven or meeting of gargoyles. 'You have to admit that we *are* funny looking,' Finnegan said to himself.

There were the four senior gargoyles from the Brunhilde: Saxon X. Seaworthy who now showed the *pherea* or protuberances on the neck (one sign of ageing in the species); William Gerecke who was wiry as a spider; Peter Wirt with the mind of a wolverine; Orestes Gonof, the largest and most menacing of them, now that Papadiabolous was gone. With these four were seven Devils more evil than themselves. Eleven of them, all of them men or whatever of some age and authority.

Finnegan was pleased that there were no young men with them, though he knew that there would be some outside the doors of the meeting room. The old monsters would not be expecting an attack from a sixth floor window, not from an opponent they had not heard from in several years and who was not likely to be in that part of the world. Or would they?

One old fox could hardly have been expected to guess an attack from the landward side on the Brunhilde, not at the very moment when the impossible seaward attack had been launched, not on Naxos, the most peaceful island in the world. It is all right to underrate the Devil, but do not underrate the man who is smarter than the Devil.

Finnegan had located the thesaurus, the treasure, the chrysus, and he knew it was not in a classical case. It was in an unnoticed corner of the room, trying to look dingy and unimportant. It was one focus for the attack of Finnegan. The *pherea*-grown throat of Saxon X. Seaworthy was the other. He would have to achieve them both.

It was quite cold; and the mist was beginning to ice on the stones, making them dangerous, even for an ape-cat of a man. Finnegan had two things with him, and he meant to leave them both behind him in that glimpsed room. He had a lead weight marked with certain cabalistic markings, meaningless, and of his own invention. And he had a short hand knife.

Finnegan had opened one window noiselessly and easily. He was a cat that could climb, he was an ape that could open anything. He left the opened window and moved dangerously and swiftly to the window the length of the room away. Both of these windows were sheer above the street.

There was, however, in the side of the building (in the back of the room) a third window. Finnegan would not enter this, but he hoped to come out of it. Below this third window, and some nine feet out, was the roof of a four-story building.

An animal on the surge does not consider. It strikes. Finnegan smashed the window in front of him with the lead weight, letting it fall heavily inside.

"Stand and wait!" he called powerfully in the strong voice of Papadiabolous. "It is myself returned again." That voice of Papadiabolous had always scared Finnegan, and it scared him a little now, even though he did it himself.

Those in the room stood and waited, apparently, startled dumb by the voice. Then one of them turned out the lights, and not with the wall switch. Look out! Someone was well-aware inside.

Finnegan was around to the previously opened window while the Papadiabolous voice he had launched still echoed in the air. He came noiselessly into the room whose darkness was modified only by a slight neon ambient from outside.

Two foci, neither of them to be seen in the dark, both of them to be remembered from observations of seconds before. Finnegan grappled the man where the man should have been, found him, and drove the knife into his throat, leaving it there. There was a death groan and a fall. And yet there was something the matter with that death groan.

Then Finnegan had his hand on the handle of the thesaurus, the chrysus. He leapt to the sill with it and surged. He shattered that third window, crashing spread-eagled through it, leaping twenty feet down and nine feet outward. It would have killed a man to hit the way he hit on the edge of that roof.

And there had been a wrong laugh in the dark room behind him just as he leaped.

The man Finnegan was on a fourth floor roof, and there was gunshot behind him. So Finnegan was a man again; but a swift and sudden man who went quickly down the iron fire-ladders into an alley, and thought as swiftly as he could with his man's brain. But what he had just done he could not have done as a man. Only as the ape-cat that he had become when he climbed and invaded could he have done it.

Finnegan moved quickly, angling from alley into street and into another alley, abruptly into a cluttered space between buildings, through another alley, into another street. He was elated about one thing, disconsolate about another.

"Got it!" he exulted to himself. "But I killed the wrong man. Ah, well, I'll kill him yet. I'm a trick ahead of him now, even though it's his pursuit."

The dying moan in the room had been that of William Gerecke. The wrong laugh in the room had been that of Saxon X. Seaworthy. That granite-faced old fox was still smarter than the Devil.

"He's a steady one," Finnegan told himself. "If he believed that Papadiabolous was indeed alive for the third time, that he had come into the room after him, he welcomed the encounter. Finnegan, you must track this smart old killer fox till one of you dies."

Finnegan walked rapidly, but not in outward panic, with the chrysus in his hand. The chrysus was a heavy and shabby suitcase, and Finnegan guessed that it was probably the most valuable suitcase in the world. He knew what he had.

He had a suitcase full of paper. There were thirty-six thousand pieces of paper in it, each of them two and one half inches wide and six and one eighth inches long. They were in bundles of one hundreds, tightly wrapped with rubber bands. They were laid in flat, three bundles lengthwise to take up the bottom length of the suitcase, and six bundles wide. They were stacked twenty bundles high.

The suitcase was broad and heavy. It weighed eighty pounds.

To improvise now, to improvise. The man who was smarter than the Devil would be after him with considerable resources. This man had killers who could follow a trail.

Finnegan had little cuts about his face and hands. It was odd that one could go through a sheet of glass and receive only small cuts like that. The freezing rain had turned to a noisy sleet. Finnegan had only small change in his pocket and it was necessary that he get off the street at once. A siren sounded, and it shook him, though he knew it could not be for him yet. A dog pursued him, noisily and relentlessly, and that could be more serious. A bum fastened onto him, and Finnegan gave him all his pocket change to be rid of him. A policeman bore down dourly on him, and Finnegan just as dourly continued on past.

He tried a car and found the door unlocked. He threw the suitcase in the back seat and sat in the front, waiting for a girl to walk past before he jumped the ignition. But she didn't walk past. Instead, she stopped at the car window.

"I'm not hustling, mister," she said. "I'm freezing. I'm locked out and you can die on a night like this. Just a dollar. I can get a place to sleep for a dollar."

Finnegan saw a whole new picture. "Get in the car," he said, "and you drive the car."

"You misunderstand me. I said I wasn't hustling. I'm freezing and starving."

"I've done both, girl. It isn't a time to be timid. I told you to get in the car. No. In the driver's seat."

She got in.

"Don't you have any friends?" Finnegan asked her.

"None. None in this town. None anywhere any more."

"Do you have anything to keep you in New York then?"

"I don't even have anything to keep me alive. I've given up."

"I'm starting south right now. You have to go along with me. I need you for disguise. Wait here till I get the motor started. I wonder if all those sirens are necessary."

"Somebody said that somebody just killed a man in the next street."

"Oh yes. I'd forgotten about him."

Finnegan lifted the hood and jumped the ignition.

"Now you drive right on and through the tunnel," he told her. "I'm going to sit in the back seat. I have a few things to do."

"I'm scared. I'm scared of you."

"That's the way to be. I'm dangerous, and you have to drive for me. And if I slip down on the floor whenever we come under the lights, think nothing of it. It's an oddity of mine. I'll let you loose and give you a tip when we get to New Jersey if you want to leave the show there."

She drove, and Finnegan was in back. She seemed more puzzled than scared now. She was a girl who would recover fast. While she drove he opened the suitcase and abstracted one of the three hundred and sixty bundles. He put the bundle in his pocket.

"Hand me everything in the glove compartment," he told the girl.

"This too?"

"Yes. That especially." She passed the things back to him.

"Did you have a gun before I passed you that?" she asked him.

"No, but I have now. You drive along like a good girl."

He went through the papers and gave her an address in Newark to drive to.

"If anyone asks who you are, you are Mrs. George Brubaker," he told her. "And you are driving home. For the rest, just look innocent."

"I am innocent. Are you George Brubaker?"

"I may have to be old George momentarily. But do not, if we are stopped for any reason, burden people with the knowledge that your husband is lying on the floor between the seats of the car. It's a habit that I may outgrow someday. Wake me up when we get to that address." He pulled one piece of paper from the bundle, gave it to the girl, and put the other ninety-nine back in his pocket.

"It's for you. I'll give you another when we get there if you're good."

"A fifty! You must be a crook. I don't think this is even your car either."

"It is mine for a while under an obscure bit of Common Law known as the Lien of Extreme Need."

Finnegan slept lightly and with great determination not to waken. He lay on the floor between the seats curled up with the great suitcase. He believed that they were stopped once and the girl was questioned. Somewhere in his sleep was her voice telling a flashlight that she was Mrs. George Brubaker and that she was driving home to Newark. She was a good girl.

And after some time, the car pulled up in front of George Brubaker's house in Newark. Finnegan wrote a note to George Brubaker cautioning him about leaving his car unlocked with the many people of an unsettled type about in the country, and he signed it Roving Magistrate Number Sixteen. He also wrote that George was to report at nine o'clock the next morning (that morning actually) to room 101 of the Epimetheos Building. Finnegan did not write the address of the building, for he did not know it. If there were such a building, then the address should be in some directory. If there were not, then George would not have been able to find it anyhow.

Finnegan and the girl left the car in front of the Brubaker house, and quickly walked away carrying the suitcase.

"Won't George be surprised when he gets home and finds his car already here!" said Finnegan. "I worry about people like George."

"What if Mrs. George is waiting up for him?" the girl asked. "When she finds his car came home without him she'll be worried. She'll think it threw him and ran off from him."

"Did you see a bus station?" Finnegan asked.

"About five blocks back the way we came."

"Take this suitcase and put it in a big locker there. Do that before you do anything else. Then see when the next bus goes to Baltimore and get two tickets. Walk back here then and wake me up. I'll be sleeping behind this hedge. Oh, and after you've got the tickets to Baltimore, go to the jane a while, and then go to a different window and get two tickets for Pittsburgh."

"Which tickets will we use? What if I keep the fifty dollars and don't come back?"

"That's yours. Wait, this is for the tickets. And do come back. I need you."

2.

The girl came back.

"Is there an all-night eating place there?" he asked. "Is anyone around the station that seems to be looking for anybody?"

"Yes, the restaurant is open. I can't tell when people are looking for someone. People around bus stations always look funny anyhow. Where did you get the glasses? You didn't wear glasses before."

"I guess they belong to George Brubaker. The world looks funny through them. Ah well, it always did look funny."

They went to the restaurant at the station and had coffee and cakes. Finnegan sketched while they ate.

"Was this man around?" he asked the girl and showed her what he had drawn.

"You really can draw. No. There wasn't anybody who looked like that. No. Not like that either. The Baltimore bus is at five forty-five, the Pittsburgh bus is at six ten. Which one are we going on?"

"Do both busses go through Philadelphia?"

"No. The Pittsburgh bus goes through Allentown and Reading."

"Give me one of each of the tickets."

"Yes. All right. You sure do draw good and fast. No, I never saw any guys that looked like any of those."

"There is one more I haven't seen. I know he is left-footed. I've heard that he shoots left-handed. What is your name? I have to call you something."

"I'm Doll Delancy. Dolores, that is. Everybody calls me Doll."

"Everybody calls me Finnegan, but I had better not go by that now. It is possible that none of them remember my real name. I tore it out of the ship's list on impulse the last day before I left, and the three most likely to remember it are dead."

Doll got the big suitcase out of the locker at the last minute, and they took the Baltimore bus. Doll checked the suitcase through to Baltimore.

They got off the bus in Philadelphia, took a taxi across town, got out and walked back part way along their trail. They stopped at a place for another breakfast, this at a more normal time for them.

"Shall I go buy another suitcase so you can switch some of the stuff, and so it won't be spotted so easy?" Doll asked.

"No. I'll steal one," Finnegan said. "A new suitcase isn't what I want."

They got back to the station just in time. Finnegan stole a suitcase to carry with him, and they lined up to get back on the bus.

"Oh my God, don't look!" Doll said suddenly. "One of the men you drew, he's standing ahead. He's where he can see anyone getting on the busses."

They faded away from there, out through a side door, and down the street. They took a taxi to the railway station. Finnegan kept the stolen suitcase in one hand, held a time table up to his face with the other, and kept his eyes on Doll's heels as he followed her around. She got tickets for the Baltimore train, and they were aboard and under way.

They exchanged wildly false accounts of themselves during the trip. They became friends. They got off the train at Baltimore, registered at a middling hotel; but they did not yet pick up the original heavy suitcase at the bus station.

Ah well, they would see what was in the stolen suitcase. Though large and tacky, it was a lady's suitcase from the irrational neatness within. Everything was separated into small packages with shipping tags attached, each covered completely with small writing.

On the first tag, attached by a cord to the handle and just inside the suitcase, was written: "This suitcase belongs to Phoebe Anne Ankerson. If I lose my suitcase, send it to my sister Minnie MacMasters of Walnut Bottom, Pennsylvania where I will be till a week from next Friday. If it is after a week from next Friday that you find it, then send it home to me in Hammonton, New Jersey. Thank you."

There was a little sack of marbles with a tag: "Marbles to give to Harold Michael, these marbles used to belong to Aaron and are all of them good ones and some of them are agates, but he is too old for them now." And another one: "Seeds for Minnie, it is almost time to plant them in a little over a month, only some of them may not grow, they are too old." There were quite a few other things in it, but nothing of use to them.

"We'd better send it to her today," Finnegan said. "We can always steal another suitcase."

They did various things. Finnegan slept all afternoon, and Doll went shopping. She got some things for Finnegan also. She was new costumed when she returned, so they went out on the town.

Finnegan was delighted with himself. He had always liked to draw a little fire. When he was a boxer he had always carried his left low just to draw right hands. He had Doll, though he hadn't asked himself the never-to-be-answered question, who was Doll? She had a broad face. She had bright gray eyes that had grown amused as the surprise and immediacy of the situation had lessened. She was nice looking, though a little large. And placid, like a slumbering volcano.

They went to a supper club and had seafood of the town; and danced. They went to another place and danced quite a while and boozed it up. "They will believe me hidden," Finnegan told himself, "if they have followed me to this town. They will not look for me out on the town. I lie. It is that, after my tension, I *have* to be out on the town."

They livened up as they went along, they had several small skirmishes, and then Doll had come to the talky stage.

"I walked out on one life after it got where I couldn't live it any more," she said. "You say that this is what you do after you are dead. I thought it would be like that with me, but for two dead people we sure do have a lot of fun. I wish that little string of torpedos would come around again, Finn. I bet we could take them all. That one was right, though. You *do* look like a hooked-nosed ape. And I just hope these people here caution us just one more time about making so much noise. I just thought of something to come back on them with. We weren't *either* dancing rowdy. We were just having fun."

"A while ago you told me it wasn't prudent to draw so much attention, Doll. Who is not being prudent now? But you sure are pretty when you get fired up. I'd like to do you in oil."

"I'd like to boil you in oil, Finn, thinking about painting when we're having so much fun. Where do these people get off, telling us that we can't carry on like that?"

"Ah, let them throw us out, and it'll be the noisest exit they ever had here. Let's order another meal first, though, Doll. We don't want to be caught short on crockery to throw when it comes to the crisis."

Finnegan and Doll Delancy were no longer alone. There was a comical little drunk with them. It seemed as though he'd materialized gradually; he hadn't been there all at once.

"You are the cutest little man I ever did see," Doll told the little drunk. "We are going to adopt you and you will travel with us, aren't we going to, Finnegan? We are going to go all over the country and live like unobtrusive princes. We will keep it gaudy but not let it get out of hand. We've got a million dollars in a suitcase, and we'll give you all you want, won't we, Finnegan? Will you go with us, little man?"

Although Finnegan realized that the little man was not really drunk, and that he and Doll were, yet he was not alarmed. Finnegan had an instinct for friendship, and he always knew a right man from a wrong one.

But it was odd that it took him so long to recognize his old friend Mr. X.

Chapter Twelve
CREST AND SHATTER

There are but two sciences, the Science of God, and the Science of Man. Perhaps the soundest scientist who ever studied and produced amongst us was John de Yepes (St. John of the Cross). He studied the highest subject (Divinity) by the direct experimental method applicable (mysticism). Yet there are those who say that he was the very opposite of scientist; even those who say that mysticism is the opposite of the scientific method. Latterly there are those who thrust back as 'soft sciences' these two basic sciences, and who bring forward as 'hard science' a distant derivative with no sound claim to reality—the Science of Things.
—WIMBISH A. MCDEARMOTT, *Panegyrica*

1.

"This is an old acquaintance of mine, Doll," Finnegan said. "He is a little sheep dog who has come to lead us out of the woods."

Mr. X rose and bowed.

"The car is outside, Mr. Solli," he said. "You had better be Mr. Solli now. Finnegan is being pursued."

"I guess so, X. What car?"

"I bought it from our common fund today. It has a D.C. plate on it. Now, if you two are tired dancing and drinking, we will be off."

"X, you are either way ahead of me or way behind. You cannot know the situation."

"Of course I know the situation, Finnegan. I am, as always, onto everything. I have decided to join forces with you for your own protection. *Diavolo,* Finnegan, you have had some close calls in the last few hours. They have been missing you by seconds and feet only. It could only happen in an old comedy, the way they have been missing you."

"Close, has it been, X? I thought I'd lost them completely, if they were even onto me this far."

"Oh, very close, Finnegan, ah, Mr. Solli. And they are about to miss you very close again. A man in this room is to be kidnapped within seconds. And if he will not tell things that he cannot possibly know, he will be killed. What do you notice about that man over there?"

"What would anyone notice about him? He has a nose even bigger than mine, though with less character to it."

"You are saved by a nose. You were correctly reported in this town, and in this place. And now the finger men have been told that yours is a nose they could not possibly miss. Out of here with me, you two, easy but swiftly now."

And in a very few seconds they were in the car of X and working their way out of town to the South.

"I hate to leave town without the suitcase," Finnegan said. "Its time will run out in the locker, and someone will look into it then."

"Let it be known that I took the liberty of lifting a certain claim check from Miss Doll's bag while she was shopping this afternoon. I have the suitcase now, of course, and I could have been off with it long ago. You will see that my mixing in this is not purely selfish. I am rather proud of the way I did it, though.

"After I picked up your prime suitcase, I left another bewildered conveyance of the same sort in the locker there, and I planted a trail that would lead them to it. Mr. Solli, those two battered suitcases are alike as triplets. They must have been whelped at the same time.

"And in the other one also there are thirty-six thousand pieces of paper, but not the same thirty-six thousand. They will be bewildered when they find it, thirty-six thousand little pieces cut out of newspapers and banded together and stacked tightly. They will wonder how we are so clever.

"Those suitcases are very heavy, Mr. Solli. I don't see how Miss Doll could have handled it so easily."

X drove rapidly South, Doll Delancy chattered, Finnegan slept.

It was beginning to be daylight when Finnegan got the

unaccountable feeling that he was traveling on the inside of a rainbow. The dawn was coming up, but there was a hint of a color fringe that didn't belong to the dawn. Yet there was no real riot of color visible to him—nothing except the conventional black and green rosettes of the leopard-skin upholstery; the mauve, pearl, and violet shades of the dashboard or instrument panel; gold where you might expect chrome; beige charcoal, purple pastel, livid lilac, shades like that.

"Signor X, what color is this crate?" Finnegan asked, "on the outside, I mean."

"Signor Solli, I do not understand the word. A crate? That would be a *cesto*, a *paniera*, a *casetta*, a *scatola?*"

"No it would not be, Signor X. It would be this *faeton*, this *drozhe*, this *vettura*, this *carrozza*, called by the vulgar an automobile, this celestial omnibus, this purring panther in which we are riding."

"Signor Solli, it is a little bit *giallo*, and a little *turchino*."

"I am waiting."

"You have heard of two-toned cars. You may even have seen three-toned. But this is the only eight-toned vehicle they had in the agency. They had ordered it in the expectation of selling it to a blind man; but when he cancelled the order on being persuaded by his family that he was too nervous to drive, they were glad to sell it to me for an exorbitant figure."

"What a hurtling rainbow!" Doll breathed.

"Pardon the doubt gnawing at my kidneys, but isn't this conspicuous?" Finnegan asked.

"There is no other word for it," said X. "The first step would be for us to take a klunker and go inconspicuous in that. But we are, and they know we are, too smart for that; so we take the butterfly. So they will watch for a butterfly. But we being smart beyond this, go beyond a butterfly to a klunker again. And they, realizing we are clever beyond what they guessed, will (after thinking it over) look for us in a klunker. Then, going beyond everything, we take a butterfly after all."

"The truth is that you fell in love with the butterfly and had to take it," Doll said.

"Yes. That is the truth. The rest is rationale. But soon we will split in three parts. We will have a klunker, and we will have another thing that is neither hot nor cold. Meanwhile I have split up the boodle. The old original suitcase is now derelict and empty, and it will be some days before they find it. The nondescript travel bag is mine. The sturdy old cowhide is yours, Signor Solli, and yours is much the heaviest. The chic little overnight is yours, Miss Doll. We have shorted you a little, Miss Doll, but you haven't been in this like we have. And it does contain more than you could earn honestly in a lifetime."

2.

Another day. They had talked conspiratorial talk; they had explored eschatological themes; they had discussed essence, whether they were man or teras or what ("I'm a woman," Doll said, "I'm pretty sure of that"); they had plotted the murder of Saxon X. Seaworthy and his crew; and they had told some funny stories.

Now they were in the Florida lake country. The three of them were richly installed.

This was a fisherman's paradise, though there was something artificial about it. Finnegan said that the crux of the matter was that there was something wrong with the fish. They weren't the honest fish that he had known in Louisiana rivers, swamps, and bayous. These were contrived fish made especially for the tourist trade.

Oh, they were live enough, and they bled blood and serum when you cut them open. But they weren't fish as Finnegan had known them. Doll said that Finnegan was incurably provincial, that he knew only his own little backwater. It wasn't true. He knew the fish of the midland rivers and streams, and of many coasts; he knew the fish of the great ocean itself. But he didn't know these strange fish.

We will leave it to any honest man: Are those fish like the fish you knew anywhere else?

The lake they were on was about eleven miles long and from three hundred yards to two miles wide. It was one of those finger lakes that are really links of one of the underground rivers, and it had river currents in it. It was grassy, like most of the lakes in that country, weed and reed grown.

"This is my kind of lake," Doll said, "where I can always get out and walk."

"Push the boat, girl," Finnegan would tell her. "Don't talk so much."

The little boat often got stuck in the mud, for land and water were hopelessly mixed here; and Doll always got out and pushed. Finnegan would gladly have done it, but he was too lazy. There were many things he would gladly have done in those days except for the delicious lassitude that had devoured him completely.

The weeds were full of fish; and Doll, who practiced the ancient art of noodling, pitched them into the boat by the dozens, while Finnegan could take only an occasional one with the hook. Fish? They were young whales, blowholes and all. Where else do you say, 'No, not that one, he's too big. He'd swamp us.'

They wore rubber boots and swimsuits. They went out where it was clear of grass and swam in the four foot deep water. They thought of putting up a sign 'Deepest Water in the State of Florida, Four Feet.' Some of the fish were nearly that thick, and had calluses on their bellies from dragging on the bottom.

Often they would empty the boat after they had it full. The noodled fish would come back to life and swim off no worse for the experience. And after such pleasures, Finnegan and Doll would go back to the shady bait house to drink beer.

"What are you always kind of afraid of?" Doll asked him once when they were loafing there, "that people don't like you?"

"What is who afraid of, Doll?"

"Why, the things like you, Finnegan; and X, I think; and I knew another one once; whatever you are. Are you afraid people won't like you? I like you."

"No, Doll, I'm afraid that I won't like people. It is very bad when we don't like them, Doll; we set them on fire."

The three little outlaws, Finnegan (Solli), Doll, and X, drew no attention here. All the fishermen were complacently rich. All of them went around like brightly-colored tramps, with fish and bait blood soaked into twenty dollar sport shirts, and with casting equipment whose cost would feed a family for years. And there were menages as unorthodox as that of Finnegan and Doll and X.

The bait house was a pleasant shady building, long and low, with whitewashed rafters, and water sloshing under the planks of the floor and sometimes squishing through. The walls were covered with the pictures of notables who had caught fish here. There was a caste system: the grander the notables, the bigger the fish they had taken, and the pictures proved it. A lot of them sat in the bait house and drank beer on the warm afternoons.

"There was a man asking for you this morning," said a man from Minneapolis. "Not by name, of course, and not by very good description, but I know he was looking for you. I didn't think you'd want to see him. I flubbed him off, I think."

"A left-footed man?" Finnegan asked.

"As a matter of fact he was. I thought I was the only one who noticed things like that about a fellow. What does he want with you?"

"He wants to kill me," said Finnegan. "I hope he doesn't."

"But which is he, Finn?" Doll asked. "He doesn't sound like any of them that X talks about."

"No. He isn't. He isn't from this last ruckus. He's on an earlier assignment."

Later, when it had come on evening, after they had showered and cleaned up, and after X had made a few long-distance telephone calls, they would drive around through the citrus and scrub to Orlando and Kissimee and Pine Castle and Apopka. And sometimes to Daytona.

"Doll, you have never told me your story," Finnegan said one day. "You haven't told me who you are, or how you happened to be clear down. You haven't told me why you once said that we were the most peaceful company you had known for a long time, us a couple of refugee killers."

"Well, I will tell you then," Doll said. "I'll tell you right now. I never had the chance before really. I will begin a ways back...."

But Finnegan wasn't there; he had wandered off somewhere.

Another day he also asked her to tell it, and again he disappeared before she could get into it. And she *did* want to tell her story.

Even X showed a momentary curiosity once:

"Miss Doll, I believe I know the basic facts about nearly everyone in the world except yourself. Kindly give me a précis of your life and leave out nothing. It may be that the details which you would be inclined to leave out would be the most interesting ones to me."

"I'd be glad to, X. I've wanted to tell my story to someone for a long time, and nobody will listen. I will begin a ways back...."

But X was telephoning. He telephoned a lot in the evenings and night.

"Xochilmileo," he said. "Listen carefully. Vinschoten, Vlissinger, Spink, Tineo, Abo, Imazu, Ligueria, Sheboygan—hell, I don't know how to spell it. How do you spell Sheboygan, Doll? Absecon, Xania. No, with an X. Oquawka, Neffs. Well, what did you *do* with your code book? Y has one. Y, Y, *i grec* yet. I'll call you tomorrow."

Doll never did get to tell her story to either of them, and she wanted to.

"The next move is up to them," X said. "We could stay here as long as a month. My operatives have nothing new to report. In fact, I am not sure that I have any operatives left to report anything. The last one had lately been fired from his job and cannot now be located."

"What was his job?" Doll asked.

"Dishwasher," said X. So they drifted on.

X now made fewer than a dozen long-distance calls a day. He had let down his guard. He no longer insisted that all three of them wear sunglasses day and night so as to be inconspicuous. To be sure, they had obtained a second and much older car, with a Georgia license plate, in case they need ride off in two directions at once. X also insisted that each of them carry a police whistle and never be out of blast distance from each other. And naturally they had a code of whistle signals, but this was all routine for him. He wasn't concerned, and Finnegan wasn't concerned. Only Doll was a little.

"It isn't any of my business, outside of me being in it up to my neck," she said, "but why aren't you guys worried?"

"Miss Doll," said X patiently, "it is a truism in my business that a worried man is a conspicuous man. Therefore, as we do not wish to be conspicuous, we do not worry."

"I see. Now isn't it a fact that, from whatever motives, personal and high-minded though they be, you have stolen quite a sum of money?"

"I wouldn't call it stealing, Miss Doll," said X. "Besides, it was Finnegan who stole it."

"But the law would consider it stealing, X dear. From what I can gather, Finnegan is guilty of stealing something over a million dollars, and of killing a man while he did it. And you are guilty of abetting him. I abet him a little myself."

"Well, yes, if you put it that way."

"Then why isn't it in the papers?"

"Who'd want it in the papers? We wouldn't. And they wouldn't."

"Finnegan wants to buy that passionate little road crawler he's been looking at. Then we will have a stable of three. We could take our chances from a hat, the Celestial Omnibus, the Little Road Crawler, and the Georgia Klunker. Then at a signal we could disappear in three directions. We could also draw for the weapons, the rifle, the derringer, and the pop pistol, or we could procure anything we wanted. We might have a stash for a certain sum, and each take enough travel money to keep up our newly acquired standards of luxury."

"*Non licet omnibus adire Corinthum*, Miss Doll," said X, "and yet we will travel."

"X dear, what did you say?" Doll asked him.

"I will not repeat. For a long time I have suspected that your hearing is not of the best, but I would not have it changed. I once knew a woman who built a reputation of being quizzical, fascinating, unfathomable, all from a certain exciting way she had of peering at a person. Yet she was none of those things. She was only hard of hearing."

"Thank you," said Doll.

"But your ideas are good ones. We will set up our signals and our channels of communication. Then we will scatter. We will rendezvous in a year and a day and some odd weeks at a certain point. I will do the staff work and set up the spring."

"And where will we rendezvous, staff?"

"If we three are in accord, and I believe we are, we will all know intuitively the time and the place. It will develop in us. But to give you a little help, I believe it will be in another southern city, and beside the grave of one Ifreann Noonan Gregorovitch, though that may not be the name that appears on the headstone."

"You are immeasurable, X. I condign you."

"Is it not a rich name he has, Miss Doll, and I am sure there is much more to it. And by the time we meet there, I should have a little story to tell you and Finn. I have a way of telling these stories, Miss Doll. I put a lot of thought and research into them. The truth in them is always interesting, but there is a wide selection of truths. Sometimes the characters do not come out the way they should, due to the perversity of people. Neither you nor the Finn satisfy me too well; I will fictionize you a little, as I will other things. There are capable people who will pass up opportunity after opportunity to have interesting incidents happen to them. Then I have to, not tamper with facts, but arrange and select a little. There are so many damned inartistic characters who creep in. It will all be worked out by the appointed time, however. I promise you that."

"Finnegan is fixing to go on another bender, I think," said Doll.

"Yes. The little benders aren't his difficulty. It is the big benders superimposed on the little benders that hurt him. We must be patient with him, but not too patient. Were I of your size, Miss Doll, I'd turn him over my knee and belabor him. I worry about his soul when he does these things. Yet the drink is more effort than cause. He first suffers a change. Then he drinks to soften it."

"We will adjust our time to his, I think," said Doll. "I think we should take it when he crests the next time. Then we will scatter."

3.

Finnegan was shaving one morning. There was nothing strange about that; he often shaved. But the funny thing was that he was shaving the face of Dopey the seaman. It wasn't illusion. It was the face of Doppio di Pinne, the seaman known as Dopey. Nor did it act like a mirror image. Finnegan was wide awake, and Dopey was plainly in a daze. He showed, for a moment, some fear of the razor (Finnegan used a straight razor), and was then reassured. It wasn't Finnegan's face. The follicles were different, slightly coarser; the complexion was made up differently, though coming out about the same color.

"Dopey, how did you die?" Finnegan asked the face in the mirror.

"Ga—I am not dead," Dopey said as if drugged.

"Dopey, where are you?" Finnegan asked him.

"Ga—I don't know. I guess I am right here."

Finnegan finished shaving. He felt his own face and it seemed to be coming along all right. He scanned Dopey carefully, and got small places he had missed.

"I am not a stable person," Finnegan said, "and I don't mean that I'm a looney. It is just that I have indefinite boundaries. I don't know where I begin, and I sure don't know where I will end."

He finished. He washed. He put his shaving things away. Then he shattered the mirror with a jar of Doll's ointment. He was still curious. He picked up one of the broken pieces and looked into it. It will still the face of Dopey the seaman, with eyes closed now in torturous sleep.

"Enough of that," Finnegan said. He had cut himself. He went out and left it.

X sometimes tried to get a little more information from Finnegan, and he found it incredible that Finnegan had no more to give.

"When you went through the appurtenances and desks of Saxon Seaworthy and his cronies on the Brunhilde, you surely must have picked up bits of information that we should now be able to evaluate. Dredge into your memory and recite, and I will take it all down. It will not matter if some of the papers were in code. Recall them to me. I can break any code."

"I went through no desks."

"Incredible! Why did you not? Always go through desks wherever you are, Finnegan, always. The information may be valuable to you years later if you have a retentive memory. But their very lockers must have been full of clues. You have the gift of recall. Let us put it to work, and now."

"I rifled no lockers."

"Astounding. But tell me at least what valuable information you obtained by cleverly questioning the evil giantess Marie. What tracings did you make in the chart room? What excerpts from the log? What interception on the wireless?"

"None at all, X. I was not then enough interested. I haven't that turn of mind."

"Everybody has that turn of mind, if only he will dig deeply enough in himself. What did Don Lewis tell you before he was murdered? What did Joe Cross confide in you? And Manuel? And the Pseudopapadiabolous? How much did the beautiful Anastasia really know, and how much of it did she tell you?"

"Nothing, X, nothing at all. You are far ahead of me on all the information. I have told you all that I know."

"*Bizarro*," said X.

It was a little before the middle of March that Finnegan had a tailor make him a tuxedo with green lapels for St. Patrick's Day. Then he began to celebrate.

"I am Finnegan the Irish crock," he said when the logorrhea was upon him. "One Finnegan is worth a dozen of those pirates. I am the salt of the earth. You do not toss the salt under a bushel. You put it in a saltcaster and set it on the table for the whole world to see. I am the only perfectly spherical saltcaster in the world; I am the grandfather of all the saltshakers; I am the cerulean saltcellar. Did you know that saltcellar is an anachronism?"

"An anachronism, dear?" Doll asked.

"That other thing, whatever it is, when you say the same thing twice. Cellar is saliere, from sal, salt. The word already has salt in it, so the salt in saltcellar is in excess, too damned much salt. 'If it be not salted with salt, it will be salted with sulphur,' as the prophet says. You didn't know I was educated, did you, Doll?"

"It is a shock."

"Ask me what you call a conic section when e is less

than one. Ask me what is an Exterior Proletariat. Ask me about Elective Affinities and the Categorical Imperative. Go ahead, ask me."

"With you it is two fingers of the stuff in the bottom of a glass. That is the imperative. The ice and the soda are the categorical."

"Right, Doll, right. Ask me how many legs has an arachnid? What you call the cosine of the angle of lag between voltage and current in an AC circuit? What is the equator of a parabola? Ask me how you say 'I ordered cucumbers, I sure did not order that stuff' in Russian. A lot of people think I'm dumb just because I don't have any brains."

"They aren't necessary, Finn dear. On you brains would be grotesque. How much better to have that little trap door into your brain pan where you can lay the hidden quart and always have it handy. People with brains would never think of a thing like that; and even if they did they wouldn't have room for the bottle there."

They were in the Marine Room in Orlando when they talked that talk. Doll would park Finnegan in a bar early every morning so he could get a good start, and would leave him there with a bunch of little Florida crackers. She would come back about eleven at night and start checking the bars. She might locate him by midnight and would usually go around with him for several hours to private parties. When he was too far gone she'd load him on her shoulder and carry him to the car.

But he had amazing resilience in the early days of his bouts. He would bounce up in a couple of hours and be booming in the shower. Then she would take him to town again and leave him, and come back to bed.

"Do you know his time table?" she asked X. "How long will he go on."

"Another week, I guess. Then he will crest and shatter. By then the staff work will be finished. We will have a briefing. Then we will part."

"Will it be safe to let him go in his bad shape?"

"Yes. He won't be in bad shape. He has been tortured. It concerns his morphosis. He drinks when he comes up from the shock of it. He will drive by instinct, and then he will hole up in some distant place. But he will remember all the instructions. They will work in him like a barrel of barm, and next year we will meet him again."

4.

It was about nine days before Finnegan crested and shattered. He went on a fighting binge. He started it in one of the little towns. He was pretty good.

"I whipped Harry Greb, and I can whip you too," he would tell the big little-town boys. He was a devastating little chopper, and he could whip most of them.

"I went ninety rounds with Joe Gans," he'd tell them. "Who'll go a fast twenty with me?"

He got whipped by some of them, but he always kept getting up.

"I fought Tom Sharky nine times," he'd tell them. "There's a lot of you here that never even fought him once, and you think *I'm* punchy!"

He would fight the local boys in series, but there were too many of them who kept coming up to try him. He was in bad shape when Doll found him that last day. He was still wearing his tuxedo coat with the green lapels, but it was shredded vow.

"How in the world did it happen, Finnegan?" she asked him. "Your nice coat!"

"That's from dragging it on the ground, Doll. That's the way we start fights in Ireland."

"You never were in Ireland."

"It's a lie. I was in Bantry a day and a half. We unloaded a cargo there once. There's a song you sing when you drag it:

His name it was Christy O'Malley,
And his ears were the ears of a goat,
But I weathered him with my shillelagh
When he trod on the tail of my coat.

I sure can sing good, can't I, Doll?"
"You sure can, boy."

"There's a chorus but I don't know how it goes. I make up the verses because I only know two lines of it."

"Is your nose broken, Finnegan?"

"Yes. But the man who did it said that it would be an improvement. He was a real smart man; he wasn't one of the kids; he said he was a railroad man. 'I can take two to give one all day,' I told him. 'Not with me, you can't,' he said. He was right. With him I couldn't. I like a man who knows what he's talking about. He whipped me worse than a lot of them did.

"But you know, that first day I won thirteen straight fights before I lost one. I fight kind of like Harry Wills. I fight kind of like Battling Siki too. You want to go a couple of rounds, Doll? We'll just slug a while and quit after the first few knockdowns. We won't try for a knockout."

"When I fight, I always try for a knockout. Why do you do it all, Finnegan?"

"I have this character defect. I'm a slob."

Finnegan was washed and patched. They poured wine and oil, or some goop, in his wounds and taped his swollen hands. Then, for his sins, he had to listen to X who talked and talked. Finnegan lay on the sofa while X went through the briefing, for now the time of action was at hand.

"Do you follow me, Signor Solli?" X would ask. "Do you understand the details?"

"Yes. Can you have an ingrown nose like an ingrown nail? That left-footed killer was asking for me in Winter Garden yesterday. I may have an ingrown nose. Can you still see it from the side?"

"We can still see it from this side, Signor. Pay attention to the briefing." It was interminable, and much of it merely cautionary. X went through the rite of burning some old papers, though they hadn't any papers of importance to burn. Doll cried a little bit. She was a rich doll now, but she would miss them for the year and somewhat. X made his last half dozen long-distance phone calls, and they were ready to scatter.

Finnegan got dazedly into the Georgia Klunker and chugged off in the pre-dawn. Half an hour later, from a point about twelve miles distant, a left-footed killer and companion followed after him.

About mid-morning, Doll went away in the little Road Runner.

Mr. X disappeared that afternoon in the Celestial Omnibus.

And another bunch of sporty fishermen came down to take their places, and things went on there much as before.

Chapter Thirteen

BILOXI BRANNAGAN

From the gall of infants strangled and the moans of the guiltless slain
I turn and seek for a greenery beyond the smouldering plain.

I dream in the great avoidance, I opt for a life that will scan,
I harry the bulking horror and hide in the hide of a man.

To sleep in the guise of waking, to make an innocuous me,
To live in a shadowy brightness, and die on an isle in the sea.

Forgetting, the blessed forgetting, of bones on a cavern shelf,
Veiling the hopeless haunting that the nameless thing is myself.

I pray that the cup may pass me, I pray that I fight me free
From the surge of abysmal terror: that I should awake unto me!
—MELCHISEDECH DUFFY, *The Alien Awakens*

When a man shoots at you once it can be an accident. When he shoots at you a second time he is still entitled to the doubt. But when he keeps it up the doubt gradually fades, and a certainty develops.

Some people are patient with this type of treatment, and Finnegan was a patient man. He was still without animosity when he suddenly ditched the Klunker, rolled out into the ditch himself, and brought the pursuing car to a careening halt with a sudden sharp volley of his own.

He shot out both the front lights, broke the windshield, let down the two front tires, and painfully winged each of the flustered men fleeing from it. Finnegan had always been a good rifle shot.

Then he drove away in the Klunker again, but the Klunker was crippled and sad now, and the bloom was off the night for Finnegan. He was very nervous when he was in the clear, and he sniffled and sobbed.

Violence had always made Finnegan nervous after it was over with. He was not an unperturbable man, though often he acted the part. Now, moreover, he was in a very low mood and was gripped by a moral revulsion from his last orgy.

Physically he was mended and was like a lean cat ready to start out on a new night's foray. He had traveled for three days, casually, and with a feeling of safety. Then, driving after dark the evening before, he had felt the sharp menace the moment they were clearly onto him. They'd spent the night at it then, over bad roads and good, and they had been crowding him intolerably when he turned on them.

Entering the town now, Finnegan parked the Klunker in front of the police station. This was an old trick that X had told him. The pursuers will always fall back and regroup when they see it there. It is a manoeuvre that worries them. They will spend half a day waiting around and devising contacts to the inside to find if the squealer has squealed and how the land lies.

So Finnegan left it there and went to see the town. He had to find cover, and rapidly.

It was very early in the morning and the bars were not yet open. But there was a small beer garden, providentially before him, and it seemed to be open for business. Finnegan vaulted over the little fence with his suitcase and sat down opposite a man who seemed familiar, or at least friendly.

"I believe I will just have the same thing," Finnegan said. "Where's the barmaid?"

"Gertrude, bring the pitcher!" the man called. And soon she brought out a tremendous pitcher full of beer.

"Oh, we have company," said Gertrude. "Such a nice looking young man! Do we know him?"

"My name is Finnegan," said Finnegan.

"My name is Fogazzaro," said the man with a touch of truculence, and Finnegan knew that it couldn't be.

"Why, it is not, Biloxi," said Gertrude. "Why do you want to tell the young man a thing like that? That isn't his name at all."

"My real name is Solli," said Finnegan.

"My real name is Brannagan," said Brannagan. Brannagan had sandy hair with quite a bit of gray mixed in it. He had the tremendous forearms and clear eyes of an old seaman. He was weighing Finnegan with his eyes, but he didn't cast him away as too light. Finnegan was half accepted already. And he did need a haven.

"You seldom see beer served in a pitcher like this," Finnegan said. "I've known it only as an Australian custom."

"My husband is another Australian custom," said Gertrude, "and we won't have it any other way. Now let us get things straight. Not that you aren't welcome, young man, but are you under the impression that this is a beer garden?"

"I thought it was an oasis, and you will tell me that it is only a mirage? And yet it tastes real enough."

"This is our kitchen garden," she said, "and my husband is drinking his breakfast."

"Oh. I am sorry that I presumed," Finnegan said, "but I do not offer to leave. That I have a place to stay is a matter of life and death—mine."

"I wouldn't let you leave now," Gertrude said. "I have adopted you on sight."

"There was a little shooting down the road a few miles a little earlier," Brannagan said. "Did you hear any talk about it?"

"No. I didn't hear any talk. You're the first ones in town I've talked to. There were some men shooting at me a while ago, and then I was shooting at them. It was possibly the same incident."

"Likely. Are they still after you?"

"I think so. Forever."

"What do they want with you, Finnegan?"

"They want to kill me."

"But why? You don't appear to be worth much alive. How would you be any more valuable dead?"

"They want my suitcase."

"I like a man who gives straight answers, even if they don't tell anything, Finnegan. But I do understand. Go inside the house and we can talk and drink together through this window. I will keep the predators off."

"Ah—they are not the kind to fool with," said Finnegan.

"Neither am I," said Brannagan.

Inside with Gertrude, Finnegan felt safe. She was herself a fortress. She was a gulf-state lady of forty-five, give or take fifteen years either way. It was hard to tell how old Gertrude was. She was full-built and pretty, dark and a little frenchy, curly of hair and smile, voluted and parapetted. Finnegan knew a little about architecture from his studies of art and related subjects, and he had always been partial to the Living Gothic.

"We should know you, Finnegan," said Gertrude. "How could we have missed such an interesting young man? We haven't many visitors, but we do have interesting ones. My husband will abide no other kind."

"And I ought to know you people," Finnegan said. He didn't say it just to be saying it. He half remembered them as friends of friends in his other life. He'd have it in a minute. "Gertrude," he asked, "what town is this anyhow?"

"Biloxi, of course. You didn't know that? You lost little shoat!"

"Is the goat in the garden Biloxi Brannagan?"

"He is indeed, dear, though more properly John Joseph. Is there some connection?"

"Yes. But I've always believed that when you surprise a coincidence uncovered the only decent thing is to turn away and leave it. You'll never have it, Aunt Gertrude. I came to you by blessed fate. It was imperative that I have a place. I claim this place as a right, and I will not even tell you why."

"Oh, I'll have it, Finnegan? Who do you know? Who knows us?"

Marie, in St. Louis, had often told tall stories of her Aunt Gertrude and of Biloxi Brannagan. And also she had often told tall stories of Finnegan, a catch-all for curious episodes in their group. Finnegan never spoke of any connection again, nor did Aunt Gertrude or Biloxi; but Biloxi did several times refer to these mutual acquaintances as though he would know they were mutual.

This was a breezy house, full of gulf winds and two breezy people, with just enough mystery about them to sauce it up. They were people who told Finnegan everything about themselves except the cold details. It was never clear to Finnegan how Brannagan had managed to retire from the sea and sit for a third of a century drinking beer and watching ships from his garden table. But he had done exactly that, Gertrude said. It isn't known why he never went back to sea, though he would not leave the sight of it.

But somewhere along the line he had acquired a rich windfall. Also, he gave the impression that he was a fugitive with much of the world barred to him. Brannagan would not, in fact, leave his private beer garden, though he seemed safe there. And 'they' would not cross the line after him.

"How did you happen to think of the nose, Finnegan?" he asked. "It's good. Most of them wear a goatee, or go to great lengths to emphasize some facial aspect. But the nose is really good."

"Dammit, Biloxi, what's it good for?"

"With a nose like yours, who notices the other thing?"

"What other thing?"

"That you're chinless."

Finnegan sat at the table just inside the kitchen window, and Brannagan sat at the table just outside; and there they talked for the most part of four days and four nights. But with so many things to talk about, they never did get down to asking the particular secret of the other. Or *did* Brannagan guess that of Finnegan?

"Do you know what the world most suffers with, Finnegan?" Brannagan asked. "Brain damage. It's a selective idiocy. Aye, it's from an epidemic, a recurring infection. Do you know the germ that carries the infection, Finnegan?"

"On one level I do, but we're not thinking of the same thing."

"Yes we are, Finnegan. This germ, in size, is at the

opposite end of the scale from the virus. In fact, it's a man-sized germ, and it repeatedly infects. It is endemic at all times; but it was several times epidemic: in ancient times, in the low Middle Ages, about six hundred and fifty years ago, and from a hundred and fifty years ago to the present. It is the attacking parasite, the alien within. And it is no less completely alien because it is within. I don't see anything that will keep it from destroying its host and itself this time."

Brannagan had been to more places than Finnegan had, including the same places. He had not only skirted the d'Entre-Casteau Islands, he had walked all over them. He had not only sailed through the China Straits, he had dived in them for old wrecks. He had not only climbed the Cloudy Mountains, but had panned gold in their streams and dips.

"I've lived in the interior of Java, Finnegan. I've lived in any number of wonderful places. Then I came to Biloxi, the most romantic spot on Earth, and I stayed here, though it is not even an island. Ah, but there's small islands I could swim to if it ever gets dangerous. But now that I mention it, there are no bad islands, and there are no unromantic places. Biloxi is on a continent, but I overlook that for the love I bear it. I've always felt that the continents were unsafe and impermanent. When the cosmic catastrophe comes, and I expect it any day, I believe that all the continents will sink and only the islands will stand fast.

"A cosmic student to whom I confided my theory does not share my fear of the impermanence of the continents. Or rather he thinks that when the continents sink the islands will not be far behind.

"But here I fell in love with Biloxi, a port just warm enough for gracious living, in a wild fresh country that is cousin of my own. And here I met a French girl, Gertrude, and I wondered how I would go about the thing. I had much against me. I was an unhandsome and awkward seaman, and moreover I was Australian.

"I had never proposed to a girl before except in fun. I didn't know how to do it, and nobody could tell me. Consequently it was never done. The first definite knowledge I had of it was when Gertrude's mother told me they had picked out the date. I married her, but I'm damned if

I ever proposed to her. Other men I've talked to say that they don't remember proposing either."

"You are an old goat and luckier than you deserve to be," Finnegan said.

"Ah, you love her. All the young men love her and she loves them. As I say, I settled down here and have been sitting in this chair for twenty-five years. There was an old chair that I used before that for ten years, but it wasn't comfortable and I disposed of it. I sometimes get up to go to the bathroom, but that's about all. I don't have to go as often as I used to.

"I'm content to sit and look at the sea. You can see four little islands from here. They are Deer Island, Horn Island, Ship Island, and Cat Island. I could swim to all of them, but I've never been to any of them. High tide comes to just about seven feet from my chair, but in thirty-five years the only salt water to touch me has been the actual spray when it reaches out. It's just that when I'm sitting down I don't like to get up."

"How do you manage it, financially, I mean?" Finnegan asked.

"When I first came here, thirty-five years ago, I brought along a sea bag of about the importance of your own suitcase. I have always liked to carry everything I need in a sea bag; this one was packed to carry everything I would ever need. I hope I don't make myself too clear. I like to pose as a man with a secret.

"I doubt that I would have gotten Gertrude without such a valuable baggage. She was better looking than I was in those days; I tell her now that the situation has reversed. But while I was trying to work up my courage to propose, the contents of my sea bag made themselves known to her by a sort of osmosis, and soon we were married.

"I might add that my wife has a sense of things like that, and even now she has divined the great value of your own luggage, even though it is securely locked and she hasn't been into it. Not that she is honorable, but she cannot fathom locks.

"This makes for a tricky situation. For, while she would rather be torn by wild horses (I think she'd like that, she uses the phrase often) than breathe a word of your secret (she does not breathe such things, she tells them breathlessly), yet the odds are that by tomorrow, if I do not throttle her or exgloss her, the neighborhood will know that the young man staying with us has a suitcase with over half a million dollars in it."

"You've a deeper reason for settling in Biloxi than looking at the sea," Finnegan said.

"Sometimes I look at the neighborhood also. When I first came here there was a most attractive lady living in that white house. She was such a pretty lady, with a husband and a young daughter. I used to sit here just to catch five or six glimpses of her every day. This went on for several very pleasant years.

"Then she disappeared. She had run off with a fast-talking man, and she should not have. Now my days were empty as I sat here, and I really believe that I would have packed and left town had I not finally noticed something very interesting. Her daughter of about fourteen was staying with papa and had not gone off with my lady and the fast-talking man. And her daughter was her very image.

" 'I am set here for a long time,' I said. They had the same sweep of the hips, the same dip of the shoulders, a certain wonderful sameness about the knees. So I pleasantly enjoyed the view of the daughter for twenty years while she married and in turn had a daughter. And then what would you guess happened?"

"She also ran off with a fast-talking man."

"She did that. She left her good husband and fifteen-year-old daughter behind. Now, with her to look at no longer, there was surely nothing to keep me in Biloxi."

"Unless it was that her fifteen-year-old daughter in turn had a wonderful likeness to her."

"And that is the truth of the matter, Finnegan. For you saw her not half an hour ago, Finnegan (she is now a few years beyond fifteen), and you noticed her closely though you said nothing. Her own daughter is now about six years old. If the trend holds, she should be of sufficient age when the next fast-talking man comes along and the mother leaves. I believe that I will have this beautiful scenery here forever."

Finnegan was at a disadvantage in judging the stories of Brannagan. He could not tell when Brannagan lied. He was not able to appraise just how tall the stories were. It would seem chronologically impossible for one man to have done all that Brannagan said he had done, and still have time left over to sit for thirty-five years on a chair on the shore in Biloxi. But there was no trapping the man.

Finnegan knew history of the usual sort. He did not know the details of history of Brannagan's sort. He did not know what skirmishes the Australian irregulars had been in, for Brannagan was Australian. He did not know how many times a man can move in and out of the various branches of the Empire armament; and he did not know the names of the main actions on the Afghan border.

There was a strange familiarity to the sound of some of the adventures, almost as if they had once been told by other men; and Finnegan was often on the verge of remembering where and when.

He was willing to admit that a man could get rich by trading in Circassian slave-girl futures on the Aden market, a canny man who watched the trends. He would allow that the brown stone statues of Sjahrir were men petrified standing by the Seti darts and the quick-acting juices in which they were dipped. He could accept that Prester John still lived in the interior of Madagascar, a rather foppish little man in the center of a static culture. But he took it with a low degree of credit that among the Simuka the men bear the children, even though Brannagan himself had witnessed such parturitions. And he would not believe that Brannagan had himself handled raw diamonds the size of ducks' eggs.

"They must be small ducks in that country," he said, "I wonder what species they are."

"No, they're not particularly small ducks, Finnegan. Why? *Anas Paludosa* is their species, and they're rather large for *paludosae*. I said duck egg only for comparison. A little larger, really. I've heard of much larger ones, but I credit only those I've held in my hand."

"Then this would seem rather small to you," Finnegan said. It was a foolish thing to do but he couldn't resist it. From a little sack around his neck he slipped out the largest stone he had, one that would have bugged the eyes of a real expert.

"Yes, a little small, Finnegan, though I'm surprised that you would have such. From Sierra Leone, is it not? One can tell, of course, by the vestigial clay still in the faults of it."

Well dammit how did he know that! Oh well, you couldn't catch that man, and you sure couldn't top him, but it was an experience trying.

Finnegan himself had lived some pretty good stories, and he now borrowed shamelessly from high experts he had known. They passed the days and nights pleasantly. Both of them liked to talk.

"Were you ever to Naxos?" Finnegan asked Brannagan on the third day.

"Sure. They mine emery there. It's their best known export. And their least known is mermaids' hair. They don't sell it on Naxos itself, out of some ancient reluctance, but you can get it from Naxos in little shops on Siros and Tinos and Kea. It is not, as is popularly supposed, fine of texture and light of color. It is rather—"

"I have seen it and handled it," Finnegan said. "Blue sparks would jump two inches whenever she combed it. It's black, but there are lavender lights in it. I cry inside when I remember how I handled it, the short-cropped electric stuff."

But there was more to the days and nights than just high talk. Aunt Gertrude cooked with as much extravagance as Brannagan talked. There were things about her cooking that you might not believe, but you couldn't afford not to eat. When she made rice ribby, the whole world gaped amazed. She had to be French and something a little darker also to cook it like that. She had huckleberry wine and greenberry wine and perry. She put pecans in everything, even pancakes. She roasted pork so opulent that it was a scandal.

Turtle chowder! Brannagan said that he had the turtles flown in special from Galapagos, but it was a lie. They were turtles from the local fishermen, but when Aunt Gertrude had finished with them they were turtles from Heaven. This was a southern home untouched by the curse of southern fried chicken and corn bread, and Finnegan offered thanksgiving at finding a citadel of sanity.

He gained in weight and wisdom when he was with them, and added the place to his index of nostalgias forever.

Finnegan got a long-distance phone call early one

morning, after he had been there three days and three nights.

"Are you Signor Solli y Gordonasco?" Gertrude called out to him.

"I probably am. I'm almost sure that I am." He took it. It sounded like a man speaking from a badly ventilated grave.

"The goats are staked out and bleat near the delta," said the sepulchral voice. "But the hunters are in cover and waiting for the tiger."

"Oh hell, X, what are you trying to tell me?"

"How did you know it was I? I was disguising my voice. Or rather, what makes you think this is X, whoever or whatever that may be? Stay away from your old haunts in New Orleans if it was your idea of returning there. Stay away from your old haunts everywhere; they watch for you everywhere. And you can stay no longer where you are. It is time to flee. I see your luck running out on you like sand. Be steadfast. There may be a role for you to play in the affair but I can't imagine what it is. I'd better ring off. This call may be monitored."

"Oh, come off that, X!" Finnegan exclaimed, but X had already hung up.

"Who was that?" Brannagan was curious through the window.

"My antipodal ghost. We're just alike only a world apart."

"I just think I know that fellow," Brannagan said, "even though I am some feet from the phone, even though the voice was disguised. I bet I know him."

"I bet he knows you," Finnegan said. "I have to go, he says. They'll be onto me here, and everywhere."

"Do you want to take Gertrude's car?"

"Yes."

"She'll fix up the title. And she can go around and get yours from the police pond. They're both about equally worthless. Gertrude, go take care of things! What I like about my wife is that she takes care of things." And Gertrude did.

"Brannagan, have you the double blood in you?" Finnegan asked suddenly.

"I won't pretend that I don't know what you mean, Finnegan. I will only say that *you* don't know what you mean. I have it a little, and you have it a little. There are several recensions of it. It saves time to have it. We have the entire conflict within ourselves."

It was all over with and Finnegan had to go. Gertrude had taken over, and the coast was clear—except for two little girls playing on it about a hundred yards down. Finnegan shook hands with Brannagan, kissed Gertrude, did it four or five more times when he found it was fun, threw his suitcase in and got in the car.

"It's been all too short," said Brannagan in parting. "Brannagan and Finnegan make a nice novelty act. If you're not killed, and if you ever get back to Biloxi, stay again and we can talk some more. Hear Brannagan's outré theory, the Procession of the Epics. The part about the Kalevala will absolutely make the hairs on your head rise up."

Chapter Fourteen

COMPANY OF FIFTY

There were giants on the earth in those days, and also afterward, when the sons of God had relations with the daughters of men, who bore children to them. These were the mighty men of old, the men of renown.

GENESIS, 6-4

1.

"These are the mighty men of right now," Finnegan said truculently, and he felt mighty. "But its seeming has been inverted. Who was it who went into whose daughters?"

Something came over Finnegan then. And this was the Transport of Finnegan upon certain shadowy history.

"Ah, we were a short stubby folk, bandy-legged and a little stooped. How is it then that even God remembers us as giants?

"'We were the people of the earth itself. We were here at the making of the hills. And how can we be called aliens?

"We adored in caves, and buried our dead with boughs of yew and elder. And how can they say that we are devils?

"We were a Childhood in the deep fimbul-winter, and we invented all childhood inventions. How then have we become the boogermen?

"We were the brothers of animals, of the giant stag, of the nobler bison, of the cave bear and the wooly rhinoceros. And how has animality become a dirty thing?

"We were a Valley; and our name is Valley of the New Men, not of the old. But how have they denied us every valley?

"We were the people before the people, and how is it said that we are not people at all?

"We labored the million years to raise ourselves. And who were these ganglers who arrived full-blown and full-brained to supercede us? Are not *they* the aliens?

"Was Cain of ourselves? Which of us bears the mark, plain on the face, that lower protuberance like another nose?

"Who made the blood, out of salinity and iron and all elementals? Who remembers the deep cisterns of the earth? Who remembers the blue ice of our childhood? It is not those summer sojourners upon the earth.

"What if ghostliness and prodigies and dual manifestations are a part of us? Must we cut out that part of ourselves?

"What if the parasite is older than the host? How then is it parasite?

"What of the deep rivers and streams in the earth? What of the deep rivers and streams in the people? Shall the deepest river of them be cursed?

"What if we be the sword inside, the sword of God? Is it right that we should stay this sword?

" 'Show mercy to the victors,' said our own prophet. But how has our mercy been answered?

"Which is the treason for us of the double blood?

"Is it then some of ourselves who must protect the people from ourselves? And what have the people done for us?"

A Transport cannot last long. Then it goes into vague rhapsody.

"The thing is biologically and genetically impossible. Was Mendel wrong? Were Morgan and Galton and Painter? Was even the great Asimov wrong? How is it possible to throw an angry primordial after a thousand generations? How is it possible to do it again and again?

"Where did we primordial aliens vanish when we were defeated and harried from the face of the earth? Into deep caves or swamps, into forests or inaccessible mountains, to distant sea islands like Tasmania? Some of us did, for a few thousand years. But many hid cannily in the bloodstream of the victors. They became the Aliens Within, and they had vowed a vengeance. And now and again, at intervals of centuries, they erupt in numbers, establish centers, and carry on the war to near death. This time, this time, they swear it will be to final overthrow and extermination."

The rhapsody had left Finnegan, but it left him weak. He came back to the world. Le Marin was with him there, reading a magazine with a gaudy cover. It was full of stories of monstrous aliens from the stars, written by Van Vogt and Leinster and such.

"Le Marin, you read about aliens from the stars who invade," Finnegan said. "Did you not know that there are nearer monsters and aliens?"

"I know it, Monster, and you know it," said Le Marin, "but we do not want everyone to know it."

They were in the Old Wooden Ship, a rambling building of four stories.

"Three," said Le Marin. Frenchmen do not count the same as do other people. You can count the stories of every building in town, and a Frenchman will always come up with one story less. Nevertheless, the Old Wooden Ship had four stories. It was unpainted and pungent, the last building in a garlic block, with raked shells for a sidewalk. It had dozens of doors; inside and outside stairways climbing all over it; loose slat shutters; and an uncanny swaying creaking motion like that of an old ship indeed.

Finnegan and Le Marin had been hanging around the Ship. It was in the town where Finnegan had first met Seaworthy and the Devil and Anastasia and the other ghosts. It was the first time since then that Finnegan had been back to the town. He had set a death trap there. He was waiting for reappearances.

Le Marin, however, was not entranced with the Old Wooden Ship.

"The people here are decadent," he said. "They are fragmented; they are episodical. There is no overall pattern to their lives, no clean strong lines to them."

"I knew a bunch with clean strong lines to them, and an overall pattern," Finnegan said, "and I love them less than my blood requires me to. I've about decided to opt for the humans. They're full of humanity, I tell you, and I've got a hunger for it. I have a need to immerse myself in these people, fragmented and decadent though they be."

The first story of the Old Wooden Ship (which Le Marin said was not a story at all, how can it be a story if it's on the ground) was the bar. And these were the people who might be found in the bar, besides Le Marin and those you will meet again; those are the regulars:

Tippio (George Tibeau), Freddy Tin-Horn Forca, Sulphur-Bottom Sullivan, Swede Aansen, Swede Kristjanses, Swede Bjork, Swede Bergen, Big Swede Swanson, John (Little Alcohol) Indelecio, John (Big Alcohol) Jereboam, Russ, Smokehouse, Bill (Buffalo Chips) Dugan, Bob, Charley (-horse) Heckel, Harold (Shrimp Boat) Gordon, Tom, Barney, Dotty Danvers, Dotty Peisson, Dotty Hulme, Little Dotty Nesbitt, Nelly Leakley, Violet, Little Eva Vickers, Mary, Avril Aaron, Frieda, Jeannie, Mae, Dutch Duquesne, Little Dutch Eckel, Art (One Shot) Yoder, Art (Two Shot) Welch, John Sourwine (Sour John), Tommy (Cow Town) Borger, Jake (-Leg) Lewis, Sebastian (Shot Gun) Schaeffer, George (Basin Street) Becaud, Catherine Cadensus, Giuseppe (Raviola Joe) Gabrielangelo, Vivian Gilligan, Sammy (Saddle Sore) Sanders, Soft-Talk Susie Kutz, Benny (Bay Rum) Boerum, Ouida (Cotton Picker) Garrard, Harold A. (Honeybucket) Kincaid, Mercedes Morrero, Aloysius (Basket Weaver) McGivern.

One is forgot! One is forgot! There should be fifty in that brave company.

Others like Finnegan and Le Marin and the boys from the beach might come in three or four times a day. Some, like Dry Gulch Cavaldos, came in twenty times a day. But they were not like these regulars who, living there, were always there.

Each of the fifty regulars had an interesting story. Had we but the time we would tell them all, but we cannot. Not even tell the story of the proprietor Lazarus Reilly who had taken to heart the story about entertaining angels unaware. So he never turned down anyone, lest he be an angel in disguise, and Lazarus be guilty of slighting him. "A man of my sort can't be too careful," Lazarus would say. "I have so much to make up for."

So to anyone who came along Lazarus would give a room and a bed, and beer credit, and a loan of money. These were the only credentials that any of the fifty had on their first coming to the Old Wooden Ship, that they might be an angel unaware. But many of them made good guests, and enough of them now paid part of the time that it wasn't necessary that all of them pay all the time.

In reality the only one of them who was an angel unaware was Soft-Talk Susie Kutz the barmaid of the Ship. She made irregular reports to the Lord, and made them a little better than they should have been; for which reason those at the Old Wooden Ship prospered more than they deserved. And if, the next time the world is destroyed, you should find that the Old Wooden Ship is one of the places spared, do not be surprised. This will be the reason.

We cannot stop to tell the story of the five Swedes who were one of them Norse, one Danish, one an Icelander, one German, one from the Orkney Islands, and none of them Swedes at all. But they were all very like Swedes, they were all valiant Viking seamen, except Swede Bergen. Bergen had sailed once, and he never would again.

He had been sick all the way over on the ship. When he got to land he swore that he would never leave it. He wrote his wife to come across and join him, for he could not walk back, and to go by sea again would kill him. But his wife as a little girl had also been on a ship and had been sick. She would not come. They have been writing letters for twenty years, each begging the other to cross, but they will be separated forever unless someone builds a bridge across the Atlantic.

Nor can we tell the story about Sulphur-Bottom Sullivan and how he got his name. He had been baptized Clarence, and his parents had never called him anything else. And yet it's a remarkable story how he came by his name of Sulphur-Bottom.

We cannot tell the story of Tippio, though Tippio told a lot of stories about Tippio, like this one:

Tippio got on a scales in the bus station and put a penny in and got a card: 'Your name is Tippio, you weigh 168 pounds, you're going to Port Arthur, and you forgot to shave this morning.'

"I didn't forget, I just didn't do it," he said. He knew that the scales was fallible then, and he thought he'd get ahead of it. He tore up his ticket to Port Arthur and bought one to the Valley. He turned up his collar and put his hat on backwards and got on the scales again. This time the card said, 'Your name is still Tippio and you weigh 168 pounds. You tore up your first ticket like a fool and now you're going to the Valley.'

Tippio tore up his second ticket and went and got a crew cut and a pair of sun glasses. He went and traded clothes with a bum in the men's room, and came back to fool the scales. This time the card said, 'Your name is still Tippio and you aren't going anywhere. You left your money in your pants when you traded with the bum, and you can't buy another ticket. And you look like hell in a crew cut.' So Tippio never did leave town; he hadn't the money to go on, so he's still there.

We cannot tell the story of Freddy Tin-Horn Forca who was called that because that is the kind of sport he was. And we haven't the nerve to chronicle the doings of John (Little Alcohol) Indelecio and John (Big Alcohol) Jereboam. These were a raw pair. They were burglars. Little Alcohol did the climbing and the high window work. Big Alcohol was the drill, saw, chisel, and pry-bar man. But they didn't work very hard at their trade. Only when they were very far in debt to Lazarus Reilly would they do a job.

Nor can we tell you here about the multi-billion dollar idea of Harry A. (Honeybucket) Kincaid. Honeybucket was in trouble with the Corporation Commission following his application to incorporate and sell seventy-five billion dollars worth of stock. "Haven't you a few too many zeros there?" a commissioner asked him.

"I don't see where I can shave a nickel off the thing," Honeybucket said resolutely.

"Just what is the billion dollar idea?" the commissioner asked.

"I will take plankton from the ocean and feed it to livestock," said Honeybucket. "Doesn't that astonish you? It astonished me when I first thought of it. At once all the habits of the globe are changed. Famine is demolished. All industry is realigned. We have a limitless source, and we can harvest our plankton, by any system of costs, at a tenth of the expense of corn or any fodder. We dip screens, charged at certain voltages and frequencies, into the ocean. The plankton settle on the screens inches thick in seconds. We haul it in, cut the charge, dump it. It's like loading scrap iron with a magnet."

"How does it taste?" the commissioner asked him.

"It tastes terrible. At first even the hogs wouldn't eat it, nor the cattle. They took some working on. Camels are the only animals to eat it willingly at first. We have twenty good milk camels now. The present name of our company is the Ancient Syrian Cheese Company. Nobody would guess that a firm with a name like that was about to change the world. We will feed the stuff to everything, now that we've got everything liking it. We will raise, slaughter, pack, and market the meat from hogs, cattle, sheep, goats, camels, alpacas, llamas, rabbits, chickens, turkeys, ducks, geese, guineas, ostriches. Naturally we will be the biggest butter and egg people in the world also."

"Why do you want to make so much money?" the commissioner asked him.

"I'll tell you why," said Honeybucket. "Someday I'll be in a barroom popping off, and there will be a little man down at the end of the bar who won't like me. And when I'm finally putting it on good, what do you think the little man will say? He'll say, 'If you're so damned smart why aren't you rich.' Yes, that's just what he'll say. That'll be the moment I've lived for. I'll say 'I *am* rich.' And the way I say it, he'll know that I am. But you can't fake a thing like that. I've got to get rich first."

And yet the commissioner turned down the request, and he shouldn't have. It wasn't that Honeybucket had actually tried the idea; he didn't even know what plankton looked like. But his story wasn't entirely a lie. He *did* own a camel. He had once operated a camel ride at the amusement park, but riding a camel makes people seasick, and the concession was a failure. He still has the camel. It lives on weeds in the weed patch behind the Old Wooden Ship. The Ship is the only barroom in town with a camel in the weed patch behind it.

We cannot tell you about Russ unless we also tell you about Smokehouse and Buffalo Chips Dugan, and Bob, and Charleyhorse Heckel, for these five were all cut from the same side of the animal. Smokehouse and Bill worked in the same garage. Originally they had worked there at the same time, but the proprietor had always got them mixed up though they were no more than passing similar in appearance. They had a great idea:

One of them quit his job, no matter which one. After that, they worked on alternate days, and the manager never did catch on. At the end of the week they split the pay. This gave them only half as much money as they had before, but it gave them twice as much time off.

Russ and Bob and Charleyhorse were steerers. They would scour the town looking for a live one, and they would steer him to the Old Wooden Ship. A man thirty blocks away could arrive at that state where he wanted to buy drinks for everybody, and instantly one of them was at his side to guide him to the Ship. They had an instinct for it.

They also were rollers, but that did not concern the Ship. They always did it in the camel-lot out back, if a man had spent all he was going to spend and was still loaded. Nobody loves a hoarder.

Shrimp Boat Gordon, Tom, and Barney were commercial fishermen, but they didn't fish very often. Every morning they would look at the sea and sky, and smell the air. "What do you think?" Shrimp Boat would ask.

"What do you think?" Tom would ask.

"What do you think?" Barney would ask. And oftener than not they would decide that it was a poor day for fishing, and would stay in the Old Ship to drink.

A lot of people got Dotty Danvers, Dotty Peisson, Dotty Hulme, and Little Dotty Nesbitt mixed up. For one thing, they had married a lot of the same people. Dotty Danvers and Dotty Hulme had both been married to Buffalo Chips Dugan. Dotty Danvers and Little Dotty Nesbitt had also been married to two brothers in Sugarland, Texas, to one of whom Dotty Hulme had previously been married. And Dotty Danvers had also been married to a man of the same name as the first husband of Little Dotty Nesbitt. Dotty Peisson didn't get married very often, and only by association was she classed with the other Dottys in this. Dotty Peisson, as you may already know, was the best Galveston-style piano player in the world.

Most of the girls who lived at the Ship were married to seamen. They were called salt water widows: Nelly Leakley, Violet, Little Eva Vickers, Mary, Avril Aaron, Frieda, Jeannie, Mae.

Dutch Duquesne looked like a snapping turtle. He was a waiter at the Balinese Room, or else one of those other places at the end of the pier, anyway the swankiest place in town. He said he made a hundred dollars a night in tips, but nobody ever saw any of that money. He always went to the clubs as soon as he was off work and lost it on the games. 'Easy come, easy go,' he would say.

But Mary who worked at the clubs said that Dutch never lost more than five dollars at the game, that he never had more than five dollars, that mostly he just stood around and watched the games. He wasn't a waiter, and nobody ever tipped him. He was a kitchen boy who cleaned fish and shucked oysters.

Little Dutch Eckel was an engineer who worked at one of the refineries in Texas City. But he still lived at the Old Ship because they had let him live there when he was poor. He was the prince of the place and he spent more money there than anyone else did.

Art (One Shot) Yodel and Art (Two Shot) Welch were card sharps and tricksters, but they weren't very good ones. It took a very sharp pair to keep ahead of the marks now, and the field was so crowded that they were always being taken by sharpies better than themselves.

We cannot tell you the story of John Sourwine here. But how that Sour John could tell stories!

Tommy Cow-Town Borger and Jake-Leg Lewis were salt water cowboys. The only things they ever rode were cattle boats. But live cattle shipments were getting very rare and they had very long times between voyages. They always wore boots and spurs and chaps and gauntlets, although they did not use horses in their business.

2.

If only it weren't so near to evening we could have the story of Sebastian (Shot Gun) Schaeffer. It goes like this:

A beautiful lady approached him once. "Aren't you Shot Gun?" she asked him.

"Indeed I am," he said, for he was. But the lady had him mixed up with some of the other Shot Guns in town. Schaeffer's name had no connection with the weapon. He was called Shot Gun because he had invented a drink of that name.

"Well come along," said the lady to Shot Gun, "and

let's see what kind of job you've done. I'll have to be satisfied with it before I pay you."

They got in a car; she drove him out to a lovely estate; they entered a mansion. Upstairs in the mansion they found a distinguished looking gentleman with his head pretty well blown off.

"That's a real nice job," said the lady. "It must take a special talent to do a job like that."

"Indeed it does, ma'am," said Shot Gun, for he could think of nothing else to say.

"And if I ever need another job like this I will call you."

"Thank you, ma'am. And I also do yard work."

"Well a bargain is a bargain," said the lady. "I believe you said five on the phone." And she gave him five thousand dollars.

"Thank you, ma'am," said Shot Gun, and he touched his cap and left. He was too embarrassed to refuse the tip, even though he knew that the lady had made a mistake.

That's the story we would have told of Shot Gun Schaeffer, had we but the time. But, as he often told it himself, you may already have heard it. One at least who had heard it was George (Basin Street) Becaud. Basin Street played a bull fiddle in an orchestra, and he carried it in a large case.

"What is that thing anyhow?" Shot Gun Schaeffer asked him once.

"How come your name's Shot Gun, and you don't know a shot gun when you see it in its proper case?" Basin Street asked him. "This is an 800-gauge shot gun. I can decapitate a bull elephant with this.

"By the way, Shot Gun, somebody got us mixed up a couple of years ago and you collected for one of my jobs. I'm sure you didn't mean to, but there's one way you can square it if you do it at once. I'm short on cash tonight, so run up and get the five thousand dollars. I'm kind of in a hurry."

"Yes sir, right away sir," Shot Gun Schaeffer would always say. And he would scuttle up to his room and lock the door and put a chair against it. And every night Basin Street would dog him again.

"I had to leave on another job last night, Shot Gun, so I couldn't wait for you to bring me the money," Basin Street would say. "Ah, it was a messy job, but it's a life. Run up and get the five right now. I'm a little short and pretty edgy."

"Yes sir, right away sir," Schaeffer would say. Then he would go tearing up one of the old outside stairways to his pidgeon-roost at the top, and lock himself in.

Basin Street looked very sinister, as do all bull fiddle players; and Shot Gun Schaeffer spent many terrified hours. If it were not for the consuming of the shot guns themselves, life would have been intolerable for him.

Catherine Cadensus was the prettiest girl who stayed at the Old Ship, and it was to look at her that many a stranger lingered in the bar. It was on account of her also that Finnegan came in more and more often. She ran around with Vivian Gilligan and Ouida (Cotton Picker) Garrard and Mercedes Morrero. Nowhere in the world had there ever been four such pretty girls together at once. They were class.

Vivian was a stunner with so much hair that she couldn't keep it all on top of her head. There was always a lot of it down around her lovely neck and wonderful shoulders. Cotton Picker was a Cajun girl who liked to be taken dancing and riding by strangers. Hey, she did make them feel welcome around that town! Mercedes Morrero was very dark and she had gold jangles hung all over her, around her neck, and from ears, fingers, wrists, and ankles. She was habit-forming. She was like salted peanuts; she made one stay and drink more and more. And if Finnegan came into the bar to look at Catherine Cadensus, he stayed to look at Mercedes.

But she worried about herself.

"Everyone thinks I'm kind of dumb just because I never say anything," she complained. "Hell, Finnegan, if I say something they'll know for sure how dumb I am. Wottle I do?"

"Keep them guessing, darling. Three or four words are enough for a woman to speak in any one day."

Raviola, Saddle Sore, and Bay Rum were unkempt and uncouth, and not at all up to the high standards maintained by the other folks at the Ship. It takes all kinds though.

Aloysius (Basket Weaver) McGivern was paid a stipend by his family to stay out of their way. There is the story that they were ashamed of him. They were red-dog rich and could afford it, and it was mutually advantageous. Basket Weaver agreed to remain peacefully at the Old Ship and to embarrass them not at all, if they would pay him for it, and would promise not to send him to the sanitorium again.

"It's the damned baskets," he would say. "I could stand it in any of them if it weren't for the basket weaving. 'The Devil finds work for idle hands to do,' they say. 'Let's learn to weave the nice baskets. It will keep you happy and busy.' Why the devil don't they put the Devil to basket weaving if he's so worried about idle hands? Why can't they let an honest man go to pieces in peace?"

After Catherine Cadensus, the prettiest girl at the Old Ship was Soft-Talk Susie Kutz the barmaid and angel unaware. An angel should be prettier than any human; but we have heard this discussed by really competent judges, and they all agreed that Catherine had it on Soft-Talk by just a little.

A lot of this material here is copied from Soft-Talk Susie's own reports, which is why these people appear so much better than they really were. If someone had tried to tell you what they are actually like, it would take a long time, and you would be disgusted with them and would turn away. And then you couldn't be sure that you were any nearer the truth than was Soft-Talk Susie Kutz.

But if you really want the tote on them, come down to the Ship tonight. Only you will have to buy.

Finnegan immersed himself in the Company of Fifty for some time. He felt a crying need for assurance in the reality of humanity. And, guys, humanity was what those folks had!

The reason we haven't told you more about Le Marin, or about Don Barnaby, is that they went with Finnegan when he left town, and you will see them again.

But these noble fifty you may never see any more.

Chapter Fifteen

BASSE-TERRE

"You probably don't know that we had a hard time of it after you died," Finnegan told him. "You almost didn't get buried. And mama changed a lot. When you have a hard time of it, it makes you lose patience."
The old peasant Giulio Solli began to cry, deeply and silently. Then he went away. That was the first that Finnegan knew that his father had loved them all very much. And they had all derided him, and perhaps they had killed him.

—*Archipelago*, Chapter Ten

1.

Well, maybe Finnegan's father had loved them very much, but there was something he didn't love. Finnegan now realized that Giulio had been a part of a monstrous apparatus, and he had died The Monster Forgotten. 'I wonder how I would have turned out if I had had a father of the human sort?' Finnegan wondered ironically.

We forgot Hildegarde Katt! How could we have forgotten her? We love Hildegarde.

One day, in the Ship, Finnegan asked her who her husband was.

"But you know him, dear," she said. "He's the cop with the little moustache named Tommy."

"It's an odd name for a moustache," said Finnegan.

"It *is* unusual," said Le Marin who was there also. "I knew an Englishman who had a moustache named Tankersley. I knew a Nigerian who called his Cecil. Myself, in my salad days, had one christened Pierre. But Tommy I had not heard."

"No, I mean Tommy's name is Tommy, not the moustache's," said Hildegarde.

"Well, what is the moustache's name?" Finnegan persisted.

"It doesn't have any name."

"How old is it that it doesn't have any name?"

"About two years old. Oh, you guys are kidding."

One day Finnegan looked up, and the very person who caught his eye was the cop with the little moustache named Tommy.

Finnegan had seen Art Emery standing on a street corner and picking his nose, and in sudden hatred had knocked him flat. Finnegan had been overcome with fear (not of Art, of course) and defeat and confusion. Then he looked up, and that cop was eyeing him icily, and Tommy seemed to have an unfamiliar twitch.

For the record, Tommy Katt was the toughest cop in that town. Not mean, just tough.

"I wouldn't have done that, Finnegan, unless I had a good reason," he said.

They were not particular friends. The cop did not necessarily love everyone who loved his wife. To many of them he was cool. Some people said that he shouldn't have married a playgirl in the first place.

"I had a good reason," Finnegan said. "I hate him. If he is in town, maybe the Brunhilde is in port."

"She is in port, Finnegan," said the cop with the moustache, "and the boys are betting that you will not be alive to answer the rooster in the morning."

Ah, that was wrong. Finnegan had been in that town to trap *them* coming in. He had a web spun out to take them, and more delicate spider silks strung to signal him when they should touch. But Finnegan would never be a good retiarius, a net man.

He had, in fact, been about to leave town. Certain conflagrations, insurrections, and slaughters in the Caribbean region had convinced him that he could better intercept their course there.

They could not be here! And he could not be the last to know it. He had lost every advantage. An old net man named Saxon X. Seaworthy had already thrown a net over him and intended to entangle him in it this night.

It wasn't for fear that Finnegan left town, however. He had said that he was tired of running, that he would not run any more. He was going to leave town anyhow. That is the truth. In a little while it will be seen that it is the truth.

For oddly he and Le Marin and a fellow named Don Barnaby already had their passage. And now, after scouting the town a little, Le Marin said that he believed they might just as well leave the way and time they had decided. So they left that night.

But before they left, Finnegan went fox hunting. He planned in a hurry. He told Le Marin and Don Barnaby to go ahead. "Hurry it," Barnaby said, "we can just make it now." "Go ahead," Finnegan said, "I'll be at the dock as soon as you are." They thought he was going to say goodbye to some girl. They said "Hurry it, Finn."

And Finnegan made a savage detour that delayed him less than three minutes. He went feral. As a surging animal he performed incredible feats in seconds. He had his own intelligence, once over the surprise of being slipped up on. He knew where they were.

He struck. Right on the sidewalk he killed two of their guards. This was right downtown, on Church Street, in the early evening. No longer man, but werecat, he went up the outside of the building; he struck at an upper level into the prepared fortress, the Pirate Hotel; he sent a shock of terror through them, as a tiger sends through a grass-hut village.

He struck death there. He got, he believed, his primary prey. He left in a splatter of gunfire; and he was hit. He came out shatteringly through a second story window, over a false balcony, dropping many feet to the street.

And he heard a sour laugh as he left!

The laugh of the man who was smarter than the Devil, who (it seemed to Finnegan) skipped from body to body at the moment of striking and let another inherit his death. Whomever Finnegan had killed in his animal wrath, it was not yet Saxon Seaworthy.

The bleeding Finnegan ran into the tough cop Tommy Katt in the side street across from the Church. Less than three minutes for it all!

Tommy Katt always came to gunfire like iron filings to a magnet. He enjoyed wading into the middle of it. But he had just watched something that scared him: an erupting creature too strong and swift and sure to be human, a werecat. He watched in stunned amazement when it struck death and then fled; when it was shot and only snarled at the shot.

Then, when he grappled it (for he was cop, scared or not) the werecat turned into the winged and bleeding kid with the big nose named Finnegan, the very one he had been following and had lost.

"Get in the buggy fast, fast," he ordered. "I'm not taking you in, I'm getting you out of here fast. Dammit, Finnegan, you can't go around killing people. If I did not know what people they were, I *would* take you in. I'm putting my neck on the block for you now. Do you expect people to hold an umbrella over you forever?"

Tommy Katt got Finnegan to the dock just in time. Winged or not, he made it by jumping. He had jumped for boats before. The seamen gave him a little cheer there, not knowing what had happened.

2.

Finnegan had been beginning to write a letter. It had been several years since he had answered a letter from Theresa and Vincent in St. Louis, and he was going to do it now. He had even started it. He wrote a salutation:

'Mon tres bon hote et ma tres douce hotesse—'

"Is that right?" he asked Le Marin who was French. "I read it somewhere. Is it all spelled right?"

"Right enough, Finn boy. They aren't either of them French, though, are they? Now go ahead and write the letter to your friends."

"I'd better wait for tomorrow. The heading is enough for one day, a real good day's work. I sure do like that heading."

So Finnegan put the letter aside to finish writing it another day. He never did finish it, but he often meant to.

Finnegan was in high clover, or in high oyster shells. The shells were deeper and cleaner and more beautiful and better raked than had been those at the Old Ship. The sea was like a blue dream. Finnegan had money. He did not know how much, but he had got nowhere near the bottom of it. And when that was gone, he knew where there was more, and still more, and still more, seven stashes of it in all.

Finnegan was in Paradise, he and Charles Le Marin and Don Barnaby and Johnny Duckwalk. And the way he happened to go to Paradise was this:

He had been sitting one afternoon in the Old Wooden Ship with Le Marin, reading a book. He had been reading about Paradise in St. Francis de Sales. And it said:

'Oh how lovely, how desirable is this place! Oh how precious is this City!' And again it said: 'let us go, my dead soul, let us go toward this blessed land which is promised us! What are we doing in Egypt?'

"I would go," said Finnegan, "if I knew where it was."

"I know where it is," said Le Marin who had been reading the passages over Finnegan's nose, "and I will go with you. I am a little tired of lingering in Egypt myself."

So they checked the boats and counted their immediate money, and converted their vendible furniture, and took passage.

"You are sure it is the place all right?" Finnegan asked. "Nobody else has offered such a location for Paradise. From what I had read, I did not even suspect that Paradise was on an island."

"Yes it is," Le Marin insisted. "You gotta read writ right. Scripture tells of it being in the middle of four rivers. This is a riddle for its being surrounded by water, an island. If you were giving the theory to me, instead of me to you, I know you could find a dozen old bishops and old Jews to support it."

"Why yes, I wouldn't have to go much further than St. John Chrysostom, and if not he, then Jerome. But none of them placed it in your part of the world. They looked for it all over the Near East."

"That's why they didn't find it," said Le Marin.

Paradise is actually in the Antilles. That is why they haven't found it in Persia or Mesopotamia or such unlikely places. The great ones have read the old sources with curiosity, but without real devotion, and they have missed it.

Pay attention now. *Here is exact information!* Write it down, the location of this Heaven on Earth. And then settle your affairs and go there. Go tonight.

Nobody else has ever given the exact location of Paradise.

Paradise has a longitude of sixty-one degrees, forty-four minutes, and forty-two seconds West. And a latitude of exactly sixteen degrees North. This is the Terrestrial Paradise.

The other has a more difficult reckoning and is reached by a longer and more dangerous voyage.

It was the Terrestrial one they went to, but St. Francis had meant the Heavenly.

There is a beatitude about the Earthly one also. But in it there are yet a few small snakes. In the end, it was the snakes, of one sort or another, that drove them out of it.

Finnegan lived cheaply here, from habit, not from need. Fifty cents would always get a bottle. He went barefoot like a boy. It wasn't that he didn't have shoes: he *did* have a pair of shoes. One of his friends was keeping them for him so they wouldn't get lost. Finnegan could have them any time he wanted them.

They were at Basse-Terre. Now this is tricky. There is a Basseterre and a Basse-Terre, and they are about a hundred and fifty miles apart as the sea tern flies. One is British and one is French, or they were so then.

Finnegan himself did not know which one he was at, and he later said that he didn't even know there were two of them. This was not the one he had long wanted to go to. He had always meant to go to the Basseterre that is on St. Kitts. Reaching the other one, he arrived at Paradise by accident, the only way it is ever arrived at.

Whatever place it was, it was in the Antilles and below the Tropic. You have the bearings; do not be confused by the names.

Here was a place that Finnegan and his friends—he had three of them—called Sloppy Joe's. In point of fact it was named either the Imperial Bar, or the Royal. It was called Sloppy Joe's only in fun, for it was a clean, even fastidious place.

It was joy to be there. There was greenery in front of it to cut down the glare, and a light blue breeze ruffled the golden air when it came in. The air itself smelled like good rum with a touch of lime, and there was always that almost inaudible tinkle coming from just above and beyond. The music of the spheres, when analyzed, has proved to be the same sound as the tinkle of ice in a glass, heard faintly and hardly recognized.

Quite near to Sloppy Joe's the four friends had four hammocks strung up, these in a slightly secluded spot where they spent endless long hours and days and weeks.

They drank the rum of the islands, and they had beer and gin. They even had good Danish beer, though that cost more than the island rum. They had no care for cost of that or of anything. The four friends all had money. Money is one of the requirements of a Paradise, especially for the undeserving.

You would naturally think that four adventurers set down in a haven like this would do a lot of drinking and talking and lying around and chasing. They did what was expected of them.

Two of them, the Duke of Moule (who was duke only by nickname, and was named Don Barnaby) and Johnny Duckwalk (it was spelled on his ships' papers Doekvalk), chased the girls, the chocolate, high mahogany, almond, and chestnut-colored girls. Chased them and caught them too. Finnegan and Charles Le Marin did not, or not to quite the same extent. In all other ways the Four lived the same life.

(About that Don Barnaby, now, there was a peculiarity. He reminded of another man. We will come back to this and come back to it, but we will never get around it.)

If Finnegan was the most addicted to the drinking, yet his gauged consumption was not greater than that of any of the rest of them, and certainly was not up to that of Johnny Duckwalk.

Johnny Duckwalk was a classic drinker, an old champion. There was nobody on Basse-Terre who could outdrink him. There were not a dozen men in all the Antilles who could; there were fewer than a hundred men in the whole world who could do it.

Finnegan had never been a heavyweight drinker like that, but he was one of the most durable welterweights around. They all of them stayed with it without faltering, night and morning.

And they didn't entirely vegetate there. Besides chasing

the girls, they swam and fished, walked the island, went out on the boats, played poker, told lies (mostly seafaring and other-land lies), and brewed and blended a saltwater philosophy.

If paradises were easy to come by, they would have them everywhere, and they don't. There are requirements. It must be below the frost line, and have a breeze and a bloom. Thre must be at least one ship a week to break the monotony. The Negroes must speak French, and the Frenchmen must speak English. There must be a history several centuries deep, a legend of the Lost Dauphin, and a volcano named Soufriere. And the place must have been discovered by Columbus himself. Also required are three friends, to be, Charles Le Marin, Johnny Duckwalk, and Don Barnaby the Duke of Moule (and there is something amiss about that duke, we tell you, though there was never a finer fellow).

With these, and a little money, paradise can be achieved. And it can last for months on end if nothing untoward comes to wreck it.

Finnegan now examined his own situation. 'There is a certain entertainment in this life after death,' he said. 'I need not keep to a pattern. The pattern I have lived by, I believe, was a people pattern, and it should not have applied to one like myself. Why should I have Wordsworthian Intimations of a Beginning, Baconian Turgidity in the Middle, and Bierceian Irony at the End? I am not thus. I know I have not come to the end here, but I have come to something.

'Did we ourselves ever find it in the old days? We must have. We left the legends of it. Have people ever been able to find it? No, no, not ever. But might a mixed company, of myself and choice people, find it for a little while? Yes. We seem to have. We have. We are all four of us, I know it now, people of the double blood.'

"I wonder if you know," he said loudly to Johnny Duckwalk who was sleeping in the hammock beside him, "that we have found it. Wake up! The waves are leaping like wallobies and the shores have all turned into assay gold. Wake up, Johnny, you're in Heaven! You can do anything you want to now."

"Maybe we can, but you had better not. You had better

not wake me up again or I'll trample you from one end of your nose to the other. Stuff it, Finnegan."

"This life can be a ramble, Johnny. We can have perfect freedom."

"You will find, Finn boy, that our freedom becomes a little abridged."

That Johnny Duckwalk fell asleep again. Let him, let him. He was a prince of a fellow and he deserved his sleep; he was so active at night.

And Don Barnaby the Duke of Moule was asleep in the hammock on the other side, breathing vigorously and regularly. And Finnegan himself, for a while, fell into the sleep of the blessed.

"Finnegan," came a low voice from Don Barnaby's hammock, "I owed Anastasia fifty dollars when I died. Pay her back for me, will you?"

Electrified, Finnegan sat up and gaped. Don Barnaby the Duke of Moule was solidly asleep, and Finnegan knew that the vigorous and regular breathing had not been broken.

And it hadn't been Don Barnaby's voice, but it had come from him.

Chapter Sixteen

LIAR'S PARADISE

THE RETURN OF THE NEANDERTHAL, subtitled THE ALIEN WITHIN. *Royce Rollins. 211 pp. $5.95 Carlson-Shipman Press.*

Not since the palmy days of the Shaver Mystery and the exudations of Immanuel Velikovsky have we had such a taradiddle as this. The unacademic author, widely known as a crank, has put together an insane creed more indicative of his own pathological state than of the objective world.

The thesis, if it may be called such, is that the Neanderthals (the other human race) have not forgotten their defeat and replacement by Homo Sapiens fifty thousand years ago; that they were not entirely obliterated; that they still exist as pure elites in isolated regions of the earth; that another recension of them hide in the human blood stream as in caves or underground rivers, and that these periodically (possibly by prodigious siring of an elite run amok, though this is not clear) produce authentic Neanderthal primordials; and that these organize and devote themselves to the destruction of the human race. The author believes that we are now on the verge of a teeming return of the Neanderthals, and that the human race is in actual danger. All the well-known animosity of the author toward progressive elements and movements is brought into play here. He sees valid revolutionary movements and liquidations of obstructive populations as incendiarism and massacre, and he ascribes many of them to these interior aliens. But this is not his greatest departure from sanity. He ascribes poltergeistic manifestations, apparitions, doubles or fetches, second sight, and 'poetic immediacy as life dynamic' to his aliens, stating that such phenomena are normal aspects of the species.

In his closing words, at which one hardly knows whether to laugh or cry, he appeals to Neanderthals of good will to block the evil inclinations of their savage brethren and to live in accord with the human species. In an appendix he proposes that these returnees might not be Neanderthal at all, but Grimaldi or some other species of early man.

Be careful of this! Things nearly as silly have been the beginning of cults.
   CHARLES O.A. HARRINGTON, Review in *Science for Today*

1.

Charles Le Marin was telling this story during one of their hammock sessions:

"Castleman was the last of the grand pirates. He is still alive and still working at his trade. I have heard people say that piracy is no more. That is like saying that burglary and shop-lifting are no more. Men do not become honest at sea when they are not so on land. A thing like that isn't going to die out completely, not when the cargoes are richer than ever before.

"Castleman broke in during the twenties as a rum-runner. Then he decided to feast on the rum-runners. An illegal cargo is always the easiest to take. He still works this side. But enough of that.

"You have all heard the story of the derelict ship. It's been reported in a lot of places and under a lot of names. But it is always a ship in clear water and calm weather, with tables set in the galley, and the coffee still warm, and all the seamen's things in order or in standard disorder, with a cigar still smoking in the tray in the wardroom, and with nobody at all on board. Well, sometimes the ship's cat, sometimes not.

"Once at least this thing really did happen, and only about three hundred miles from here. The ship was the Sarcophagus, and I was one of the seamen who disappeared and was never seen again."

"I knew another man who disappeared and was never seen again," said Finnegan from his own hammock, "but

he was around for a while to tell me about it. Whoof! I have the strongest feeling that he's still around right now. But go on, Le Marin."
"I will *not* go on. You have a bottle, and it's time to crack. Mine was the last."
Finnegan cracked a bottle and they started it around. "Here's to Hildegarde," he said.
They named their daily bottles, like the hurricanes, after the ladies. This day the four had drunk more than usual. It was late at night and they had got down to Hildegarde. They seldom got so far.
They had enjoyed Agatha, Bathildes, Clotilda, Delphina, Etheldreda, Faustina, Georgina, beautiful names all, liquid music, liquid ladies.
"Now tell us how you disappeared and were never seen again," said Don Barnaby, and to Finnegan Don's words had a mocking quality as though there was a double meaning.
"The Sarcophagus was a little tub and shaped like a coffin," said Le Marin, "which is how it got its name. We came up from Paramaribo and we had several stops. We had a standard cargo which the authorities said was intact and undisturbed when the ship was found derelict. This was not strictly true; the records had been falsified, and much of it had been taken.
"We had another cargo not on the manifest. It was well worth stealing, so it was stolen. But now I hear you asking in amazed voices how this could happen in charted waters, and no radio warning given, no nothing."
"I did not hear anybody ask anything," said Johnny Duckwalk.
"And the answer is that it didn't really happen there," Le Marin continued. "It happened earlier. Castleman, for it was he, had our ship infiltrated before we left Paramaribo. Then, at every port, Buxton, Morrow Hanna, Port of Spain, one of our men apparently jumped ship, and a dock rat was signed on in his place. But here is the peculiar part. In every case, the dock rat signed on looked just like the seaman who had disappeared. Nobody could tell the difference."
"How about yourself?" asked Don Barnaby the Duke of Moule.
"I apparently jumped ship at Fort-de-France," said Le

Marin, "and a dock rat who looked exactly like me was signed on in my place. But to continue—"

"Then you aren't you?" Finnegan asked.

"No. I never did know what happened to me. To continue, the dock rats raised hell and got us all in a turmoil. Then we took it over, and of course the radio shack was taken over first of all."

"I knew a world that was taken over that way," Finnegan said. "This one. And the communications shack was taken over first of all. One of the things took over each person of the world, and I never did know what became of myself either. And quite soon the world will be found derelict."

"Shut up, Finnegan," said Le Marin. "You interrupt once more and I'll kill you. I did that to a fellow once, but that's the story for tomorrow. After we had taken over the strategic spots, lo and behold, the Tercel Hawk appeared on the seascape and ran us down. And Castleman came on board like a king. We herded our captain and the faithful crewmen onto the Tercel Hawk; there they were all bound and shackled and weighted and dropped overboard.

"Now here it was that I got the sudden feeling that everything was not exactly right. There was a sick wind blowing and I got a whiff of it. 'Do we have them all?' Castleman howled. 'Drowned, all drowned,' I answered in another voice, and hid myself. 'Did we get Le Marin?' he asked. 'I never did trust him. I never was sure we made the switch on him.' 'Got him, got him first of all,' I answered in the other voice from my hiding.

"I concealed myself for three days. Then I swam ashore as we hove to, and I was in Florida. Castleman, that is not the name he goes by, made his report. It was a classic. The Sarcophagus had been found derelict, he reported, with everything in perfect shape, coffee still warm in the cups and cigarette butts yet smouldering, and not a soul to be found on board. Fellows, were a cat to report that he had come on a canary's cage, open and empty, with the perch still swaying, and the half-eaten birdseed still warm, with tiny feathers drifting in the air, but with the canary not to be found in Heaven or on Earth, it would be a great mystery. Yet, a very canny man might catch a glint of the answer.

"Castleman had lifted a great cargo, and I a small one. I myself had taken a portion wisely, and when I swam ashore I had fifteen pounds of the raw stuff that is worth more than gold."

"And of course you met Castleman again some years later," Don Barnaby suggested.

"I did. And it was in a respectable stateside bar and he couldn't touch me. 'Castleman,' I cried out with a ring in my voice, for I was pretty well filled with the Courage, 'You're a bugger and a Turk.' (That is not the words I used).

" 'Ah little Le Marin,' he said. 'I always thought that we had miscounted. I preach care and I preach it, but a man has to attend to everything himself. I never did trust you. I never was sure that we made the switch on you.'

"He was a large and dangerous man, and I let him alone then. I never let my courage carry me to extremes."

"Why, it's only the story of the Marie Celeste," said Johnny Duckwalk. "You miss a drink. You pass us a counterfeit story."

"I do *not* miss a drink," Le Marin insisted. "The story is nothing like. And please, I'm a purist, the name of your ship was the Mary Celeste."

2.

"The same thing happened to me," said Johnny Duckwalk, "exactly the same thing."

Johnny always started his stories like that, though what happened to him was never anything like what happened to the fellow in the previous story. Hildegarde had now declined by one quarter.

"This was in Lisbon, or possibly it was in Stockholm," said Johnny Duckwalk. "There was this girl. Her name was Marie. No it wasn't. It was Kristine. Marie was a different girl. 'I need a strong smart man,' she said, and I jumped when she said it. I thought she must have heard of my reputation to spot me so perfectly. I know I don't look it, but I'm strong as a bull and smart as a sheep and horny as a toad. 'I have a proposition,' she told me. 'We can both collect a lot of money, and you can win a beautiful wife—me.' 'But why do you ask me, a stranger,' I inquired.

" 'Right away I saw what a wonderful man you were,' she said, and I had to admit she was right. She was not very pretty, but if she thought she was I didn't want to tell her different. 'I have insured my husband for a fortune,' she said. 'I hocked everything I could put my hands on and bet it all on him. Now if something were to happen to him, we could collect it all.' 'What do you have in mind?' I asked. I was feeling my way here, being the cautious type. 'I'm a pretty good man with either a gun or a knife,' I said, 'or do you have some other suggestion?' 'I thought it would be nice if an axe fell on his head,' Kristine told me. 'We could tell the insurance people it was an accident, and then collect the insurance money and get married.'

"She outlined the details of time and space, which was to be right then and right there. Being a sport, I naturally said all right. I downed a fast one to appear cool. Then I took the axe and went upstairs to the little darkened room to tempt fate. 'Fling open the door and do it fast,' she said. 'It's always better to do it fast.'

"I bumped open the door and raised the axe. It was dim in there, and for a minute I thought I was looking into a mirror. There was my shipmate, Mike Merganser, with an axe raised opposite to me. He is left-handed and I am right-handed, and we are of the same great size, and at that time we were bearded the same. We looked at each other and started to laugh. We were good friends; but for a minute there I thought I'd let him have it anyhow just for the hell of it. I saw that he was considering doing the same thing to me, and he saw that I saw it. Finally we lowered our axes and fell into each others' arms, but it had been close, I tell you.

"We went back down to the bar and cornered Kristine. 'I knew you each had a roll,' she said, 'and I thought that if I got you both in a dark room swinging axes, somebody would get it. I ought to be able to get one roll out of it, and probably two. But I had to go pick two damned smart alecs who knew each other and knew that neither of you was my husband. You two sure messed it up. What I want to know now is: Who's going to pay for this room?'

" 'I'm not going to pay for it,' I said. 'It wasn't my

idea.' 'I'm not going to pay for it either,' said Mike Merganser. 'I didn't rent it, and I didn't use it very long.' 'By God, I'm not going to pay for it either,' said Kristine. 'I didn't get any good out of it. I had to go pick a couple of smart alecs. But somebody owes three *kroner* for rent on this room, and somebody had better pay up.'

"We were around that town for another week but we didn't have much to do with Kristine. She was too tricky, and besides she held a grudge against us. But I can't honestly see where we wronged her."

3.

"Exactly the same thing happened to me," said Don Barnaby the Duke of Moule. Johnny Duckwalk winced at this, but he didn't know why he did it.

"Exactly the same thing," said Don, "only to me it happened different." And Hildegarde had now declined to one half. "Now first a question," said Don. "Did any of you ever take joy pills? Yes, you of course, Johnny; but I do not mean just any joy pills. There are all kinds.

"There are Haiti hoodoo joy pills. There are High Harry joy pills that you can get in Jamaica. There are Deep Romany joy pills, and Dead Frenchman, and Black Rooster, any number of varieties. All have their devotees and also their scoffers. I can understand the skepticism of most intelligent persons to many of them. After all, there is nothing to even the best of them except sawdust and honey and the urine of a black cat. I see something worse coming: the goddess Mageia will be replaced by the false goddess Narkos. Then all the joy will be gone out of them.

"The general distrust, however, should not apply to Madame Le Mourcheor's Old Original Juju Joy Pills. These *do* have an amazing effect. It is so. I cannot explain it. And these are made, not in Black Africa nor in Black Haiti, not in coffee-colored Jamaica nor on the Gullah Coast; they are made in the most enlightened quarter of the most dazzling city of the brightest land in the world, in the city of the nativity of our beloved brother Count

Finnegan; they are made in noble New Orleans herself, in the heart of the quarter that is in all ways distinctive.

"And the curious thing is that the efficacy of Madame Le Mourcheor's pills is not due to the strangeness of their additives, but to the omission and simplification. She does not use the stone from the stomach of the red-eyed goat; there is no such thing as a red-eyed goat outside of bock beer ads. She does not use the gall bladder of a deranged alligator; the alligator, being reptilian, has no gall bladder. Nor does she draw blood from the third toe of a swamp dragon; the swamp dragon, being legendary, has neither blood nor a third toe.

"Madame threw away all the tainted additives. Her methods were like a breath of spring bursting into the musty halls of the Juju Joy fabrique. She returned to pristine sources. She used sawdust, but only sawdust from the Arabian Frankincense Tree. She employed honey, but only the honey of the bees of the meadows around Megapolis in Arcady. And the black cat that she used had the glanders. Her pills are like no others."

'There is something the matter with this clown,' Finnegan mused. 'He is not the other man, he cannot be. He is larger and rougher. The other man is fearful, and this man is afraid of nothing. This is a foul-mouthed lecher, and it is for homicide that he has fled here. But he is also a genuine poet from the shaggy days, and such men may have ghostly extensions. And they are both dark and handsome. He is as the other man would be if he let himself expand, physically and personally.'

"I was in port only three days," said Don Barnaby. "On second morning I had a terrible hangover and I went to find a joy pill dispenser to cure me. But in the whole town at that hour of the morning I could find none: all were in jail, or dead, or deaf, or moved, or not yet awake. Nobody would answer my knock at that hour of the morning, except Madame Le Mourcheor. From her I bought one pill only (I had not the habit), and by this simple bit of business I discovered a new magnitude of the world.

"There was a small courtyard or interior garden to her establishment, and I went there to sit down when I had taken the pill. It was small, as I said, but beautifully greened and flowered. But not so small either! One now learns how to look. Quite large, really. Very large. Boundless would be the word. In fact, the entire world was contained in this garden, and not this world only.

"The garden was filled with a multitude of wonderful people, all of whom I knew intimately if intuitively. I may have stayed in that garden for many years. It was there that I met and married a chameleon-like creature who did not always have the same name nor appearance, and yet I knew that she was always the same one.

"This beautiful wife bore me a number of children. These were not like children as you might know them, nor were they born at so early an age. They were ambulant and cognizant from the first, and completely charming. Like their mother, they had the changeable quality. Though they always preserved the threads of their identities, they did not always have the same names or appearances, and there were not always the same number of them.

"That life was multi-faceted, a cosmic kaleidoscope. Thus a conversational friend who began a sentence might be an entirely different person by the time he had ended it. It made for complexity, but it also made for joy. So an apple that you started to eat might not be exactly an apple all the time that you were eating it. It would grow sweeter or sharper or cooler or more bracing. It would be an unknown mountain fruit or a valley fruit of matchless flavor. And yet it would be the same all the time, in its essence and its soul.

"It was the same with sleep in that garden. You would be asleep. Then you would be not so much asleep as dead, but not inextricably dead; only dead for the moment. And then not dead, but transported, disembodied, detached. This is the amoral hypnosis.

"Teleportation was possible there also. I would be in that garden: then, instantly, I could be in Scollay Square, or Hyde Park, or Ringstrasse, or in the old cow meadow of my home town. I sailed in many ships while I was in the garden. I was in Campeche and Paraiso, in Freetown and on the Grand Canary. I was at Tangier."

"And how did you get out of Tangier?" Finnegan asked out of an angry daze.

"By the efficacy of the joy pill, Count Finnegan. And yet that was part of it, as this is part of it. All that, and all this here present, Basse-Terre and you the company, are but episodes I experienced in the garden. I traveled a lot there. I went where few men have been before, down in the caves in the middle of the earth, and up on the mountains that are brothers of Everest. Then do you know what spoiled everything?"

"No, three times no," said the three.

"It was my damned goodheartedness, my cursed, contemptible, moronic, wretched magnanimity. I was full of bedamned benignity then and I let it trick me. In my perfect pleasure, I felt sorry for the most unhappy man in the world. Naturally the most unhappy man in the world is John Sourwine whom we call Sour John. In my warmheartedness I thought I would go to John and get him to take one of Madame's Old Original Juju Joy Pills, that he might be as happy as I.

"No sooner imagined than done. I was at the side of Sour John. We were in a bar, and it was the same day that I had taken the joy pill, and not fifteen minutes later. 'Sour John!' I cried, folding him in my arms, though ordinarily I can't abide him, 'Come across the street with me and have a joy pill and be as happy as I am. I have lived a hundred lives in fifteen minutes, and the hangover I had in my previous existence is gone.'

"Sour John would not go with me. He had a look that would wither weeds and he gave it to me. 'You and me ain't going nowhere except to the ship,' he said to me. 'I'm going to take you to the ship and put you in your bunk and strap you in. Your eyes look like a hoppy, and you're not fit to be on the street.'

"But I am happy, Sour John,' I told him, 'and my hangover is cured.' 'I'd rather have a hangover than be in your shape,' Sour John told me. 'I don't mind having a hangover. I kind of like to have a hangover.' Sour John took me to the ship and put me in my bunk and tied me down. And he stayed with me till the ship sailed. That was three years ago. I have not been back.

"But I will go back there if I ever leave here. I will get the secret of the mixture from Madame if she is still alive. And if she is dead I will still get it from her somehow."

That was the story of Don Barnaby the Duke of Moule. Hildegarde had now declined to one quarter of her original state.

4.

"Exactly the same thing happened to me," said Finnegan, "and this is the way it went:
"I had been studying with some other young painters under the great master Van Ghi in Firenze. He had taught us nearly everything that could be taught.
" 'You have learned your trade as a plumber learns his,' he told us. 'You are now able to do a workmanlike job. You can draw, you can limn, you can color, and shade, and copy. The worst of you is not too bad, and the best of you' (doubtless he meant me) 'should go a long ways.' Then he went on to tell us about inspiration, and whether or not we should court it. 'This is not a vague idea,' he said. 'It is real. It is something that comes. It is, in fact, a person, a spirit. It may be that for some of you it would not be a pure spirit. I do not know what it is, but I will tell you this: *Do not court it if you do not want it to come.* There are many uninspired painters in the world. They make more money and have more peace of mind than do the inspired; and they do not get burned. But if you must have it, seek it!'
"I had sought it for a long time. And I suspected that for me it would be an impure spirit when it came. There is no accounting for certain elements in Art if we except Diabolism. I dabbled in it, I dabbled. I would sit at night by my canvas, and it would gradually come to me. You are all familiar with *planchette*?"
"No. What is *planchette*?" asked Don Barnaby.
"To Americans, the ouija board," Finnegan explained.
"To Americans. What are you, a Hindu?"
"I use the continental term," said Finnegan. "As I say, the influence was like *planchette*; my hand was guided. I painted under the influence, and the results were not too fortunate.
"I talked it over with my friends and fellow students. They advised me to try an experiment. I would try to paint that spirit itself. I would paint that daemon, that devil. I did it. I painted this devil."
"I remember one Devil you painted on the Brunhilde,

Finnegan," Don Barnaby said absentmindedly. "Oh, oh, that was a slip! That wasn't me. I never heard of the thing. Go on, Finnegan."

"It took eleven nights," said Finnegan, talking a little nervously. Don Barnaby sometimes made him nervous. "I would just piddle around with the black and red shades a while. Then a jerky sort of nervousness would seize me and I would make bewildering marks. Another painted by my hand. I could not see what was coming from it; I could not see how it would ever turn into a form or a face recognizable.

"It was on the eleventh night and all my friends the former students were there to watch. The picture was still completely formless. *And then it was there!* I say that I could not consciously have done this, for I was the last one to recognize it: that face staring out of the canvas, that face that was real and had no connection with the canvas.

" 'There he is; he's coming out!' my friends had cried. 'One more stroke and he'll emerge!' I made the stroke, but I could not see the pattern yet. 'One more,' they cried. I made it. 'There he is!' they cried. He was there.

"Believe me, he was an odd little devil that I had painted, or who had painted himself with my hand. Crawling evil, of course, but not too threatening. Just unpleasant and mean. He reminded me of a toad, not in appearance, but in a sort of misguided earnestness. I understood then that the poltergeist is not a creature with a macabre sense of humor. He is the only creature in Heaven, Hell, or Earth with no sense of humor at all. He is deadly serious. This is his scope and his higher life. When he buffets and pinches he is serious.

" 'Is he anybody we know?' my companions exclaimed. 'An ectoplasm with acne!' 'Finnegan, however did you get that dead fish color?' one asked. 'I have seen him before, I will remember where I saw him,' said another. We all treated it as a joke, but we were impressed. This was the picture of a devil. Finally I covered it, and we thought about breakfast.

"About seven in the morning, as we were ready to leave to get something to eat, a priest, a Father Le Faye S.J. arrived and introduced himself.

" 'First the Devil, and then the Jebbies,' said one of my

friends, an anticlerical. Then Father Le Faye explained his visit. He had just got off the train, he said. He had ridden all night and had come direct to our rooms.

" 'Who called you?' we asked him. 'There is no point in waiting to be called,' he said. He talked a while on diabolism in general. He was an exorcist of some fame. I had six or seven pictures in the room, all covered. He went direct to *that* picture and uncovered it.

" 'Oh, it is only he,' said the Jesuit. 'Do you know him?' I asked. 'Oh, yes. It's almost a shame to waste ceremony on him. Well, burn the thing, and sweep out the ashes! I don't think you'll have any more trouble after that, but in case you do. . . .' And he performed the short form of exorcism.

" 'Well, burn it and sweep the ashes out,' he said crisply once more after he had performed the exorcism. 'I'd like for the master, Van Ghi, to see it first,' I said. 'He was interested in the experiment.' 'Is that old mountebank still in town?' the Jebbie asked. 'Well, send for him and get it over with.' Van Ghi came, and he said exactly the same thing and in the same voice: 'Oh, it's only him.' 'You kmow him too?' we asked.

" 'Yes. He's an old repeater,' said Van Ghi. 'He's in the background of many otherwise fine paintings. "The Night Watch," for instance. And Peter Bruegel did him often. He's in the "Betrayal" of Giotto, and he's in the "Burial" of Count Ortega. He was in a lot of El Grecos, often painted over, and nearly as often uncovered again. He has been painted out of many pictures for their betterment. He's on Notre Dame in stone. He's on Etruscan vases and Aztec statuettes. Let's burn him as the Father says. You had better paint without inspiration from now on, Finnegan. You have drawn the Joker instead of the Queen.'

"That is the story of how I painted a picture of a devil when I was a student under the great Van Ghi in Florence. And if anyone wants to know what a devil looks like, let him go to a library and look up reproductions of the pictures that Van Ghi named. In each of them there is a minor face in the background, and it is the same face in all of them. If looked at long enough, it ceases to be minor and dominates the picture. It does not itself become significant; it draws everything else down to its level. You will spot that mean little face and figure that is common to them all, and you will know what one of the devils looks like."

The story wasn't entirely a lie. Finnegan *had* painted the picture of the Devil, but not under those circumstances. Finnegan thought much of the Devil now, since he had killed several men. He thought about a hundred cities burning along curious shore-hugging routes, and he wondered how long it would be till hellfire should consume all the earth.

Hildegarde was completely emptied by this time.

They uncorked Idabel, and each took one gulp for good fellowship, and to show that they all appreciated the high lies they had told each other. Then, as it was very late, and as even gentlemen of the beach must keep some hours, they fell to sleep in their hammocks.

"Finnegan!" sounded a remembered voice from Don Barnaby's hammock an hour later. "I'm lost and scared. I'm dead in the sand for three years now. *Get me out of here!*"

But the strong and even breathing of Don Barnaby had not been broken. It was not his voice, but it had come from him.

Chapter Seventeen

ANGELA COSQUIN

*There we saw Monsters, Giants, the sons of Enac ...
And the whole multitude crying wept that night ... fear
not the people of this land, for we are able to eat them
up like bread.*

—NUMBERS

1.

There is one other requirement of Paradise that hasn't been mentioned: a beautiful barmaid or factotum.

"Factota," said Don Barnaby the Duke of Moule, "for if anyone is feminine, she is."

There is a thing about Don Barnaby that is not easily explained. Finnegan did not remember when he first met him. Finnegan and Le Marin would be together, the two of them, and gradually there came the feeling that the two of them were three. The third presence had coalesced into Don Barnaby. This was mere impression, however. The first time Finnegan actually saw Don Barnaby, he near jumped out of his frame. Finnegan had taken him for someone else, someone not really very much like him.

We were about to talk of Angela, however, and not of Don Barnaby.

Feminine, but she was feminine in an old island fashion. She was womanly but not weak. She could carry two hundred pounds on her head as she went swaying along the rocky roads. She could launch a six-man boat by herself. She was always in dazzling color, and often she broke into music.

Angela Cosquin was French, of course, but more than French. She had in her everything that had ever been on that island, from the Carib Indian to the English. Some of her forebears had been noblemen, and some had been slaves. It is a little hard to explain just how pretty she was. She was never silent in any language that she possessed, and she told quite a few stories herself.

"The only difference in mine," she would say to the four topers, "is that mine are all true, and yours, I believe, are sometimes loosely detailed."

Most of her stories had to do with her father and his interesting occupation.

"He was a cartographer and antiquarian," she said. "He made maps by hand. He did this beautifully upon old leather and vellum and parchment. He was an exquisite artist and imitator, and he was unsurpassed in the imagination that he put into his detail work.

"Originally he made these maps for showpieces, for the clubrooms and dens of rich men, for their libraries and showcases. It was quite by accident that he learned that one of his maps had been passed off as an old pirate treasure map. This amused him, but he immediately saw possibilities in it.

"On many of them that he had not yet sold, he put the *signatura del tesoro*. This is the *baul* or *arca*, and above it the *azadon* and *pala*, the treasure chest under the pick-axe and shovel crossed. And on the *baul* or chest he would often put a lettering or brand, as T or K or BP, which the simple-minded might take to mean, if it were suggested to them so subtly that they thought they had discovered it themselves, that of Teach, or of Kidd, or of Bartolomo Portuguese, or one of the other old pirates.

"He made a lot of these old maps, and he penned a lot of ancient affidavits on the backs of them. And the con men would buy all that he could draw. Yet he never let down on the quality or did sloppy work, however great the demand. His maps were always authentic in detail, whether they were intended to represent the sixteenth or seventeenth or eighteenth century hand of Englishman, Spaniard, Frenchman, or Colonial. A tetteraglot from childhood, my father was an expert on archaic spelling and handwriting.

"A second sort of treasure map he now devised at the demand of the con men, the *naufrage* signature maps, those of the shipwrecked treasure as opposed to the land-buried treasure. In the plotting of these, he also used unusual imagination. He put himself in the place of the ship. He said to himself, If I were a ship, where would I go to be shipwrecked?

"As you may know, there are seven true passages through the Antilles, and seven false or shoal passages. The seven true passages are: Anegada; Guadelupe; Windward; Mona; Martinique; Ste. Lucia; and St. Vincent. And the seven false or shoal passages are: Jardines Banks; Cabo Rojo; Vieques; St. Barthelemy; the pass between Basseterre and Nevis; the pass between Basse-Terre and Marie Galante; and the Grenadines. These seven false passages were where the wrecks piled up, or where they should have piled up if they were ships of any logic and had mistaken a false passage for a true one.

"My father made a master map, the most beautiful of all his maps. It hung on the wall in his study in my old childhood home. On this great map he represented fifty or more sunken ships, real or imaginary. The fame of this map went out, and the con men came to visit him on our island. They came from all over the world. There were Spanish-Trunk Swindlers, Custom-House-Gambit Workers, Mexican-Prisoner-Story Dealers. All kinds of them. For them, he made maps and half-maps.

"You may not appreciate all the tricks that can be done with a half-map. You cannot just cut a map in two and have two maps. It must appear to have been torn or cut in two a hundred or more years ago. This takes art. Of course, one half-map is useless without the other half. The cons stake out their two half-maps at a good price to two victims a thousand miles apart. Then, by devious tricks, they bring the owners together, collecting again and again as they came nearer each other. There is a fascination about two matching half-maps that a complete map can never have."

"Do you have any of them left?" asked Johnny Duckwalk. "I just believe I know a few ways I could work those map tricks after I leave here."

"Of a certainty I have a few left," Angela said, "and I will always let them go at an immodest figure. The buyers used to gather around the old master map of my father. There, from a selection of fifty or more, they would choose a sunken ship that they fancied, choose also a new location for it if they did not like it where it was; and they would commission my father to do the detailed treasure map and supporting papers. He would draw, compose, age, and deliver. There is money enough in treasure, if you can fine it; and there is very good money in treasure maps.

"Oh the ships on that big map! The Mary Jane, the Red Fox, the Halcon, the Loutre, the Jabali, the Moonraker. There were Spanish ships like the litany of the Blessed Virgin: Estrella del Mar, Torre del Marfil, Virgen la mas Benigna, Casa del Oro.

"There were old English venturers: the Golden Mastiff, the Indiaman, the Hind, the Crane. And the French: the Blaireau, the Megère, the Renard Volante. All noble ships, and they all had two things in common: they were loaded with treasure; and they went down.

"My father's maps still have a wide currency. In fact, he died of overwork after he had put an ad in *Variety* and had so many confidence men come to him for maps that he could not do them all. And every year the treasure hunters come down to the Antilles and dive and sound. Some of them are dashed to pieces and drowned in the shoal passages, and some of them spend all their money on the search and then leave.

"They even come to this very island and look for the twin ships that my father depicted as sunken here, the *St. Marc*, and the *Sangre del Cristo*. These two ships are supposedly sunken one on top of the other. This account, of course, is the most complete fabrication, even though some of the other ships in the other maps may have their ounce of truth."

In this last sentence only did Angela lie a little. For the nearby *St. Marc* and *Sangre del Cristo* were solid fact, even though some of the others may have been mostly legend. Angela said these things to throw even these her good friends off the track. For the two ships were really there, not over three hundred yards from where she spoke. They were sunken, and were so full of gold that it passes understanding how they could ever have floated.

Angela often dived down to the two ships and luxuriated in their hoard. At one time she had brought up a great lot of it; but she found that people were suspicious when she spent gold coins of such ancient mintage. And they looked at her as if she herself were morally implicated when she wore too many of the diamonds of the ship.

After that, she brought all the treasure she had gathered back down to the old ships again, as being the safest place of all to keep it. Later she had a copper box made, and on it was inscribed: *Angela Cosquin sa Caisse.* Into this she put all the money that she had in the world, and dived with it down to the two old ships to leave it for safe-keeping.

And after that, once a month, she would go down and add to it one gold sovereign that she had saved; for she thought that her money would be safest there with so many millions of old dead men's money to keep it company.

There is an interesting sidelight to this. All four of the beach gentlemen had followed her, and all knew where the treasure ships were and had explored them. But they had never taken anything up from their diving except a few interesting samples, having no need.

Except Johnny Duckwalk, who had a mean streak in him. Every month, as long as he was on the island, and on the day after Angela had deposited her gold sovereign, he would dive down and steal that sovereign from the box of Angela Cosquin, and touch nothing else of all the millions there.

But Angela had another series of treasure maps that worried Finnegan. Only he of the four topers had seen this latter series of maps; Angela had arranged that only he should see them. There were seven maps in this series, and they were beautifully drawn by the hand of Angela Cosquin in imitation of that of her father.

Each of these showed, not a shipwrecked treasure, but a land-buried treasure. The treasure symbol on these was not the *baul,* but the *maleta* (the suitcase). And on each of these were the initials S X S, and below these, *robado por* C F. It seemed very likely that this might indicate: Saxon X. Seaworthy's, stolen by Count Finnegan. And the seven maps were accurate. They showed correctly the seven cities of the seven treasure stashes, and they seemed to indicate an even finer detail.

It was possible that Finnegan's enemies might have discovered one or two of the stashes. But they could not have discovered all seven. And Angela was not his enemy. She could have got the information only from the mind of

Count Finnegan himself (it was she who first called him that). But when and how had she read him?

"Who will you sell these seven maps to, Angela?" Finnegan had asked her.

"Oh my heart, I will not sell them! I will keep them for memory of one who scattered his treasure too widely and had none left for me."

2.

In the Haggada there are passages about the forbidden fruit, and there is one thing mentioned there that isn't generally known. The fruit, whether pomme or drupe, we will still call the apple, the apple of the first offense, that apple was wormy anyhow.

St. Augustine also seems to refer to this, and others. Anyhow, the apple was wormy. This was also the case with the golden apples of the Hesperides, which were a cross from the same tree of Eden and a small sweet yellow apple of the Western Islands.

It was on these golden apples, among other things, that the four tired topers had been living; and now the worm began to stir. The taste of it appeared first to one of them, then to another.

Johnny Duckwalk, who appeared to be a man without a conscience, now was taken with the sickness of repentance. He announced one day that he had decided to give up the cheerful life and to enter on another condition of existence. He would return to a shabby mainland site. He would confess to the appropriation of a sum of money which (due to involved reasons) had never been missed. And for this offense and confession he would spend from six to ten years in confinement or durance vile. He had already been in touch with someone, and he had that estimate of the length of his servitude.

"So that is the end of it with me," he told them, "the plain end of the stick. Well, there isn't any other thing I can do, what with the apprehension that has come over me. It's the end of me, though."

"But you are still a young man," said Le Marin, "and six, or even ten years won't last forever. You might get time off for good behavior, and when you get out you can still have a long and happy life ahead of you."

"It isn't so," said Johnny. "You all know me well enough to know that I will never get time off anywhere for good behavior. So much I will do of what I am obliged to do, but I will not behave well when they have me. And I am not as young as I appear, though I'm still a boy to myself. I'm in my forties. With six years or more, I will be in my fifties when I come out, and I will be an old man. A fellow like me, who's followed the rogue roads a long while, will age all at once. I remember my father. One day he was old: and he had not been old before."

Johnny Duckwalk went home on the next ship, and he wrote to them from prison. He told them all to get off that damned island before it ruined them. There is nothing like prison to give a man a changed outlook, he said.

And then it was Don Barnaby the Duke of Moule who became restless in the middle of Eden. ("You ever hear anything from Manuel?" Don asked Finnegan one day. "He was the only one out of our bunch, besides you, who got through it alive, wasn't he? Ah, ah, I forgot. That wasn't me there." This Don was an odd one. He couldn't have been the other Don, but he seemed to carry some of his memories.)

Yes, the next of them was Don Barnaby who decided to go farther and do worse. He would be back, he would be back, he said. "Oh, he will *not* be back," said Angela Cosquin to Finnegan, "they are all fools, they never come back."

"There is something a little bit wrong about this Don Barnaby," Finnegan said to her.

"Whhooff! There is something a little bit wrong with the Count Finnegan, he says," said Angela. "He says you are mixed in the head, that you mix him up with another Don. He says he has not been that other Don for several years."

Well, Don Barnaby had gone now, a man so open that he left the very lid off himself, and you still couldn't solve his mystery when you looked inside.

And in a few days (you could see it coming on him, you could see it coming) it was Charles Le Marin who took to the sea again. He had developed a trouble with his stomach, he said, and he was convinced that he would never be whole again till there was a ship under his feet. He said he would be back; they all said that. He left it all there and he didn't know what he was leaving. "He is a fool, a fool, a nine kinds of fool," said Angela Cosquin.

"Well, I will stay," said Finnegan. "I, at least, am not such a fool as to go wandering off after I have found a den. I will stay here if I have to drink sea water and eat sand."

"No, you will not stay," said Joseph Chastaigne (Sloppy Joe). "You'll leave within a month. I can see it on you, too. I thought that you, at least, would measure up to this place, but I see you have the same weakness as the others. You'll leave on the next boat."

When the three other topers were gone, Finnegan had no friends left except this Joseph Chastaigne, and Angela Cosquin the girl who worked for him at the Imperial Bar or whatsoever it was called. All the other people on the island were acquaintances that Finnegan didn't know very well, or friends that he didn't like much, or beings with whom he would not associate at all.

Besides, there was the taint of smoke in the air, even here. Finnegan had tried to insulate himself from the world, but news kept creeping in. They were still burning down the world, bit by bit. They were still fomenting riots and massacres. The people of the world were still being destroyed, or were being led on to destroy themselves.

Finnegan got the idea that he might go back to the States for just a little while. One thing had gone seriously wrong with Basse-Terre. He was no longer safe there, as he was not safe anywhere. He was being hunted even here.

A Negro friend had told him that he had been asked for. The Negro friend had even been paid a certain sum to find him and to put an end to him.

"It was a left-footed man who asked?" Finnegan inquired.

"Aya, sor, it was."

Finnegan, of course, was obliged to pay a larger sum to the friend not to put an end to him. He did not mind this, except that it wouldn't stop there. "But I will have to have something to show," said the friend. "I will have to have some of your old clothes."

Finnegan didn't understand, but he gave the friend some of his old clothes. The next day, he understood it a little, when a stray seaman, of appearance not too far from his own, turned up shot dead on the beach in the old clothes of Finnegan.

They were getting close to him. The left-footed man would not be fooled by anything so simple as this. The friend would play it along further, as far as it would go, and collect something again. But he could not be expected to warn Finnegan a second time, or even to stay bought if he did warn him. Johnny Duckwalk had once spoken of friendship with a difference, and this was too different.

Finnegan began to rationalize his reasons for leaving Paradise.

"There are, I am sure, letters lying for me in a call box that have not been forwarded. There is a man to whom I owe ten dollars that I had forgotten about. He may need it, and I cannot reach him from this distance. There is a bundle of merchandise that I should market and realize upon; my partner will believe that I have forgotten our agreement. I will go and take care of these things. And I will be back in a week or a month."

"If you go away, you will never come back," Angela told him.

"But of course I will be back. I am not the same kind of fool as the others."

"I will give you everything if you stay," Angela told him. "I clasp you. I do not want you to go. I give you two ships full of gold, and other things."

"Oh, them! I would not stay for them, Angela, but I would stay. I will be gone only a few short weeks. Then I will be back."

She clasped him. She lifted him off his feet.

"Count Finnegan, we will not let them get the people. We will always protect the poor people," Angela said. "We are the strongest ones and we can protect a little."

"We will not let them get the people, Angela," Finnegan said.

He sat on the strong knees of Angela Cosquin in the shade there and told her goodbye. But he never came back.

Chapter Eighteen
FUN IN THE GRAVEYARD

The brain of the Neanderthals must have been slightly larger than that of modern men (cranial capacity 1,400–1,600 c.c.) and apparently well developed. It was not, however, the same brain. The development and shape is different. Modern man is the high-brow of the animal kingdom with the fore-brain greatly developed. Neanderthal was the low-brow, with the fore-brain less than ours, and with a great back-brain forming a bulge at the base of the skull. We understand most of the functions of the fore-brain; these are the functions that make us what we are. We do not well understand the functions of that back-brain which in the Neanderthals must have been six times the size of ours, a difference that is frightening. It is partly the site of the unconscious, we know; of the subliminal, of certain psychical phenomena, of parapsychological manifestations, of what we can only call ghostliness.

Modern humans with heads of the Neanderthal type (pumpkin heads, with the bulbous nose and the basal bulge) are often absolute criminals. But they may also be religious pathfinders, seers, inflamatory leaders, spiritualists, humorists, poets, inventors.

Consider Plato who was named for his curious broad head as well as his broad shoulders. Consider the Ambrosian bust of Homer; the fifth century representations of Attila the Hun. Consider Aquinas the angelic ox: what things he did spin out of his massive back-brain, tedious to most, it is true, but it is said that God understood him. Consider Rabelais, Luther, Christopher Smart, Rasputin, Toussaint L'Ouverture, Steinmetz, the twelve children studied by Washita as poltergeist hosts, the levitators, the stigmatists. Consider Santana's wonder that the mystics of such singing and beautiful thoughts were all facially ugly. And they were ugly in a certain type. Their brains differed from ours, their concepts must have been different, and therefore they lived in a different world.

Could we understand that world, we would understand ourselves better; for we also are part of that back-brain world to some degree. It was the 'other people', the 'Ugly' people who gave to us whatever ghostliness we have, and whatever imagination. We gave only forebrain consciousness.

The back-brain type is also found in the Grimaldi, the Aurignacian, and other related types of early man.
—CARMODY OVERLARK, *Studies in the Imagination*

1.

There are a few months or seasons missing here. Finnegan had been into his other life, what might have been called his human life. He had been in New Orleans and St. Louis and Chicago, seeing his friends from that set. He had had long visits with Casey and Vincent and Hans and Henry. He had been in a sanitorium for six weeks. It was not his idea, but that of his friends. He knew that what was wrong with him did not come from a bottle, however much he enjoyed that.

He had worked for Hillary Hilton, really exciting work for which he had a special talent. All that, however, had pertained to Finnegan's normal life, not to his under-life here. He had been passing for a human, albeit a strange one. Then he had the call from inside his head that the time was nearly at hand.

He had begun now to wander in the direction of the meeting, but with many stopovers. It was an early morning with some country-type friends after a night with the coon dogs.

"I have eleven days," said Finnegan. "Then I must attend a meeting."

"Hereabouts?" asked one of his friends.

"No, not hereabouts. A few hundred miles. I have to

207

meet a middling old gentleman and a tolerably young lady in a graveyard."

"At midnight?"

"No. No, that came before. This one will be at high noon. There I will hear a story from an old master, exchange a few remarks on the destruction of the world, and then scatter again to see if we can do something about that destruction."

"Where will you scatter to then?"

"If I don't find a road sign pointing elsewhere, I may go to St. Kitts."

"You ever been there before?"

"There is only a slight chance that I have been. I once intended to go there but was confused by names. Sometimes it seems that I have been there very recently, though there is a dispute about this.

"It is like the night that we have just passed. Some of you say that we have been in the Chosky Bottoms, and some of you say that we weren't within fifty miles of those bottoms. There is something here that transcends geography. Old Pop Potter here says that the Chosky Bottoms is just a sort of general name for a spook place, that they are always over the ridge and in the valley of the next river from where you are. The Chosky Bottoms are where the man-killing panther lives, and where the swamp ghost is; it's where the old masked riders rode from; and where the Northern Platoon went down in the quicksand. It's where the grandfather of all the big coons and big fish live; it's where the Bloody Mulligans shacked, and where eighteen-foot-long bull snakes have been seen."

"How come you know so much about the Chosky Bottoms when you're not from around here?"

"The Chosky Bottoms are everywhere, or just over the next hill from everywhere. St. Kitts is a little like that to me."

"They got big coons and snakes there?"

"No. That's not what I mean. But that is where I will go. The name is loosely applied to several islands, by myself, at least. If it doesn't turn out to be the end of the rainbow for me this time, the chances are going to be a lot slimmer for me ever finding it."

They had breakfast of flapjacks and roast possum, and popskull from a distressed stock that the sheriff had confiscated in an accidental encounter during the night. Finnegan himself had shot a boar coon that would have weighed sixty pounds. He told them that it would be considered little where he came from.

"Now, now, boy, now, now," they told him. They knew it wouldn't have been considered little anywhere.

Then the men scattered to their patches and farms and towns. And Finnegan set off for his rendezvous eleven days away. He had been immersing himself in humanity again. Often he had to convince himself of its reality all over.

2.

Finnegan had hitched a ride on a produce truck, over the causeway and onto the island and into the city. He was inside the net now; he could feel it. Likely his old ship was in port; very certainly his old antagonist was in town. He could feel the grizzled evil of that fox and hear his sour laugh. It was a congregation of powers here. The left-footed tracker was here, as well as his employer. It was showdown time today.

"Oh my odd uncle!" Finnegan cried out. "It is our confrontation again today, the last time in either of our lives!"

Finnegan went to the club across from the graveyard. Yes, they remembered him there; but there was a certain iciness in their looks as well as a certain compassion; such a look as they turn on one who is about to die, on one they are bound to disassociate themselves from.

Oh yes, the old master and the doll had been looking for him. You could see them from there, across the boulevard and inside the graveyard. Ah, the secret meeting was well heralded.

Finnegan crossed over to meet his fellow conspirators, in bright daylight, and with many eyes upon him. He kissed Doll with great vigor and pleasure when he came up to them. She had always been an undemanding friend of his.

"And how many have you kissed since we parted?" she asked.

"I could count them without using any of the fingers of any of my hands," Finnegan said, "except when I did it just for fun. It doesn't count when you do it for fun."

Finnegan had brought along a portable radio to follow the Indianapolis race. They had chosen that day for the meeting in the graveyard so as not to be conspicuous, though here in the South the day was not so much observed as elsewhere. Doll had brought a hamper of food, drink, and ice, and red roses on the top of it.

X had brought only himself and a little briefcase; and an otherworldly cloak with as many pockets and concealed drops in it as a magician's cloak, which as a matter of fact it was. He had used it when he was the great X-Capo, Magician and Escape Artist. Doll Delancy and X had both been waiting for Finnegan who would have to show them the way.

"Finnegan, I have looked for it all over the hallowed place," X complained, "and I can't find a clue to it. I surely cannot be wrong, can I? I am so seldom wrong that often I do not even consider the possibility. I have not looked over all the graves, but I have looked over more than two hundred of them.

"The grave register does not seem to be complete for the earlier years, but I cannot spot the name in any form. And I know for sure that it's here. It is necessary to my theory that it be here. Please lead us to it, Finnegan."

"We are watched," said Finnegan.

"I know we are watched. Here there are traps within traps. We want them to know that we have found it. We want them to believe that we intend to open it as soon as possible. We want them to attempt to open it before we have done so. Lead us to the grave, Finnegan."

Finnegan led them, after some wandering around, to an old and neglected grave. They had to pull weeds to see the carving on the gravestone. And it meant nothing when they had cleared it, nothing to Finnegan, at least.

The carving on the stone was I.N.C.G.P. Bogovitch.

This was the grave of the Devil himself. And that was the puzzling name carved on his gravestone.

"What diabolical irony!" X exclaimed. "Finnegan, Doll, is that not true irony! Why didn't I think of it? I thought of everything else."

"It would be kind if you would explain," Doll murmured.

"Why, Bogovitch is, of course, an euphemism."

"It is?" asked Doll.

"And of what?" inquired Finnegan.

X looked at the two of them with pity. It was a look that he seldom used. Mostly he was tolerant of the ignorance of his fellow citizens of the Earth.

"Why, of Chortovitch, of course. How obvious can it be? You would hardly call a man Chortovitch in death, would you? Even the chisel of the monument man might hesitate to cut such a name. Even if this man did bear that dread name while living, it would be natural to soften it at death. We have that cleared up, I hope."

"Apparently not," said Finnegan. "If only we knew what the words meant, it would be easier."

"Oh. I didn't realize that your difficulty was on that score. Chortovitch means son of the Devil. Bogovitch means son of God. And now I will just have one of those devil's food cakes from Miss Doll's hamper, and then I will ease into my story that is also, aptly, devil's food."

"They're gingerbread, not devil's food," Doll said, but she gave him one.

"Bogovitch, as I say, means son of God," X continued. "This is the euphemism, for the man to whom it refers was really named Son of the Devil. My researches, which are extensive and could have been carried out by no other man but myself, have turned up his name to be approximately Ifreann Noonan Columkill Gregorovitch.

"The names of this family are confusing, being a mixture of the patronymic, the conventional eponymic, and a mystic sort of uionymic. We also have the alternation of generations in the names."

"How close do they want to watch us?" Finnegan asked. "The glint of the sun on the binoculars, of course."

"They try to read mouth," said X. "I face them clearly, but I am too tricky for them. I have learned a disassociation. My words say what you hear them say, but the movements of my mouth indicate that I am telling a series of humorous stories in Yiddish. Not everyone can do this.

"In other words, a family name may run all through the strand. At the same time, the son may bear as surname the first name of the father or the grandfather; or the father may be named for the son. Or the father may be named for the grandson: this is the hard part to understand. At any rate, Papadiabolous and Chortovitch run as common auxiliaries through the generations which concern us.

"Please get the picture now, you two. Sympathy and personal identification are required. These are the people and events that we must understand:

"It was in a hay field near Krakow, Poland (possibly a little nearer to Skawine) that Ifreann Noonan Columkill Gregorovitch Papadiabolous Chortovitch was born. This was in the year of Restored Salvation 1830. He had for mother an Irish girl named Noonan. For father he had the Devil.

"In the early part of my researches I was of the opinion that Katie Noonan, in a moment of exasperation, had merely said (as unfortunate girls with a child and no husband are likely to say): his father was the Devil.

"But later I came to believe that his father really was the Devil. The progeny of this devil are numerous. You may say that it was the old race still throwing angry primordials after a thousand generations. I say that it was the Devil himself come to Earth. And the son of Katie Noonan was only one of very many that he pupped.

"There is a personal note here. This manifestation of the Devil was, I am convinced, my own grandfather. He was also your own great-grandfather, Finnegan, and also that of the beautiful Anastasia. She was right when she called you *adelphos*, for *adelphos* meant cousin as well as brother in the Old Greek. So these are all of your kindred, and I believe that you have known it.

"In the records of St. Elmo, the parish nearest Krakow, it is clearly written 'The Devil' in the blank for the father. I have seen it myself. Officially, at least, likely in reality, this was the son of the Devil.

"Katie's son was baptized Columkill and was given the patronym of Gregorovitch, from a certain Gregory in whose home Katie was governess, and who adopted little Columkill. There is also the chance that Gregory was the real father, but this I do not believe. He was a kind man, and Katie was a good girl, and this would not account for the perversity that broke out in the brood. Katie called the boy Ifreann, which of course is Irish for the Devil, but she seems to have used the term affectionately.

"There is an old tendency in certain parts of Poland, as in Brazil and Italy and Spain and other places, to speak English with an Irish accent. I myself have it, and I have it from my native Milano. This was sometimes due to the English tongue being taught by Irish nuns. It was also due, in families of property, to English being taught by Irish governesses. These Irish were preferred in the last century to the English as working more cheaply; and also, for those landed Catholic families, as being able to give the true religious instruction and a grounding in manners. Katie Noonan then was a governess in a landed Polish family. She left their employ some months before the birth of Ifreann Columkill, and returned to it several weeks afterward.

"Ifreann is known from old family letters to have been a monster from the beginning. He killed cats, and he tried to kill children—twice in fact. His mother was the most placid creature in the world, but he broke her heart.

"You may wonder how I know so much of the inner emotions of obscure persons of a century or more ago. There are ways by which an off-trail historian like myself can reconstruct: a few phrases in a badly-written old letter, a rain-soaked evening in the countryside in question, old grandfathers who remember what they were told as children. One can get the feel of an unhappy old family, especially if one has a common background of belief and station and temperament.

"Ifreann was a large and brutal boy. He was possessed of an exceptional mentality (I almost said intelligence, but he had no trace of that) and an abundance of energy and purpose. He was fifteen and large for his age when he killed a man, probably not the first, but the first for which he was pursued. He escaped due to the confused state of the land.

"In that year (and that year only) there existed the Republic of Krakow, which reverted the next season to Austria. Poland herself, in that century as in most centuries, was enslaved. It is possible that Ifreann had a certain loyalty to his own region. He had a rebellion against all foreign, indeed all, authority, at least. He later appealed to patriotism for his own purpose and he proclaimed himself a citizen of Krakow all his life, though he was below the age of citizenship when he left there.

"After this punishable murder of his sixteenth year, he abandoned the Krakow region and lived thereafter in Austria proper, in Russia, in Greece, in Smyrna, in London, in Ireland, in Milano, in Sicily, in the United States, finally in this particular city.

"Ifreann had attended the Paris Commune when he was forty and had become an ironic disciple of Kropotkin. Where Kropotkin was a crooked saint, Ifreann was an honest devil. The point is that Kropotkin affected to believe in his own teaching, and Ifreann was guilty of no such dishonesty. I believe that Ifreann had a number of half-brothers at the Paris Commune. I believe that my father was one of them.

"Ifreann became one of the old line communists. He was active in the conspiracy when its sheer evil was still undiluted by nonsense and not yet weakened by Slavic imperialism; when the mentally inept had not yet found shelter on its fringes or in its half-way houses; when it still used its own name when it went about its business. Ifreann won a certain respect in the movement due to the fact that his father was the Devil. Even those who did not believe in the Devil, believed that his father was the Devil.

"Enough of that. Ifreann lived a full and pungent life. When he was seventy years old he sired twins.

"The unusual thing about these twins is that, though they were born at the same instant, they were born in different centuries, on different continents, and to different mothers."

Chapter Nineteen

THE DEVIL IS DEAD

Man, the privileged mutation, rose out of a deadly conflict, a murderous mingling, an actual cannibalism of one of the elements by another. This has not happened to any other species; there is no other case of one species totally absorbing a close kindred, nor the emerging of a fertile hybrid of such sudden ability and such stunning advance. Sharply, in an incredibly narrow instant of time, Cro Magnon man stood tall and serene and talented and dominant; but recessive in him was a reservoir as deep as the earth.

We are the taut bow. The iron-wood of the bow must never break. The twisted bull-sinew of the string cannot be cut, or we lose everything. We are born of this terrible tension and balance, and it must be maintained. But there are premonitions of more than usually savage conflict between the two misunderstood elements of ourselves. This time it goes to the conflict, and there can be no victory. The death of either of us kills all of us. We become the broken bow. Our limbs, our lives, our world become unstrung, and we die.

—HIRAM HUNT, *The Death of the Species*

Doll had wine in a picnic jug and she passed it around. She had sandwiches and coffee and cakes. They were very neat about this, and they returned all the remnants and papers to the hamper.

Finnegan had a pocket harmonica with him and he played a few bars of 'Arise, ye Saints, Arise,' but none of the dead in that yard arose. "I wanted to give them the chance," Finnegan said.

Doll put the last of the red roses on the grave of Ifreann Noonan Columkill Papadiabolous Chortovitch, which was also the grave of Gregory McIfreann.

"Will you go on with your story, X?" she asked.

"No. I will begin my story," said X. "It was with those fearsome words that Kantara fok El-Nahr began the last page but nine of his eight-thousand-page novel *El-Kamar*. He didn't write in humor; it was just that he was a slow starter. I will begin the story now. And how should one begin a story? *Il y avait une fois?*"

"That's a good way," said Doll.

"*In illo tempore—*"

"That is still better," said Finnegan, "but get with it." And softly on his harmonica he blew the first eight bars of Browne's Prelude.

"Very well," said X. "Once upon a time a septuagenarian had twins. Some may say that these were not properly twins as they were born to different mothers. But they were of the same father, conceived at the same time (for he was a lively rake), and born on the night of the turn of the century. They might not seem so old to some, but those of the Other Flesh do not age quickly. One was born in Smyrna, and one in Cork. Ifreann, as we will call the ancient father for simplicity, had in the meanwhile separated his menages.

"The Asiatic son was called Gregory McIfreann, and the Irish son was named Gregory McColum. Both of them picked up various cognomens during their lives. We will call them here, Papadiabolous I (the Asiatic one, the one you buried, Finnegan), and the Irish one, Papadiabolous II (the one you knew).

"The first was correctly named Gregory McIfreann Papadiabolous. Other names he used were Sanditen, Chrysostom, Protagoras, Hochstruwelpieter-Goltz.

"The second or Irish one was correctly named Gregory McColum Papadiabolous. And the variant names he used were Noonan, Flaherty, Christy, Clarenden, Cobbett, Malory, Ingraham, and Arbuthnot."

(On his harmonica, Finnegan was playing softly 'Oh what was your name in the States?')

"The brothers both employed variations of John as a working first name," X continued, "Ivan, Sean, Jan, Ian, Jean, Giovanni, Juan, Johannes, and Giannes; so that either of them was likely to be known at any given moment as John Gregory. The untangling of these names proved something of an obstacle to me.

"Papadiabolous I was (*horresco referens*) much like his father. He was an evil man, and evil with a purpose. He was a man of phenomenal physical power. It is doubtful whether his twin was his equal in this dark strength, though he also was a very large and powerful man. Papa II is not known to have performed great physical prodigies; here he rather traveled on the reputation of his brother as whom he was masquerading. But Papadiabolous I did have preternatural powers that cannot now be explained. He was a devil, and he had that dark power of the Devil.

"Papadiabolous II was his opposite, that is to say, a comparatively good man. Not that he was entirely free of encounters with the law before he entered police work. He was a gentleman burglar, a contrabandist, a swindler, and a forger. But at all times he was morally sound. Born in an enslaved nation, he turned in his youth to these means of self-expression. Later, when he entered police work, he found this early training valuable.

"The two brothers were identical as to build, coloring, and skull shape. Skeletally one could not tell them apart. But fleshed, there was little superficial resemblance. In the accidentals of face they differed, even though the faces hung on the same sort of facial bones. You, Finnegan, who had seen them both, and both dead, may understand how one brother was able to masquerade as the other, and why you were the only one who knew it. I myself cannot understand how he did it.

"For years the twin brothers did not know of each other's existence. In fact, Papadiabolous I did not know about it till after he was dead; and then (as I have it from my contacts) it came as quite a surprise to him.

"Papadiabolous I was a working revolutionary, as his father was. He grew up in the middle of it. His associates were a group of men, some of whom you know, several of them rumored to be his half-brothers under the bar sinister, Seaworthy, Genof, Wirt, Gerecke, Wedekind, Askadrian, Sanditen, Sorensen. While he lived, and you will notice by his gravestone here that he lived to be a hundred years old, the old man Ifreann was dominant. But Papadiabolous I was crown prince.

"We know that Papadiabolous I was in St. Petersburg on November 7, 1917. He was about eighteen years old. He was serving a practical apprenticeship. All the sons and pseudo-sons did so.

"All except Papadiabolous II (McColum) the forgotten issue in Ireland. He was not included; we do not know why this was so. His native talents were allowed to develop without guidance. When he was twenty-five, under mysterious auspices, he went into police work. I am not sure just who his superiors were. I am not even sure for whom I myself am working now. I knew him vaguely for several decades as Noonan the undercover Irish cop. He was simply N, as I was simply X."

Finnegan was harmonicaing 'A policeman's life is not a happy one.'

"I forget a lot of the people, and mix the others up before you get around to them again," said Doll.

"That is because you have a human mind, Miss Doll," X explained, "unable to comprehend the thick texture of details that make up our world. Ah, the convolutions of this police work, the counter-subversion business, are so intricate as to be incomprehensible to a layman. So intricate, in fact, that, like those of modern art, they sometimes raise the suspicion of being meaningless. It is the case of watching the wheels of a great evil machine turn relentlessly, and trying to convince the world that it is happening.

"And the world, as you know, has always insisted, not only that the wheels of the machine are not turning, but that there is no machine there at all—this against all the evidences of the senses, particularly that of smell. This we in the counter-work have never understood. The only conclusion, is that we are not getting our message across. We have not been able to alert the populace."

(And Finnegan was tootling 'Wake the town and tell the people' on the harmonica.)

"Go ahead, X," said Doll, "and when you finish, Finnegan is going to take me swimming. What are you giving me that little gun for, Finn? I already have one."

"Noonan (Papadiabolous II) kept track of his half-brothers and step-brothers who did not know of his existence," X continued. "And there is the story that he confronted the old man his father shortly before the father's death.

"The father was buried in the year 1930 in the grave on which we are sitting. After this, Papadiabolous I became the uneasy head of a regnancy that lasted for some years. The other associates revolted perpetually, and there were often clashes. Saxon X. Seaworthy, one of the half-brothers, was more or less the chief of the mutineers. He was selected to effect the murder of Papadiabolous I.

"We do not know quite how Seaworthy did this. He seems to have convinced Papadiabolous, and I believe that the thing is true, that very valuable information had been buried with the father (the father of them both), and that they should open the grave in each other's presence. Fearing treachery, Papadiabolous I had taken the precaution of getting Saxon Seaworthy very drunk, which may not have been difficult in his high-strung and near hysterical condition. You, Finnegan, may have been an accidental instrument in this. Papadiabolous I, being the larger and more vigorous, did most of the digging in opening the grave. But Saxon Seaworthy was still lucid enough to kill Papadiabolous the Devil with a small caliber weapon after the digging had gone down a ways. He is smart, that Saxon, and he can fake it. Whether they had already examined what they came to seek I am not sure. I think not, for Saxon still seems to seek an opportunity to get to it. I think that Saxon was that night incapable of getting to the bottom of the event. Something scared him. You were that something, Finnegan.

"For Saxon was about to dump the body of Papadiabolous I into the grave when our fabulous friend Finnegan came along and offered to deepen the grave out of the pure goodness of his heart.

"The feelings of Saxon may have been a little mixed at that moment. We aren't sure why Finnegan wasn't also killed. Possibly Saxon had already thrown the small caliber weapon into the grave to be rid of it. Finnegan was quite close to death when he let go the spade and fumbled with his hands in the old grave for the bones. He'd have died surely if he had not looked up when he did.

"The feelings of Saxon Seaworthy may have been even more mixed the next morning when Noonan (Papadiabolous II) the Irish cop took his quasi-twin's place in the organization. There must have been strained relations on that trip half-way around the world. Seaworthy had already been proclaimed the new leader of the band, and Papadiabolous II could not have known all the details. He felt his way, but he came in as if nothing had happened, and he carried it off. Did the relations seem strained, Finnegan?"

"They were all a cryptic bunch."

"Saxon never has figured it out. When he killed Noonan (Papadiabolous II) on Naxos Island, he did not recognize him dead as the man who had been masquerading as Papadiabolous I. Saxon is not a believing man. He *knew* that he had killed Papadiabolous. He is a total materialist. He knew that a man could not come back to life. He also kept Finnegan for confirmation that he was not out of his mind. But then the ghost *had* come back and continued to control the gang on a voyage of many months. Ah, but the deaths of the two Papa Devils are a parable of the deaths of us all. I can see nothing but destruction for us.

"They all believe that Papadiabolous is still alive. They do not know that there were two of them, and that both are now dead. One of our forgers (why should I lie about it? it is myself) sends them notes now and then in Papadiabolous' strange handwriting. It was, in truth, a taunting note in this devil's hand that brought Saxon Seaworthy to town this day and into my trap. Ah, he and Papadiabolous are to meet this night again and complete their opening of the father's grave.

"And Saxon has nerve. He has come. He isn't afraid of a man returned from the dead; he isn't afraid of the Devil. He's a cool one, Finnegan. But his group has declined, has in fact been relegated to the fringes of the conspiracy.

"Oh, they can still get funds. The funds that Finnegan once stole and shared with us were but one season's working specie for them. People enjoy contributing to these funds for their own destruction."

"X, I hear a sour laugh," said Finnegan. "I have heard it twice before, when I thought I had killed that man, and had not. He is smarter than the Devil, he is smarter than I, and he is smarter than you. X, tell me about this. I know that now we—they—are not a small group, but a million, mostly quite young. I see our reappearance every day in strange youthful faces. Will we, they, really bring down the world?"

"Likely they will, Finnegan. The feeling of Rome and such things were only boys' tricks of theirs. Now they well up in earnest. And the people, of course, are no help in the saving of the people."

"Bet we are," said Doll.

"No, Miss Doll. The people are but sheep. They graze on catch-words, and they go to their slaughter. If there is any staying the revenge of the old people, it will be done by a stubborn minority of themselves, and I haven't much faith in us.

"One thing ere we part. There is a thing, a key buried in this grave. It was that which brought Seaworthy and Papadiabolous I to open the grave in the first place. It is that which will cause the grave to be opened tonight. There is something in that document that would give one person too much power if he were the only one in the world to know its contents. Saxon may have been restrained in something by believing that Papadiabolous is still alive and possessed of the information.

"I have decided to remedy this situation by possessing this information tonight. I will need no help. I dig well and silently. This night I will have the visit with those two old devils in the grave under us. And I believe that Saxon Seaworthy will come to intercept me."

"Bet he doesn't!" said Finnegan. "Bet he'll have been intercepted before that. He did say, though, that nobody drinks at his spring three times, and I've drunk there twice."

"Bet he does," said X. "Oh, you mean your own little encounter with him? You are no match for him at all. I say it in some sorrow, Finnegan, but this is most likely the last afternoon of your life. It will not matter. You have led me to certain information, and now you are not really needed any longer. But it will also be the end of Saxon Seaworthy tonight. I bait the trap when I dig here, and he will die in that trap."

"Bet he doesn't," said Finnegan.

"Now we have had a pleasant visit here," X intoned. "It took me nearly a year—"

"Hold it, X," said Finnegan. "The glint of the sun on binoculars is one thing. The shine of a compounded rifle scope is another. I get behind this rat-leaf palm from them, you behind that other. Doll may remain in the open. Nobody wants her."

"It is their loss," said Doll.

"It took me nearly a year," X continued when he was sheltered by the rat-leaf palm, "to unravel the relationships of a father and his sons. It has unraveled other kinships. Now I will be on my own mysterious way tomorrow. And you two have a swimming date today; it may be a colorful one, Finnegan; it would be a good place to get you. The two of you may be found bobbling in the water, staining it red. In a way, I hope not."

"You make the water seem a little chilly, X," said Doll.

But Finnegan, at that moment, was thinking neither of devils nor of death. He was not even thinking of the man who is smarter than the Devil, his own disreputable uncle, as it seemed. He was rather looking at Doll Delancy and marveling at the strangeness of the human kind. The poker-faced weirdness of people came over him like a wave. 'The mystery of them,' he mused. 'What goes on in them anyhow? What do they think? How is one ever to understand the human kind. The Doll has several times tried to tell her own story, and we would not listen. But is it possible that regular people *do* have valid life stories? Who would believe it? Oh, the inscrutability of them!'

But Doll was meanwhile speaking sharply:

"Now you listen to me, you two loop-eared, bugger-nosed bums! Are you saying that people can have no effect on what happens to people? Are you saying that you old gargoyles will destroy us, unless a minority of the g's can prevent it? Why can we ourselves not prevent it? We whipped you once, I believe."

"The people are hopeless, Miss Doll," X said. "The people are sheep. All leaders everywhere, on all sides, of every sort, are either of the older people or of the double blood. Regular people are incapable."

"Bet we're not," said Doll. "I like you two. But why don't all of you just go away?"

"We were here first," said X. "Tell her, Count Finnegan."

"We were here first, Doll," Finnegan said. "Wait, wait, I have to listen in the back of my head for the rest of it ... We are the lords of the world, the people who were before the people. We arise in our primordial form and reestablish ourselves. We will cause this late-world people to destroy themselves. We will roast the people of the world and eat them up ... And I am renegade if I do not go along with it; I am traitor. So then I am renegade. But I know there is no help from the people themselves."

"Bet there is," said Doll. "This thing must be ended. Do you two not realize that it must have a climax?"

"It is only regular people who believe in climaxes, Miss Doll," X said. "It is not the other people who have fought from within for thirty thousand years who believe in such things. It is the constant gnawing down, the undercutting, the inflaming. But there will not be a climax."

"Bet there will," said Doll. "Here, I have a high thing that I've been scribbling myself. I will register it here with the devils, and you their kindred. And after that, a joyous death to you all! Tomorrow I'll be about my own way of salvaging the world. I've been in the business for years. I tried to tell you both about it, but you never listened. You didn't think that I met you by accident, did you, Finnegan?

"Get this, boys, it's good."

All the people in this history are poets, or they cannot get into this history. So Doll had written a poem, or at least some verses, and dropped it down in the great split in the grave; for the ground was always splitting there since the second burial. And the evoking paper went all the way to the bottom.

This is the poem, and the name of it is:

DIABOLIQUE

Tell us the story of one who was said
to fall like the Devil and die with the dead.

Salt him with sulphur and level his mound.
Dig him in deep in his grave in the ground.

Hound him with thunder and let him not sleep.
Pitch in another and cover them deep.

Bury the bodies all under one lid.
I never did it, but Finnegan did.

Wreathe with black roses, and case him in lead.
This is the day that the Devil is dead.

This is the pit, and the story is X's.
Those are the ashes, and these are the hexes.

Boys, it's been fun, it's a bang-up, a revel.
Finnegan soon will be dead as the Devil.

Roll out the sidewalks and paint the town red.
This is the day that the Devil is dead.

And they also tell the story of—

Colophon

This book was designed by Thomas T. Beeler. David G. Hartwell edited the introductory material and Betsy Groban and Thomas T. Beeler copyedited it. New material was phototypeset in Century Schoolbook typefaces by Trade Composition, Inc., of Springfield, Massachusetts. The book was printed and bound by Braun-Brumfield, Inc. of Ann Arbor, Michigan.